LOVING BAD

REGAN URE

Cover Design: © L.J. Anderson, Mayhem Cover Creations

Formatting by Mayhem Cover Creations

ISBN: 978-0-9932864-5-2

Thank you to my hubby and kids. Without
your love and support this wouldn't have been possible.

Table of Contents

Chapter One

TAYLOR

I took another sip and swallowed quickly before I could spit it out. The liquid burned slightly as it slid down my throat. I had no idea what I was drinking, but it tasted awful.

Beside me, my roommate, Jordan, took a gulp of the same liquid from a red plastic cup as she swung her hips in rhythm to the music pumping through the house party. We were two very different people; she was confident and flirty, and I was nervous and shy. I took another sip of the liquid and forced it down. It was the whole point of the night, to go out and have fun.

I studied the people dancing on the makeshift dance floor in the living room. Furniture had been moved to make enough space so people could move. They were throwing their arms up in the air and singing to a song that blared through the house.

A couple of girls were dancing on a wooden coffee table that had been moved against a wall. They held my attention as they danced and flirted with some of the guys who were dancing beside the table. I wanted to be a normal college student like the rest of the students who were clearly enjoying themselves. They were getting drunk and dancing without a care in the world. In a secluded corner, I noticed a couple making out heavily. Some were just flirty, but some were clearly getting lucky tonight.

As strange as it was to say, I envied them and their carefree, reckless attitude. Wasn't that part of the whole college experience? People said that college was a whole string of bad decisions best forgotten about but, for me, it would be different. I was going to learn from my experiences here. I hadn't had a chance to make any mistakes yet, but I was going to rectify that.

When Jordan had suggested we go to the party she'd heard about, I'd felt apprehensive, but I was determined to get out and experience things. Going out to a party didn't seem like much to most people but it was a big step to me.

To say I'd led a very protected life up to this point would be an understatement. But before the memories could start to cycle through my mind, I pushed them down. I didn't want to remember the things that had showed me the ugly side of life at an early age. Not all people were bad, and I had to remember that. I couldn't paint everyone with the same brush.

I'd lived such a protected life that it had suffocated me from the inside. Now that I had more control over my life, I'd decided that I wasn't going to hide away and live in fear of what could happen; instead, I was going to embrace it.

Was a life worth living if I didn't actually live it?

I took another determined sip of the alcohol that Jordan had assured me would loosen me up. She'd said I was so tightly wound that I needed something to help, hence the red plastic cup in my hand.

There were a lot of things I'd never experienced that most of the people my same age already had. To most people, it would be unbelievable that this was my first party ever and that I'd never drank alcohol before.

When I'd first met Jordan—a week ago when I'd moved into the dorm room—I'd been as nervous as hell, but Jordan had been friendly and we'd clicked. At first she'd been incredulous when I'd first begun to tell her how innocent I really was. I didn't go into the details of why and she didn't pry. When I'd told her about my decision to change that, she'd been completely on board with showing me what I'd been missing.

I pulled the tight red miniskirt I was wearing down, since the damn thing kept creeping up and, if I weren't careful, it would show my panties. As comfortable as I was in my own skin, I wasn't comfortable wearing such a revealing outfit in front of a bunch of strangers.

I'd worn the miniskirt and tight white top that Jordan had shoved into my hands because she told me that it would go with my pale skin and platinum-blond hair. But when she'd handed me a pair of high heels, I'd drawn the line. I didn't want to spend the whole night falling over my own feet.

I'd started experimenting with makeup a year earlier, so I knew how to put on a little makeup. Jordan had shaken her head at me when she'd seen me, though.

"It's too light," she'd complained and she'd gotten her own makeup out to help.

She'd been right. Once she was done, I could see the darker makeup made my pale blue eyes stand out more, and the shade of red lipstick she'd used on my lips matched the color of the miniskirt.

My mission tonight had been to dress up like some girls my age did and to go to my first party. We had been at the party for an hour, and I was still nervous, although I had to admit the alcohol was beginning to take effect, and I could feel myself start to relax.

I glanced at Jordan, and she looked at me and smiled, raising her cup. I mirrored her action and then took another sip. My eyes began to scan the party, happy to be a bystander and just watch for the moment.

The second my eyes landed on him, I felt a shiver of awareness go right through me. There was something about him that had kept me mesmerized as I'd stared at him from across the room.

It wasn't just the fact that he was the hottest guy I'd ever laid eyes on; there was a confidence about him that made it hard to pull my eyes away. Even though I'd led a very protected life, I knew he was the bad boy that people had warned me about on more than one occasion.

His hair was black and cut neatly short. I couldn't see what color his eyes were. He wore a plain shirt with faded jeans and his clothes molded a fit body that I bet hid a six-pack. Tattoos that ended at his wrist covered one of his muscular arms. I was standing too far away to get a really good look at them.

Then I took in the piercings. Both of his ears were pierced, as well as his lip. I couldn't stop myself from wondering what it felt like to kiss a guy who had a lip ring.

Who was I kidding? I wondered what it felt like to be kissed at all. It was another area I was totally innocent in.

He was like the exact opposite of me. Where I was innocent and had no experience, it was like he wore his life experience on his body with the tattoos and piercings. You had to be pretty confident in what you wanted to have it permanently inked into your skin.

Next to him was a girl flirting with him and I couldn't help the stab of jealousy I felt. The girl was pretty, and I watched as she put her hand on his arm when he leaned closer.

When Jordan noticed who'd caught my attention, she

leaned closer and said, "Don't even think about it. He'll eat you up and spit you out."

I pulled my eyes away from him to look at my friend. Her relaxed smile had been replaced with a stern expression.

"Sin Carter isn't someone you play with without knowing the rules, and you are too innocent to get caught up in that," she warned further. Sin. His name suited him.

She leaned closer.

"He has a serious reputation with women. And don't think that it's just a reputation based on rumors. I've had friends who have rotated through his bed and don't get me started on all the rumors about his past."

I knew her words were meant as a warning, but it just made me more curious about him. Despite trying to keep my attention off him after Jordan's warning, I felt my eyes drift back again to find him.

But this time his attention wasn't on the girl still flirting beside him. He was listening to what the girl was saying, but his eyes were fixed on me.

His eyes were a piercing blue that ignited a fire inside of me, and I felt myself come alive under his intense gaze as the one side of his mouth turned up in a sexy half-smile. There was a promise in his eyes of more experience than I could handle.

I groaned as I shifted slightly. My head was pounding, and it felt like someone had stuffed my head full of cotton balls. I touched my fingers to my forehead gently. My mouth was dry, and it was hard to swallow. Where the hell was I?

The pounding in my head eased up enough for me to open one eye. It was dark, but a streak of sunlight shone through a crack between the curtains, which was enough for me to be able to see that I wasn't in my own bed.

This wasn't good. Panic began to well up in me as I tried to piece together what had happened, but I couldn't remember anything. I took a deep breath to try and calm myself down. Then I felt the bed shift.

Oh. My. God.

I wasn't alone in the bed. I stayed still and closed my eyes, hoping not to wake up my bed partner. If they did wake up, I'd just pretend I was still sleeping. When the bed didn't move again after a minute of holding my breath, I opened my eyes and shifted my gaze to see who was in the bed with me.

Even in the slightly darkened room I could tell who it was. It was the guy that I'd seen at the party. I tried to remember his name, but I was coming up blank. Vaguely, I remembered Jordan had warned me about him. It took another few moments before his name came to me.

Sin.

Any thoughts of how hot he looked lying in the bed next to me evaporated at the question of why I was in bed with him in the first place. What on earth had I done last night? Had I done him? Well, there was one way to find out.

I squeezed my eyes closed for a moment to build up the courage to lift the bed cover to peer underneath. Thankfully there was enough light to see that I was still in my underwear. Should I be relieved I wasn't naked? But where were my clothes?

More questions than answers raced through my mind, and I tried to remember back to my last memory of last night. I had drunk some alcohol, but I didn't remember drinking that much. It was mystifying that the last thing I could remember was Sin eyeing me, and then everything kind of got fuzzy after that. Had I drunk too much? Is this what a hangover felt like?

I glanced back briefly to Sin sleeping peacefully beside

me. He was lying on his stomach with his arms wrapped around the pillow that his head lay on. He wasn't wearing a shirt. I had to fight the urge to lift the covers to check if he was naked but, honestly, I was too scared.

Had I slept with him last night? Had I lost my virginity and I couldn't remember it? After remembering Jordan's warning about him, he didn't sound like the type to take a girl up to his room and do nothing. Trust me to go to bed with one of the hottest guys I'd ever seen and not remember a thing.

It wasn't like I was keeping my virginity for someone special or 'the one.' I had planned on losing my virginity, but I'd at least wanted to remember the details.

I nearly groaned out loud and quickly put my hand over my mouth when I realized that I was in a stranger's bed, and the noise might wake him up. As quietly as I could, I slid out of the bed. My shirt, skirt, and shoes were strewn across the carpet, so I didn't have far to look for them. I gathered them up quickly and quietly got dressed. A couple of times I had to stop and let the pounding in my head ease before I carried on.

If this was what a hangover felt like, I swore I was never going to touch another drop of alcohol. Just the thought of it made my stomach roil. With pieces missing, I couldn't remember what had happened to Jordan. I wished that I'd brought my phone so I could call her to check that she was okay, but I'd left it in our dorm room.

Once I was dressed, I tackled my next problem. I wasn't sure where I was, and I wanted to be gone before Sin woke up. The whole situation was embarrassing enough without an audience. Shoes in hand, I walked to the door and, as slowly as I could, I opened the door and left. I didn't bothering closing the door properly; instead, I left it slightly open, too scared that I'd wake him trying to close the door behind me.

Thank goodness I didn't bump into anyone on my way

out. It was only when I descended the stairs that I recognized that I was still in the same house where the party had been held. I signed with relief. At least I knew the way back to my dorm room, and it wasn't far. Thankfully it seemed to be too early for anyone else to be awake, and I thought I was in the clear until my hand wrapped around the door handle.

"Leaving already?" someone asked in a playful tone from behind me, just as I was about to make my exit. I nearly jumped out of my skin and my heart was hammering in my chest when I turned to face the source of the voice.

I recognized him vaguely from the party, but I had no idea what his name was. He was leaning against the kitchen doorway with a bowl of what looked like cereal in his hands as he watched me with a smirk.

"I..." I was a blubbering idiot. I had no idea what to say to his question. I wished the ground would open up and swallow me whole so I could avoid the embarrassment. What did they call it? Oh yes, the walk of shame.

His grin grew as he straightened up and set the bowl of cereal down on the kitchen counter. He was taller than me, well over six feet. Like Sin, he was built but not in a bulky way, but it wasn't the only thing that he had in common with Sin.

Like Sin, he also sported a tattoo sleeve on one of his arms. The lack of shirt confirmed that was the extent of his tattoos on the top portion of his body. And I had no wish to know if he had any tattoos on the bottom half. He also had piercings but only in his eyebrow that was arched at me.

Unlike Sin, his hair was a light brown and a little longer on top with the sides shorter. He had pale blue eyes similar to mine. He was a good-looking guy, and I bet he could pull as many girls as Sin could but, despite that, he didn't have the same effect that Sin had on me. He was still smiling like he was enjoying watching me squirm with embarrassment.

"You're the girl who was with Sin last night," he said to me. This house was big enough to house a few people so maybe he was trying to place who I'd been with. The fact that he had seen me go upstairs with Sin made me question the fact that despite waking up dressed in my underwear something had happened with him.

I'd heard stories of girls being tender there afterward, but I wasn't. Did that tell me anything? I'd been determined to experience what girls my age did, but this was one I wished I'd skipped. How did I tell this guy that I had no recollection from the night before and that I wanted to get out of here before I embarrassed myself further?

"I need to go," I mumbled as I turned to leave.

"What's your name?" he asked with curiosity as my hand gripped the door handle tightly.

I kept my back to him and, for a moment, I weighed up whether it was a good idea to tell him my name. It didn't take me long to decide not to answer his question. I hoped that by keeping my identity from him I could erase this from my mind. In my rush to leave, I slammed the door closed and hurried down the street.

The air outside was cool, and I shivered. It was early morning. I glanced down at my watch and saw that it was only seven o'clock. My mind cycled through what I remembered from last night as I did my first—and hopefully last—walk of shame.

Chapter Two

TAYLOR

By the time I made it back to the dorm, I was feeling a little better. Maybe it was the fresh air that had done the trick. The pounding was gone, but there was still a dull pain in my head. No matter how much I tried, I couldn't seem to find my missing memories from the night before. At least I'd managed to get out before Sin had woken up. That could have been a lot more embarrassing than my run-in with the stranger when I was trying to sneak out. I let out a frustrated sigh. I'd lost my virginity to a hot guy, and I couldn't remember a thing.

Damn it!

The dorm was quiet as I entered the building. It was too early for most people to be awake, so hopefully no one would see me sneaking back in. I hurried up the stairs to the second floor. The elevator had been out of order since I'd arrived, and I wondered if they were ever going to fix it. Before, it hadn't really bothered me, but I was still feeling fragile, and I didn't feel like taking the stairs.

The room I shared with Jordan was quiet and dark when I entered. I tried to keep as quiet as possible so as not to wake

Jordan, who was sleeping in her bed.

"Doing the walk of shame, are you?" I heard Jordan's voice ask me as I kicked my shoes off.

I nearly jumped out of my skin at the sudden sound of her voice and clutched my chest as my heart hammered so hard it felt like it was trying to break free.

"Geez, you scared me!" I gasped as I turned to face her, trying to calm my heart down.

She was sitting up and, even though it was dark, I knew she was giving me a knowing smile. I walked over to the curtains and opened them. Light flooded into the room, and I could see Jordan sitting with her back leaning against the wall. She was smiling as she shook her head at me.

"Spill," she instructed. "I want to know what happened to you after I left?"

At the last part, she was wiggling her eyebrows suggestively at me, to which I rolled my eyes.

From the short time I'd known her, I'd discovered she said exactly what was on her mind and whatever she was thinking she blurted out. The good thing about it was that you knew exactly where you stood with her.

Not only were we different personality-wise, but we also looked like night and day. I had the blue eyes, platinum-blond hair and pale skin. Jordan was the total opposite, with short dark brown hair that she wore in a pixie cut, and olive skin. Her hazel eyes were her most striking feature. I was secure enough in myself to know that I was pretty, but Jordan was gorgeous. She was single at the moment, "in between boyfriends," she'd told me. Where I'd gotten a couple of appreciative glances from some of the guys at the party last night, Jordan had been constantly hit on.

"So, what happened?" she asked.

I sat down on my bed across from her, trying to figure out what to tell her. It was hard when I didn't remember. I rubbed my forehead a little, still feeling the headache that lingered.

"I lost my virginity last night," I revealed reluctantly. I could have admitted the truth and told her that I wasn't sure, but instead I lied.

"Oh, wow!" Jordan gasped with wide eyes. "You really went for it."

I nodded my head. I didn't want to reveal I couldn't remember anything about what was supposed to be one of the most eventful nights of my life.

"I honestly didn't think you had it in you," she admitted. Apparently I did.

She'd known that I'd wanted to have sex. I'd told her I wasn't waiting for the right one to come along. Not that there was anything wrong with that if I had.

"And? How was it?" she prodded. She hadn't been kidding when she'd told me she wanted all the details. Details I couldn't give her, so instead of answering her question I just shrugged. What I'd heard was that the first time was sore and uncomfortable, so Jordan wouldn't be expecting me to tell her that I had felt the earth move.

"Who was it with?" was her next question.

She'd warned me about Sin last night. I remembered that much, so I didn't want her to know I'd lost it with him. It wasn't like I was ever going to see him again, and even if I did, it wasn't anything more than a one-night stand that would never be repeated. It wasn't like he wanted to hang out. He was the type to get what he wanted and move on.

Lying was the easy part; remembering the lie was the hard part.

"Just some guy I met at the party," I vaguely answered. I opened and searched through my side table next to my bed looking for some painkillers.

"Was he hot?"

She just wasn't going to stop with the questions. I found the painkillers and swallowed two with a bottle of water I normally kept beside my bed.

"Yes."

I wasn't going to tell her that he was the hottest guy I'd ever seen, and all he had to do was look at me to have an effect on me. A shiver ran through at the memory of meeting his eyes across the room full of people.

"So, do you feel any different now that you've lost your V-card?" she asked.

"No, I feel exactly the same," I replied. I didn't even feel a little tender down there like some girls had told me that I'd feel after losing my virginity.

Even Jordan had relayed her first experience of sex. It had been in high school with some jock in the backseat of his car. It hadn't even lasted five minutes. Even she'd said that she had been tender there the next day.

"Was this guy just a one-night stand or are you planning on seeing him again?" she asked. I let out a sigh as I sat back down again. I had a feeling she wasn't going to let up on the questioning anytime soon.

"It was just a one-night stand. I doubt I will ever see him again," I brushed off.

It had happened the way I'd wanted it to, all except for the remembering part. I didn't have the need to get involved with someone to lose my virginity, so the fact that it had been a one-night stand with no strings attached suited me perfectly. It wasn't like I was daydreaming about a relationship with Sin. I was inexperienced in some ways and innocent in others, but I knew how a one-night stand worked, and I was okay with that. I wouldn't be shedding any tears over it.

Trying to deflect the questioning off me, I turned the tables and began to ask Jordan about a couple of the guys she'd talked to last night. We sat talking for an hour about the party before I decided I needed a shower. I got my stuff together and went to the restroom. I was still feeling a little ill by the time I made it back to my dorm room. It was a Saturday, so I didn't have to worry about getting to class or trying to concentrate. I did have an assignment to do, but I could do it later or the next day.

I was lying on my bed, reading a book, trying to get over my hangover. Jordan was dressed and busy with an assignment with some books open on her bed when someone knocked on the door. We both looked at each other with curiosity. We weren't expecting anyone. I sat up as Jordan walked over to the door and opened it.

At the sight of the person who filled the doorway, my mouth dropped open in shock.

What is he doing here?

The sight of him made me want to climb under my bed and hide. One-night stands weren't supposed to come looking for you the next morning, were they? He was dressed in a faded pair of jeans and a plain white shirt. Even in shock, I couldn't dispute that he was gorgeous.

Had I left something behind and he was here to return it? It was the only logical thing that would explain why he was here. But I couldn't remember leaving anything behind.

"Whoever you're looking for isn't here," said Jordan with hostility. I'd never heard her be so rude before.

But Sin ignored her as his gaze swept past Jordan into the room and onto me. I felt a shiver run through me at the intensity of it. It was too late to hide; he'd seen me. Jordan looked a little confused as she took a step back and looked from Sin to me. I felt a guilty blush tinge my cheeks at the fact that I hadn’t told her it had been Sin. He still had his intense gaze fixed on me when Jordan looked back to him.

It was time to take control and be an adult in this

uncomfortable situation. I'd had a one-night stand with him, and I didn't need to feel ashamed of that. The only feeling I should feel was the guilt for not telling her it had been Sin. I stood up and dropped the book I was reading onto my bed. An uncomfortable atmosphere set in as I walked over to the door, and Jordan took another step back and watched us with curiosity. He still hadn't said a word, and his gaze fixed on me as I came to a stop in front of him.

Not wanting to have this conversation in front of anyone, my eyes met his for a moment and then I stepped past him. I walked down the hallway, and I couldn't ignore the appreciative looks some of the girls were giving him as he followed me. I opened the door to the staircase and turned to see Sin follow through the door behind me. Silence settled in between us for a few moments after the door closed.

I was the first one to break the silence.

"How did you find me?" I asked.

"It really wasn't that difficult," he answered. "I asked around."

"What are you doing here?" I asked anxiously, dropping my eyes to the floor for a moment. Just spending a little time in his presence made me hyperaware of him. It also didn't help that he could remember what we'd done last night, but I couldn't.

"I wanted to check on you."

It was the first time I'd ever heard him talk, or could remember hearing his voice. It had a sexy huskiness to it that made my body tingle. I had to remind myself that as attracted to him as I was, one-night stands didn't do repeat performances.

"Why?" I asked, looking up to him as I crossed my arms.

He gave me a confused look.

"It was just one night. Why would you need to check up on me?" I asked.

He looked at me like I was talking a different language.

"What are you talking about?" he asked, shaking his head slightly.

"Last night was fun and...thanks," I said, unsure of exactly what to say. From what Jordan had said, it had sounded like he was king of one-night stands, so he would know exactly how these things worked.

He cocked his head to the side, brushing his lip ring with the tip of his tongue as he studied me for a moment.

"How much of last night do you remember?" he asked.

Should I lie to him or should I tell him the truth? I hesitated.

"You don't remember," he murmured as he saw the indecision I was wrestling with.

I pressed my lips together as I fidgeted with my hands. There was no point in lying about it. I was a grown woman, and I had nothing to feel ashamed about. I shook my head.

"No, I don't."

"Trust me—sleeping with me isn't something you'd forget," he assured me. Then it occurred to me—if we hadn't slept together, it meant I was still a virgin.

Slowly, so many of the things I'd noticed—like not being sore or tender down there—began to fall into place. He watched me as I began to piece stuff together. But if we hadn't had sex, why had I woken up in the bed with him?

"I don't understand," I said. "If we didn't sleep together, why did I wake up in bed with you?"

That is it! I'm never going to drink again.

"You were out of it last night, and you could barely stand," he revealed. I didn't remember having that much to drink, but I hadn't drunk alcohol before. Maybe I didn't have a tolerance for it.

"I'm sorry," I mumbled to him, feeling the heat of embarrassment on my face.

"Did you take a drink from someone last night?" he asked. I looked at him. I wasn't sure what he was trying to get at.

"Why would you ask that?" I asked, a little puzzled as to what he was aiming at.

"I don't think you were drunk," he answered cryptically as he folded his arms across his chest.

What exactly did that mean? Did he think someone put something in my drink? I frowned.

"Do you think someone spiked my drink?" I asked the thought out loud. He nodded his head slowly while he watched me for a reaction.

"Why would someone want to do that?" I asked, feeling shocked.

"You can't be that naive," he said, looking at me in disbelief.

I tried to hide my anger. Apparently I was naive. It came from a lack of experience, and I was trying to rectify that. Once the surprise disappeared, annoyance took its place as he took a step forward.

"There are bad people out there. People who will do really bad things given the opportunity," he tried to explain to me. It was like he was talking to a child.

"That was why I took you up to my room. I don't want to think what would have happened to you if I hadn't," he said. He dropped his arms to his sides, and turned his hands into fists.

I suddenly felt a little bad for being angry at him when evidently I should be grateful for what he'd done for me.

"Thank you," I mumbled.

He'd looked after me and, like he said, it could have been worse if he hadn't. It explained why I was in his bed, but it didn't explain why I'd been missing most of my clothes.

"You're welcome," he mumbled as he shoved his hands

into the pockets of his jeans and dropped his gaze to the floor. It was like he was unaccustomed to being thanked.

"Why was I only dressed in my underwear?" I asked, wanting to be able to piece most of what happened that night together.

"You were trying to take advantage of me," he said with a smirk as he watched me blush. He looked like he was enjoying that little piece.

So embarrassing!

"I'm sorry," I mumbled again, wishing the ground would open up and swallow me up. I felt mortified that I'd thrown myself at him.

"Don't be," he said. "If you hadn't been out of it, I probably would have taken you up on the offer."

At that information, my stomach did a flip. *Oh, wow!*

My skin tingled as his gaze swept me from head to toe. He smiled—that sexy, knowing, type of smile that told me he would make my world move if we had sex.

"Uh...well...thanks," I stuttered back, trying to get a hold of myself.

If this is what he did to me without touching me, I couldn't imagine what he was capable of if he could.

"I'd better go," he said as he turned to leave. Then he hesitated for a moment and looked back over his shoulder to me.

"If you ever want to take advantage of me when you're in a sober condition, you know where to find me," he offered as a sizzling smile tugged at his lips.

I felt my knees weaken from the effect.

Then he turned and left. I stood, trying to recover as the door slammed shut. I leaned against the wall with my back and took a deep breath. His parting remark kept cycling through my mind. Was that something that I thought I was up for? I wasn't so sure. If I had more experience, I would know if I was capable of having sex with him without attaching strings, but I wasn't sure if that was something I wanted to chance. Developing feelings for Sin would only lead to heartbreak for me, and I wasn't sure I was ready to handle that yet.

Chapter Three

TAYLOR

Jordan was sitting on her bed with her arms crossed over her chest as she watched me enter the room.

"I know. I have some explaining to do—" I began, but she cut me off with the wave of her hand.

"I warned you about him. I told you that if you got involved with him he'd break your heart," she said, her tone getting more and more upset. "I'm not trying to tell you how to live your life; I just don't want to have to pick up the pieces when he's done with you."

My eyes softened at my roommate. I understood why she was so upset with me, and I loved that she cared.

"Look, I'm sorry I lied to you," I apologized. "I shouldn't have. But the truth is, nothing happened with him."

"Then why did he show up here looking for you?" she asked, her eyes questioning.

"Well..."

In truth, it was complicated.

"He thinks someone spiked my drink last night," I started. Jordan's eyes widened, and she shot up.

"Someone spiked your drink!" she shrieked. I grabbed

her by both of her arms to try and calm her down. She was visibly upset at the thought that someone had tried to do that to me.

"I have no proof someone did that. It's just that I didn't drink that much and Sin said I could barely stand."

"You said you lost your virginity last night," she began and swallowed. "Did someone rape you?"

"No," I answered, shaking my head for extra emphasis.

"Sin is the reason nothing happened to me. He saw I was out of it, so he babysat me for the night."

Jordan looked at me like I'd grown another head.

"He babysat you," she repeated, hoping they would make more sense to her, but his actions clearly didn't coincide with the person she knew.

"I didn't remember anything from the time that you left, and when I woke up, I was in Sin's bed dressed in my underwear. That's why I thought something had happened between us, and I left before he woke up," I started to explain as I released her arms and rubbed my forehead. I was still feeling the effects of my 'hangover.'

"Why were you in your underwear?" she asked suspiciously.

"No, it wasn't like that. He said I tried to take advantage of him," I admitted, feeling a blush tinge my cheeks. I'd felt that attraction for him across the room the first time I'd ever laid eyes on him, so I didn't doubt that given the opportunity I would have tried something.

"Well I never," she murmured and sat down on her bed. It was like I'd told her Santa was real. I gave her a moment for her to wrap her mind around the thought.

"It's just he's normally the one that girls need protecting from. It just doesn't make sense that he looked after you." She was trying to explain why it was so hard to believe.

I shrugged. It was what it was, and there was no point

trying to figure it out.

"I kinda feel bad for being openly hostile toward him," she muttered as she raised her eyes to mine.

"It's fine. I don't think it bothered him," I replied. Then her face changed from sympathetic to angry.

"I told you not to take a drink from someone you don't know," she lectured. It felt like I was getting a talking to from a parent and not just a friend.

"I can't remember who gave me the drink," I said. Most people, by college, would know the dos and don'ts of going to parties and dealing with alcohol. I'd missed out on it, and I must have forgotten about Jordan's warning.

I didn't want to think of what might have happened if Sin hadn't seen me. I took a deep breath of guilt and fear and released it. There was no going back and changing it. I just had to learn from my mistakes and make sure I didn't repeat them.

"I knew I shouldn't have left you," she mumbled to me as she stood up and gave me a hug.

"It wasn't your fault, I'm a big girl," I replied as I hugged her back. She pulled away slightly and looked at me with a serious face.

"But that's the thing. You might look like a big girl, but you lack the experience that girls our age have," she said.

She was right, but this was the whole purpose of going out and experiencing all the things that life had to offer, even if some of those things were bad. I wasn't going to be scared to do the things I wanted to because I feared the bad that could happen.

"I know that you think Sin is a good guy because of what he did last night, but one good deed in among all the bad ones doesn't mean he's any less dangerous," she informed me, watching me closely to see my reaction.

"I know."

She was just telling me this because she was worried I would think he was a good guy, but I already knew that he was dangerous. If I allowed him anywhere near my heart, he would break it, and I didn't need Jordan to tell me that.

"Okay, lecture over," she announced. "Let's go and get some lunch."

"Sure."

We left the dorm and went to the cafeteria.

Later, when I got back, I realized I'd left my phone behind again. I glanced down at the screen and saw twenty missed calls from my brother, Connor. I let out a sigh before I dialed his number. I was preparing for the inevitable lecture that I was going to get when he answered on the second ring.

"Where have you been? I've been going out of my mind with worry," he lectured me in a worried tone. He'd had time to work himself up.

I rolled my eyes before I answered.

"I'm fine. I just forgot my phone behind when I went to get some something to eat," I explained to him.

"You left it behind! What if you'd needed to call for help and you didn't have your phone?" he continued in an angry tone. I bit my lip to stop myself from telling him to quit being so dramatic.

"I'm sorry," I mumbled, knowing there was no use trying to argue with him. As much as I wanted to break free from his hold, I understood why he was so protective, so I tried to put up with it. It was frustrating at times, but I knew he was doing it out of love.

I loved my brotherly dearly—he was the only family I still had left—but his overprotectiveness was suffocating me. If he had his way, he'd have me under lock and key.

"If you're going to be irresponsible I'll hire someone to watch you," he threatened. He was starting to pull out the big guns. When I'd first made the decision to go to college, he'd fought me on it. After months of arguing about it, he'd finally conceded, but he'd told me that if at any time he felt that I wasn't careful he'd hire a bodyguard to keep me safe. To an outsider, it could look overdramatic, but if you knew the truth you'd understand why he was the way he was. As much as I hated it, I understood.

"Please don't. I promise not to forget my phone again," I said, trying to reason with him. There was no way I wanted someone following me around the college. It would attract attention that I didn't want and I wanted to have a normal college experience—and normal didn't include a bodyguard.

If he knew what happened last night, he'd been on the first plane here to take me home. But home was his house, not mine, and I wanted to make my own way in life. This was my chance, and I wasn't going to let him ruin it. I was determined to be able to make my own decisions even if they led to a few mistakes in the process. He let out a big sigh, and there were a few moments of silence.

"You know I do this because I love you," he explained, sounding like he'd managed to calm down a bit.

"Yeah, I know. I love you too," I replied, sitting down on my bed and leaning against the wall as I waited for him to say more.

He worried so much. I wondered if all the stress was going to put him into an early grave one day.

"So how are things going?" he asked, trying to make conversation. He phoned me every day to check on me.

"Good."

There was no way I could tell him what happened last night, or he'd show up and drag me back home.

"You okay with the workload?" he asked.

I began to fidget with the end of the blanket that covered my bed. The stitching was coming undone.

"Yeah, so far so good," I said. I was so glad to be out

from under his protective presence that college and all the studying was easier than dealing with him.

I know it was horrible to think that, but it was the truth. Despite the fact that I knew his protectiveness came from the fact that he loved me and was scared to lose me, it was suffocating. He'd thought he'd nearly lost me once, and that fear pushed him to take every precaution he could to ensure my safety.

"I've got to go. I've got a meeting," he told me. "Please keep your phone on you."

"I will."

"I love you," he said. He said it to me every time we talked. I think it was those three words that people regretted not uttering for the last time to a loved one that they had lost.

"I love you too."

The call ended, and I dropped my phone onto my bed. I let out a sigh as I leaned my head back against the wall and closed my eyes for a moment.

"Was it that rough?" Jordan asked.

She'd been so quiet I'd forgotten she was in the room with me. I opened my eyes and found her sitting on her bed, crossed-legged with a book on her lap.

"Yes, but it was my fault. I shouldn't have forgotten my phone," I said, rubbing my forehead. I was still feeling a little fragile and, after the conversation I just had, I could feel another headache starting up.

I'd told her about my overprotective brother, but I had never told her why he was so overprotective. It wasn't something I liked to talk about, and she understood that. The problem with telling people about it was the sympathetic looks, and I just couldn't stand those anymore. This was my chance to start over, doing what I wanted, making my own mistakes without my past following me every step of the way.

For the rest of the day, I put my homework away and lay

on my bed with a book, trying to get my mind off a hot bad-boy who made my stomach flutter every time I saw him.

The next week was busy. Between classes and homework, I didn't have a lot of free time. I'd made it in just in time to my last class for the day. Still out of breath, I sat down in the first available seat and began to get my books out.

"You nearly didn't make it," said a voice from beside me.

I brushed my hair out of my face to see a guy that I'd noticed the week before smiling at me. I tried to calm my heart down as I gave him a friendly smile back.

"Yeah, tell me about it," I replied as I went back to the task of getting my notes out.

I could still feel his gaze on me, and I tried to ignore it when the class started up. Despite my best efforts, I couldn't concentrate on the teacher and what he was babbling on. It was the boy with the nice smile beside me who had kept my thoughts busy. The few times I'd snuck glances at him, he'd smiled knowingly at me.

He had blond hair with dark blue eyes, but his dimples that appeared every time he smiled were his sexiest feature. Embarrassed that I'd been caught looking at him a few times during class, I packed my bag as soon as the bell rang and tried to get out of the class before I embarrassed myself further.

"Wait," he called out to me as I exited the classroom.

I didn't want to be rude, so I stopped and turned to face him.

"I'm Caleb," he said while running a hand through his hair.

"I'm Taylor," I replied as I hitched the strap of my bag higher onto my shoulder.

"When a pretty girl sneaks in a couple of glances my way, I don't let her leave without taking her number," he said and pulled out his phone.

I was speechless.

"Are you going to give me your number?" he asked, seeming a little more serious than before.

For a moment, while his eyes held mine, I debated whether or not to give him my number. I was here to experience everything that I could. I liked him, and there was nothing wrong with that, so I decided to give him my number and he typed it into his phone.

"I'll call you, and we can go out sometime," he said as he turned to leave.

I nodded, and he gave me that killer smile with the dimples once more before he disappeared down the hallway.

For a few minutes, I stood there trying to get myself together. It had been the first time a guy had asked me for my number, and my heart was still hammering with excitement. It was precisely for these moments that I'd strived hard to experience, and it was even better than I'd ever dreamed. I smiled to myself as I turned to walk back to the dorm. I still had the stupid smile on my face when I pushed the door open to my room.

"Why are you so happy?" Jordan asked, looking at me with narrowed eyes.

“A guy asked for my number," I said, sharing my moment with her.

"That is awesome. What's his name?" she asked, closing the book she'd just been studying.

"Caleb," I said.

"Come on, I want all the details," she prompted as she patted the empty spot beside her. I dropped my bag onto the floor beside her bed, and I sat beside her. She listened intently as I gave her a brief rundown of what happened.

"So what does he look like?" she asked. My first response was to say he looked like the opposite of Sin, but I caught myself. I couldn't understand why I compared him to a boy I barely knew.

"He's tall and blond with dark blue eyes," I said, trying to describe Caleb to her. "And he has dimples."

"I have a weakness for dimples," Jordan revealed, shaking her head.

Before I could stop myself, I thought about Sin. It seemed I had a thing for bad boys who had piercings and were covered in tattoos.

"So if he calls, will you go out with him?" Jordan asked, pulling me out of my thoughts.

"Sure, he's really cute," I answered automatically. He was good-looking, and he seemed like a nice guy so I would definitely give it a chance.

I couldn't help thinking that although I'd been excited about Caleb asking me for my number, my response was still lukewarm compared to how I felt around Sin. Sin didn't seem like the type to ask a girl for her number. He seemed like the type to give her one earth-shattering night and then never look her way again. I'd been so wrapped up in my thoughts that I'd missed half of what Jordan had been saying so I only caught the end part.

"What are you going to wear?" she asked.

I frowned for a moment.

"Wear to what?" I asked, confused.

"You weren't listening to a word I was saying," she said as she smiled knowingly at me. "You daydreaming about Caleb already?"

I shrugged, not wanting to lie.

"There is a party tonight," she repeated. "So what are you going to wear?"

My first party had been an eventful one. Most girls after

experiencing what I had would steer clear of parties for the rest of their lives, but for me it was different. I didn't want to shy away from experiences even though they might be bad.

"I'm not sure I have anything to wear," I mumbled.

"It's okay, I'm sure I can find something of mine you can wear," she said as she got up and walked over to her closet.

"Just no miniskirts," I said, remembering spending half the night trying to make sure my panties didn't show the last time.

"No miniskirts," she said and began to look through her wardrobe.

Chapter Four

TAYLOR

I was a little apprehensive as we walked to the party. I was dressed in a pair of black skinny jeans that I'd paired off with a royal blue halter-top that I'd borrowed from Jordan. Black ballets finished off my outfit. Jordan had tried to talk me into heels again, but I'd refused. She was wearing a black miniskirt with a tight, black sleeveless top that showed off her narrow waist and ample cleavage. The night air was a little chilly as we walked to the party. I rubbed my arms, trying to keep the cold away as I walked alongside Jordan.

She'd given me another lecture of dos and don'ts, emphasizing the point not to take a drink from a stranger. I didn't want a repeat of the last time I'd done that, although I couldn't wish away waking up next to a sexy bad-boy who still occupied my thoughts a week later.

It was just after nine when we arrived outside the house where the party was in full swing. There were people talking and drinking outside on the patio, and some were already unsteady on their feet. Jordan nodded her head to greet a couple of them as I followed her into the house. Music blared from the living room where people were dancing. We forced our way through the jostling bodies to the kitchen to get something to drink.

After we got a couple of drinks, we went back to look over the dance floor. My eyes drifted over the crowd as I took a tentative sip of my drink. I cringed as I drank the vile liquid. A guy across the room gave me an appreciative look. The fact that I didn't have a lot of experience with guys didn't mean that I didn't know that I was attractive. I was still getting the hang of dealing with some of the attention I was receiving from boys, so I gave him a forced half smile and let my eyes keep moving over the crowd. A little while later Jordan peered into my empty cup.

"I'll go and get us some more drinks," she said as she took my empty cup and disappeared into the crowd in the direction of the kitchen.

I was swaying to the beat when I felt hands rest gently on my hips and slide around my waist. The hairs on the back of my neck rose in anticipation as I felt warm breath against my ear.

"I didn't expect to see you here," the husky voice whispered against my ear.

I closed my eyes for a moment. I didn't need to turn around to know who it was. My body's reaction to him was a telltale sign for me. For a moment, I allowed myself to enjoy the feel of his body against mine and revel it in.

Gently, he released me and turned me around to face him. I tilted my gaze upwards to meet his eyes. His eyes met mine, and I felt a flutter in my stomach as he held me gently with his hands resting lightly on my hips. He smiled, and I felt my knees weaken. His smile turned to a knowing one when he took in my reaction to him. There was no hiding it. He could see the effect he had on me.

"I hope you haven't taken any drinks from strangers tonight," he said as his eyes flickered from my lips back to my eyes.

I bit down on my lip nervously. I felt vulnerable and exposed under his intense gaze. Unable to form words because of the havoc he'd started, I shook my head. His eyes lifted and looked past me.

"I'd better go before your friend gets back," he said. Then he leaned forward, and I felt the air in my lungs lock as his warm breath caressed my cheek.

"I'll see you around, Taylor," he whispered against my ear and I felt a shiver of awareness run through me. I closed my eyes for a moment, and when I opened them, he was gone.

I scanned the room quickly, but I couldn't find him. I took a deep breath and let it out. Jordan returned moments later and pushed a drink into my hands.

"Thanks," I mumbled to her absentmindedly as I tried to pull myself together. My heart was still racing in my chest.

"Are you okay?" she asked me as she studied my face.

"Yeah," I replied. I couldn't exactly tell her the truth—that I was turned on by the bad-boy she'd warned me about.

"Are you sure? You look a little flushed," she said as she touched my cheek briefly with the back of her hand.

"I'm fine," I lied. I was so not fine. Sin, with just a few whispered words and a smile, had made me nearly combust with the heat of my hormones raging through my body.

He was lethal.

I spent the next hour trying to forget about Sin. Some guy was trying to chat me up but, as hard as I tried to pay attention to what he was saying, my mind was replaying my moment with Sin over and over again. I bet he knew exactly what he was doing when he was in the bedroom with a girl, and I couldn't help but imagine his naked body against mine, our bodies slick with sweat. A red blush tinged my cheeks at the naughty thought.

The boy who was trying to chat me up cleared his throat, which brought my focus back to him.

"So, do you want to go out sometime?" he asked, his eyes wide and expressive as he waited for my answer.

I was out to enjoy life and live it to the fullest, but spending a night in the company of a guy who couldn't even hold my attention for a short time didn't sound like my idea of fun.

"I'm sorry, I've got too much studying to do," I said, giving him the nicest brush-off I could come up with so quickly.

"Sure, I get it," he mumbled. He looked a little disappointed, so I gave him a smile. He didn't stick around.

My eyes caught sight of Sin. Just the sight of him was enough to make me come alive in ways only he could cause. A stab of jealousy stabbed through me when I noticed he wasn't alone. The girl was blond and pretty. Even though my mind was telling me to look away and ignore him, my eyes remained on the two of them. He leaned down and said something against her ear and she giggled. I watched as he took her by the hand and led her to a darkened corner by the stairs. People were too busy dancing and drinking to notice the two of them, but I couldn't pull my eyes away from them.

Jordan was still dancing next to me. Thankfully, she was too busy flirting with some hot guy to notice who had my attention. Sin leaned forward and kissed the girl. I knew I should look away, but no matter how hard I tried, I couldn't. The girl's arms wrapped around his neck, and he deepened the kiss. I felt a flutter in my stomach at the thought of him doing that to me. I watched as his hand caught her knee when she lifted a leg to wrap around him. His hand slid forward and cupped her butt as they kissed. I was so transfixed by the two of them and what they were doing that it took me a moment to realize that the girl didn't have Sin's undivided attention. His lips were still against hers, but his eyes were on me.

Look away! I told myself, but I couldn't.

He smiled against the girl's lips as his eyes held mine. I felt myself blush at the brazen way I was watching him make out with some random girl. It was Jordan who finally pulled my attention away from him.

"Do you want another drink?" she asked.

"No, I think I'm done for the night," I replied, setting my empty cup on the closest table I could find.

"Okay, then let's leave," she said.

I felt a little bad for cutting her night short. She seemed to be enjoying herself. It wasn't her fault that I couldn't keep my eyes off Sin.

"No, you stay," I insisted. "I can get a taxi back to the dorm."

"I don't mind calling it a night," she insisted.

Just before we turned to leave, I glanced back to Sin and the girl. He was pressed up against her, kissing her. I'd been forgotten, and I couldn't help feeling a little deflated.

That night, I tossed and turned. As hard as I tried to forget about Sin, I couldn't get rid of the images of him and the girl, which kept me up for most of the night. The way Sin looked at me while he'd been kissing that girl made my stomach flip. In those eyes was a promise of what I wanted: hot, mind-blowing sex.

If he could make me feel like that with just one look, I wanted what he could make me feel with the touch of his mouth and fingers. I could feel the heat in my cheeks at the naughty thought, and I felt an ache between my legs. I pressed my knees together, trying to rid myself of the physical effects of him on my body. I beat my pillow as I turned onto my stomach and tried to get some sleep, but every time I closed my eyes I saw Sin's hypnotizing eyes.

I rolled onto my back and let out a heavy sigh. For a while, I just lay there, staring at the ceiling in the darkness, trying to come to some sort of decision. He'd said if I was interested in taking advantage of him, I could let him know. I wanted to get rid of my virginity, and I wanted to experience sex. He'd offered me sex, so that left me with the choice.

I was going to lose my virginity—that much I'd already decided, but the question was who was I going to lose it with? I could meet some random guy who could help me with that, but I couldn't help thinking sex with Sin would be awesome. Did I just want sex or did I want the ground-moving type?

Jordan had warned me about him, but it wasn't like I was going to date him. I had to suppress a laugh at the thought of my brother's face if I brought Sin home and introduced him as my boyfriend. My brother would have a heart attack.

No, I wasn't interested in dating Sin. I wanted no-strings-attached sex for one night, and then I'd walk away and he would be able to move on to the next girl. I didn't have to hear all the rumors about him with tons of girls to know that he knew his way around a girl's body. I bit my bottom lip at the memory of his hand sliding up the girl's thigh to her butt.

My decision was made. I still felt a little nervous because he was so experienced, and I wondered if my inexperience would put him off. Maybe guys liked girls with some experience. I didn't have a number for him, so the only way I could talk to him was to go to his house.

I was nervous for most of the next day, trying to work up the courage to go through with my decision. It was only when I was standing outside the front door of the house he stayed in the next day that I realized how crazy my idea was. What if he laughed in my face? I took a deep breath while I wrung my hands. As I let it out, I stepped forward and knocked before I could talk myself out of my crazy idea.

Nervously, I waited. I heard sounds coming from inside the house, and before I could prepare myself, the door opened. It was the guy who had caught me trying to sneak out of the house after the first party.

"You back for more?" he asked with a smirk.

I swallowed hard, feeling my cheeks blush. It was at times like these that I wished I didn't blush so easily. I couldn't exactly explain to this stranger that I hadn't gotten any the first time.

"S-Sin..." I began to stutter. I felt like such an idiot, and I was making a total ass out of myself.

Maybe it would be better just to turn around and walk away. His eyebrows rose as he waited for me to complete my sentence.

"Never mind," I muttered and turned around. This was a bad idea.

"Wait," he said, grabbing my arm to stop me from leaving and I turned to face him. I crossed my arms over my chest.

"I'm sorry, I didn't mean to scare you off," he said. He replaced the smirk he'd worn earlier with a welcoming smile as he ushered me into the house.

"Sin!" he yelled, looking up the stairs. I held my breath, feeling more nervous now that I was standing inside his house waiting.

I turned to see two other guys that I remembered from the party where I'd first seen Sin. They were playing video games, but their attention was now focused on me, the video game having been forgotten. Just when I didn't think it could get any worse. Great, I'd have to do this with an audience! I felt the burn of embarrassment in my face as I stood there waiting for Sin under the curious looks of his friends.

My nervousness increased when Sin appeared at the top of the stairs. He looked surprised to see me. His eyes flickered to his friend, the one who answered the door and who was still standing beside me. Then Sin's gaze settled back on me as he descended the stairs. His friend walked into the living room and joined the others. I was ready to make a dash out of the door and forget I'd even considered this ludicrous idea.

"I never expected to see you again," were his first words to me as he looked at me with curiosity. He was probably trying to figure out why I was here.

"Hi..." I said. I threw a glance at the three pairs of eyes that were watching us from the living room. Sin's eyes took our audience in.

"We can talk upstairs," he suggested, shaking his head at his friends' inability to give us privacy.

I quietly followed him up the stairs and to his bedroom. Once inside, I couldn't help thinking the last time I'd left it I had never thought I would be back here again. Sin closed the door and turned to face me. One moment of silence turned into two while I wrestled with my words. He cocked his head to the side and studied me.

"You don't have to be nervous," he said as he stepped closer.

If I was nervous before I was even more nervous now standing in front of him. Up close with his eyes on me made me feel so aware of him and I struggled to put together the words I wanted to say.

"I wanted to...ask...you," I stuttered under his intense gaze.

"What do you want to ask me?" he said, standing confidently in front of me. I swallowed.

I couldn't exactly say, "I want to have sex with you" so instead I said, "I want to take advantage of you in a sober state."

He didn't look like the type who was easily shocked, but there was no mistaking it, he was shocked this time. He blinked and then he smirked at me.

"You want to take advantage of me?" he asked, his smirk widening into a smile.

Worried I'd stutter again, I just nodded my head. There, I'd told him what I wanted, and now the ball was in his court. I tried to meet his gaze without looking as nervous as I felt. His eyes slowly raked over me as he contemplated my request.

"I'm not one to turn down an offer like that," he began and I waited with butterflies fluttering in my stomach.

"But you don't look like you've ever taken advantage of anyone," he finished. How on earth did he know that? Was it written in my forehead?

"So what?" I said. I wasn't going to lie to him about it. He would eventually find out the truth, and I wanted him to go into this with his eyes wide open.

"As stunning as you are and as much as I'd like to take you up on your offer..." he started, and I felt my stomach begin to sink at the realization that he was turning me down.

"I don't do virgins," he finished.

"Okay," I mumbled as I tried to step around him and make a hasty departure, but he caught me by the arms.

"Find someone special to share it with," he suggested.

"No, it's fine. I'm sure I'll find someone who can help me," I replied, pulling out of his hold and getting out of his room as quickly as I could. He wasn't the only guy who could help me, and if he wasn't prepared to do it, I was sure I'd find someone who would.

Chapter Five

TAYLOR

It took me a few days to get over Sin's rejection. I hadn't thought that my virginity would be something that would make him turn down my offer. I knew some guys, especially the types who didn't do commitment, had a thing against screwing virgins. I wondered why. Did they feel taking someone's virginity made an emotional connection that made it harder to keep the girl's expectations in line with casual? In general, girls were more emotional about sex, and every girl remembered the guy she had sex with for the first time.

I could understand to a certain degree why Sin had turned me down, but it didn't help the feeling of being hurt. I barely knew him so I didn't know why he'd been able to bruise my ego as badly as he had.

I'd been very quiet and subdued when I'd gotten back to my dorm room. Jordan had noticed something was wrong.

"What's up?" she asked, studying me closely.

"Nothing, I'm just feeling a little under the weather," I lied. I couldn't tell her I'd asked Sin to help me get rid of my virginity and that he'd turned me down.

Finally, after a couple of days of mulling over my bruised

ego, I decided that there were plenty of guys out there who would jump at the chance to help me. I didn't need Sin. He couldn't be the only guy who was good at sex.

I was on my way to one of my classes when I heard someone shout my name. I stopped to see Caleb running down the hallway to catch up with me.

"Hi," he greeted, still sounding a little out of breath.

"Hi," I greeted back, smiling at him.

"Did you have a good weekend?" he asked, trying to make conversation as we continued to walk down the hallway side by side. We had the next class together.

"It was okay," I replied with a shrug. I couldn't help the embarrassment I still felt every time I replayed asking Sin to sleep with me.

"How was yours?" I asked. I wasn't used to talking to the opposite sex a lot, so I still got a little nervous and I struggled to think of what to say.

"Fine," he replied. I wished I could have said the same as I shook my head, trying to get rid of the memories of the rejection.

"I was going to call you this weekend," he revealed as he ran his hand through his hair. I felt my stomach dip at his words.

"So why didn't you?" I asked, smiling at him.

"Something came up," he replied as my eyes glanced down the hallway.

I was about to look at Caleb when I spotted Sin a few feet away. He was facing our direction, leaning against the wall with his shoulder, talking to a girl in front of him. I was shocked to see him. I didn't even know that he actually went to the same college. I'd never seen him around before. He did live nearby the college, and there had been a couple of college parties at his house. It shouldn't really have come as a shock, but it did, and at that moment I wished I could disappear so he wouldn't see me.

Don't look up, I begged myself while I tried to hide behind a curtain of my hair.

As I said the thought in my mind, his eyes lifted and met mine. The impact of his eyes on me was powerful. I felt like someone had punched me in the stomach, and my cheeks burned red with the embarrassment from our last encounter. I pulled my eyes from his and turned my attention to Caleb.

"You okay?" Caleb asked when he saw that I was a little distracted.

"Yeah, I'm fine," I replied, determined not to let Sin affect me. It didn't help that my body didn't get the memo and I could still feel the butterflies fluttering inside my stomach as I felt the heat of Sin's gaze on me when Caleb and I walked past him.

"You want to go to a movie sometime?" Caleb asked, and I tried to ignore the feel of Sin's eyes on me.

"Yeah, that sounds nice," I replied. I hoped Sin was within hearing distance. I don't know why it mattered, but it did. I wanted Sin to hear Caleb ask me out; I wanted him to know that I wasn't that desperate girl who couldn't find a guy.

"Great," Caleb replied as we entered our class together.

"Just let me know when," I replied as I sat down in my usual seat. Caleb sat down in the seat next to me.

"This week is a bit hectic so how about sometime next week?" he asked as he leaned back into his seat.

"Sounds good," I replied, feeling a little more confident now. One guy had turned me down, but another was asking me out, so I started to feel a little better.

Our class started, and I tried to concentrate on what the lecturer was saying, but I couldn't stop thinking about Sin. It was so frustrating that I was thinking about him and not the boy sitting beside me who'd asked me out. Deep down I knew the reason why. The attraction I had for Caleb wasn't anywhere near as powerful as the attraction I had for Sin. *Stupid hormones!*

I felt a little jealousy at the girl Sin had been talking to. I couldn't help thinking that he'd screw her if she asked. No matter how much I tried to stop thinking about him, I couldn't. Maybe it was a little unfair to go out with Caleb when I couldn't get Sin off my mind. But then I thought about it. Maybe it was exactly what I needed. I had to get out and meet more guys.

Just because I didn't feel the powerful attraction for Caleb didn't mean I couldn't have a good time. And that was part of the college experience. I wasn't really looking to find someone to start a relationship. I wanted to be young and reckless. I wanted to experience life.

After my little chat with myself, I started to feel better. But I still couldn't stop myself from scanning the hallways when I left my class. Caleb said goodbye before he rushed off to his next class. I was glad I was done for the day.

When I got back to the dorm room, I got started with my assignments and managed to forget about boys long enough to complete them. An hour later I picked up my phone to call my brother.

"Hi, Tay," he answered.

"Hi," I replied.

"Everything okay?" he asked, his tone laced with concern.

"Everything is fine. Can't a sister phone her brother just to say hi?" I asked. The truth was I knew how much he worried about me so I thought I'd call him for a change.

"Of course you can. It just doesn't happen that often," he said. He was right. I rarely phoned him. I made a mental note to phone him more often.

"So how are things?" I asked conversationally as I lay on

my bed staring at the ceiling.

"Busy. How's college?" he asked. It was the answer I often got. He was always busy.

"Good."

I kept my answer short and to the point. There was no way I was sharing more than that with my brother. He'd have a heart attack if he knew I'd propositioned a guy to take my virginity.

"How is the love life?" I asked, knowing he was way too busy wrapped up in business to actually date.

"It's okay," he lied, and I knew it.

There hadn't been anyone significant in his life since his high school sweetheart. I didn't know why they broke up, but I knew that despite them being so young they had felt very deeply for each other. That had been about six years ago. I'd asked him once a couple of years after they broke up what had happened, and he'd refused to elaborate. All he had said was that it hadn't worked out. I wished he would find someone special to share his life with. I didn't want him to be a rich guy with no one in his life. No one stuck around long enough to achieve the label of girlfriend.

For the next few days, I couldn't help looking out for glimpses of Sin everywhere I went on the college campus, but I didn't see him at all.

I was looking for my phone in my bag. I knew if my brother phoned me again and I missed the call, he would do what he'd threatened to. Unable to find it in my bag, I turned abruptly to head back to my dorm to go and get it before Connor called when I bumped into someone. Hands reached out and gripped my arms to steady me. I looked up to see the guy who had caught me sneaking out of the house after the night I spent with Sin.

"Shouldn't you be looking where you're going?" he asked me with a grin as he released my arms.

"Yeah, sorry, I was a bit distracted," I replied quickly. I made a move to walk past him, but he grabbed my wrist.

"Aren't you the girl who came to see Sin?" he asked. He cocked his head to the side and studied me for a moment. There was no getting away from the guy.

"Yeah," I answered. There was no point in lying. He grinned at me.

"How about we swap names so the next time we bump into each other I won't refer to you as 'the girl I caught sneaking out of the house after a night with Sin' and you won't have to refer to me as 'the guy who caught you sneaking out of the house'?"

I couldn't help smiling.

"Sure, my name is Taylor," I replied.

"I'm Slater," he said. It was a nice name. Then I remembered why I'd bumped into him. I needed get back to my dorm room to get my phone before my brother called.

"Well, I gotta go," I said to Slater as I moved past him.

"My company that bad?" he teased. I stopped and turned to face him.

"No, I just forgot something I need to get before my next class," I explained, shaking my head.

"Fine. Listen, we're having a party at the house on Friday. Why don't you come?" he asked out of the blue.

His request took me by surprise. I wasn't sure why he was asking me to come, but did it really matter? If the party was at their house, then there was a good chance Sin would be there, and I didn't think that was a good idea at all.

"I don't think that is such a good idea. I think it might be a little awkward," I admitted to him, trying to turn him down gently.

"It won't be awkward. Once Sin is done with a girl, he doesn't go back, so he won't care whether you're there or not," he explained with a shrug of his shoulders.

The truth was Sin never had me; in fact, he'd turned me down. Maybe this would be another way to show him that I was over his rejection, even if it was a lie. I contemplated for a moment while Slater watched me. I'd also agreed to go out with Caleb in a week, but we weren't really dating so I could still do what I wanted.

"Okay," I replied. "Can I bring a friend?"

I would feel a lot less nervous if I could drag Jordan along with me.

"Of course you can. The more, the merrier," he replied.

"Great," I said, feeling confident in the decision I'd made.

"I'll see you then, Taylor," he said with one last flash of a smile as he turned and walked away.

I'd forgotten about my phone. I rushed as fast as I could back to my dorm room to get it. Thankfully there were no missed calls when I found it on my bed.

For the rest of the week, I didn't see Slater again, but I did see Sin briefly. This time he ignored me totally, his attention fixed on another pretty girl. It reinforced that my presence didn't affect him at all so going to the party wouldn't be a problem.

Later that day when I was talking to Jordan in our dorm room, I told her about Slater and the invitation to the party.

"Slater invited you to the party?" she asked, looking at me suspiciously, like there was more to the story than I was telling her.

"Yes," I confirmed.

"Does Sin know you're going?" she asked. It felt like I was being interrogated.

"I don't know," I sighed. "This isn't about Sin. This is

about a guy inviting us to his party."

"I don't know if Slater's reputation is any better than Sin's," she muttered.

"Come on, don't be like that," I said, crossing my arms over my chest. "We're just going to his party, it's not like he's asking me to date him."

"He doesn't date, he's the same as Sin," she retorted.

I let out a heavy sigh.

"I'm not interested in dating anyone either, so let's go and see what happens," I replied. I felt a little guilty because I had made plans to go out with Caleb the following week, but it wasn't like one plan to meet up meant we were dating.

This whole dating thing could get quite confusing with what was considered a date, or what was considered just hanging out. Then you got people who dated exclusively and then there were couples who didn't. Finding someone I think was hard enough; throwing in all that stuff just made the whole process more complicated.

"Okay," she relented. "I'm sorry for giving you a hard time about it. It's just that I don't want you to get hurt."

"I get it, I'm not looking to get hurt, I just want to live a little. Is that so bad?" I replied.

"No, it isn't."

When Friday night arrived, I began to feel a little nervous about the party. I kept telling myself that I didn't care that Sin would be there probably draped over some random girl. It was time to forget about him and his rejection. I needed to move on.

Jordan and I spent a couple of hours getting ready. I was getting better at putting on my own makeup.

"Yeah, that's much better," Jordan commented as she

surveyed my made-up face.

This time I surprised myself by going for a skirt. Granted, it wasn't as short as the one Jordan had made me wear the first time I'd met Sin. This one was short enough for me to show off my slender legs and not make me feel like I was going to be flashing my panties if I wasn't careful. I was dressing to make myself feel more confident, and I wanted to look beautiful. I wanted to go to this party tonight, maybe have a few drinks, and have a good time. It was time to forget about Sin and his rejection.

By the time we made it to the party, the house was packed. This time I entered first with Jordan following behind me. My eyes scanned the living room for any signs of Slater, but I couldn't see him.

Deciding he might be in the kitchen, I began to push my way with the crowd that was dancing to the beat of the blaring music. As I got closer to the kitchen, I saw Sin. My heart skipped a beat as I watched him chat up some girl. She was pretty, and it made me feel a little deflated.

I reminded myself that coming to this party had nothing to do with Sin, and I needed to forget about him. I was at this party to act my age and to have fun. I was about to look away when he looked up, and our eyes met. The impact of his gaze was unmistakable on me as I felt my stomach flutter. He looked surprised and then I saw his lips press together as he continued to look at me.

I pulled my gaze away from his and continued my way to the kitchen. I felt the heat of Sin's gaze as my heart still hammered inside of my chest. Thankfully Slater was in the kitchen when I entered.

"You made it," he said. He actually sounded surprised to see me although I'd told him I was coming.

"Yeah. This is my friend Jordan," I said, introducing him to Jordan.

"Nice to meet you. You have pretty friends," he bluntly said, and I swear I saw Jordan blush. The thing about Slater was he was a charmer. He knew exactly what to say to get a girl to do whatever he wanted.

I shook my head at him as I smiled.

"Do you want a drink?" he asked, surveying the different bottles of alcohol that covered the kitchen counter.

"Yes, I do."

I was determined to have fun tonight, no matter what.

Chapter Six

TAYLOR

"Tequila?" he questioned mischievously.

I looked to Jordan, and we nodded our heads in agreement. He poured the liquid into three shot glasses. I'd never had a shot of alcohol before. I picked up the shot glass filled with tequila, and I was about to knock it back, but Slater stopped me.

"You need to do the salt first, and you can't forget about the lemon," he said. I gave him a confused look. What did salt and lemon have to do with drinking tequila?

"You've never had a shot of tequila, have you?" he asked, looking a little surprised. I shook my head.

Did I have everything tattooed on my forehead?

"This is how you drink a shot of tequila," he said. He licked a spot on the back of his right hand, and he took the saltshaker and sprinkled some salt over it. With his eyes still on me, he licked the salt off his hand and then knocked back the shot. Then he took a piece of lemon and sucked on it. He grimaced, then took the lemon out of his mouth.

"Does it taste that bad?" I asked, still watching his expression.

"No," he said, shaking his head with a smile.

"Your turn," he informed Jordan as he handed her the saltshaker. She licked a spot on her hand and sprinkled the salt over it, then she handed it back to Slater.

"Bottoms up," she said as she knocked the shot back. Then she swallowed it. She grabbed a slice of lemon off a plate on the kitchen counter and sucked on it.

"Your turn," Slater informed me as he handed me the saltshaker. I followed their actions except after I knocked back the tequila I began to splutter. The alcohol burned its way down my throat.

"Don't worry, you'll get the hang of it," he assured me as he patted my back. Jordan was still laughing at me.

The stuff tastes horrible!

"I'm...not sure...I want to," I muttered.

We did two more rounds of tequila shots before I called it quits. I wanted to drink and have fun; I didn't want to end up passing out and not remembering the night. Jordan and Slater did one more round without me before we all headed to the dance floor. The effects of the alcohol were taking effect, and I felt myself enjoying the sound of the music. I was probably tipsy at this point and, along with Jordan, I was singing to a song blaring through the house. Slater was dancing with us, laughing at our feeble attempts to keep in tune with the song.

Through the mass of bodies dancing against each other, I caught Sin's gaze fastened on me. The intensity of it shivered through me. For once he was standing alone. I held his gaze for a few moments before I turned away. He'd had his chance, and he'd turned me down. If the opportunity arose and I found a nice guy, I may even decide to have sex. Slater leaned closer.

"Are you having fun?" he asked as he smiled at me.

"Yes," I answered as I beamed at him.

He was about to lean closer when I felt a hand wrap around my wrist. Taken by surprise, I turned to see the owner of the hand standing beside me, glaring at his friend. The look he shot Slater made his friend back away from me and he lifted his hands in mock surrender. Even Jordan looked a little shocked at what she was witnessing.

I was still trying to figure out what was going on when Sin pulled me by the wrist off the dance floor. I didn't miss the curious looks we got as Sin led me up the stairs to his room. I could just imagine what everyone thought as they watched me disappear up the stairs.

Once inside his bedroom, he closed the door and turned to face me. My legs felt a little wobbly, so I sat down on the edge of his bed. Maybe I was more than just a little tipsy.

"What the hell are you doing?" he asked as he crossed his arms over his chest. I felt like a child being spoken to by a parent.

"Whatever I want," I shot back. I was old enough to make my own decisions and my own mistakes. I didn't have to answer to anybody, least of all him. Besides, I was having such a nice time, and he'd ruined it. I crossed my arms and glared at him.

"I told you to go and find someone special to share it with," he lectured me angrily. "Not to go to a house party, get drunk and see who you end up with."

"Who do you think you are?" I asked angrily. He remained silent.

"You know what? You don't get to lecture me," I said as I stood up. "I already have one protective brother and I don't need another one."

He said nothing, and just studied me with a glare.

"Your friend invited me to a party and I came to let loose and have a little fun. What I do and who I do it with is none of your business."

I made a move to walk past him, but he stopped me.

"I'm not trying to lecture you. It's just there are bad people out there, and you just seem so naive," he tried to explain as he ran a hand through his hair.

"I was talking to your friend," I reminded him. I couldn't understand why he was acting the way he was.

"Slater and I are not good guys," he stated cryptically. Our eyes held for a few moments in silence. His tongue flickered against his lip ring.

"I asked you to have sex with me and you told me no. That doesn't mean you get to tell me what to do," I explained. It was hard to not let my eyes drop to his tongue playing with his lip ring. I felt a flutter in my stomach as I gave him one last look before I tried to walk past him again but he grabbed my wrist gently, and I turned to face him.

"I changed my mind."

I looked at him with confusion for a moment.

"I want to take advantage of you," he whispered, the intensity of his gaze making my stomach flip.

"In a sober state," he finished as his eyes flickered to my lips as he took a step closer to me. I couldn't believe he'd changed his mind. I felt excited as I thought about what that entailed for a moment. Then I remembered the horrible sinking feeling when he'd turned me down.

"Who says the offer is still on the table?" I said, trying to stay calm even though I felt a shiver of excitement at the way he was looking at me. I had little experience with guys, so I had no idea how to handle Sin. He was lethal when he wanted something, and it seemed that he now wanted me.

Instead of answering me as I expected, he backed me up against the wall and I looked up at him nervously as he put his arms out against the wall on either side of me, effectively caging me in. For a moment his eyes held mine, then his eyes flickered to my lips. He leaned closer, and I felt a nervous shiver through me as I waited for him to kiss me. I'd never been kissed before.

The moment his lips touched mine, I swear I felt my knees quiver as I closed my eyes. The gentle pressure of his lips against mine made everything else around us disappear, and all that mattered was what he was doing to me. The kiss intensified as his tongue swept into my mouth. His tongue glided against mine as I opened my mouth wider. Unsure of what to do, I just followed his lead. The soft touch of his lip ring against my lips was strange at first, but as he kissed me harder, I forgot about it.

All thoughts fled from my mind as he wrapped his arms around me and moved his tongue against mine. His body pressed mine against the wall as my hands snaked around his neck and pulled him closer to me. I swear I felt the earth move. Then his mouth was gone, and I opened my eyes to stare up into his. I was still dazed, and he smirked at me. I was breathing hard, and so was he. There was no disputing it: I wanted him, and he wanted me.

"Tomorrow night," he stated as he reached out and caressed my cheek lightly with his knuckles.

"You've been drinking tonight, and I want you to be sober," he explained as his eyes held mine. I felt my stomach dip at his words.

"Go back downstairs and enjoy the rest of the party," he told me. "Meet me here tomorrow night."

I felt my head nod in agreement. He studied me for a moment before he pressed his lips to mine again. I left him in his room and went back downstairs. The curious looks followed me back to Slater and Jordan.

"What was that about?" Jordan asked loudly enough for me to hear over the music.

"It's complicated," I replied. I wasn't sure if I wanted to tell her what was happening between Sin and me. She wouldn't approve.

"I don't think he's done with you," Slater whispered into my ear and I gave him an awkward smile. There was no way I was going to say anything to Slater.

For the rest of the night, I enjoyed myself. I kept looking for Sin, but I never saw him again that evening.

Later when I was back in my dorm room with Jordan, she broached the subject. I let out a sigh.

"Look, I know that you don't approve, but... I'm going to give my virginity to Sin," I blurted out to her before I could change my mind. She looked at me liked I'd grown an extra head. I held up my hand because I knew what was coming next. She was going to lecture me on how bad Sin was.

"Look, it's not like I want to date or have a relationship with him. I just want to experience sex and lose my virginity. Who better to lose it to than someone who has had a lot of practice?" I argued.

"I just don't want him to hurt you," she tried to explain.

"I know you don't and he won't. It's only going to be one night," I insisted.

"Okay," she said, taking me by surprise. I hadn't expected her to say that.

That night I was restless and spent most of the night tossing and turning. The next day dragged. Time ticked by slowly and I tried to keep myself busy. I worked on an assignment, but my mind was preoccupied, and it was impossible to concentrate.

I showered and shaved my legs. It took me nearly an hour of trying to decide what to wear. I debated whether it would be better to wear a dress or not. Finally, I decided to go with a pair of jeans and a blue button-up top. The later it got, the more nervous I became.

"Good luck," Jordan said just before I left to go to Sin's

house. It was only when I was standing outside the door that I felt the nervous knots in the pit of my stomach. I took a deep breath and knocked on the door before I could change my mind. The door opened, and Sin smiled at me.

"You came," he said as if he was surprised.

"Hi," I said, unsure of what to say as he stepped back so I could enter the house. The house was quiet, and a quick scan of the living room indicated we were alone.

"Where are your roommates?" I asked as I clutched my hands together nervously.

"They're out."

We were alone. I felt my nervousness increase.

"Do you want a soda?" he offered as he kept his gaze on me. I shook my head. He studied me for a moment.

"Are you sure you want to do this?" he asked softly.

I nodded my head. I had no doubts about it even though I was nervous.

"Okay," he said as he reached for my hand. He led me up the stairs to his bedroom.

His room was neat and clean. The main bedroom lights were off, the only light coming from a side lamp on a table beside the bed. I looked at his neatly made bed. I couldn't help wondering how clean the sheets were.

"The sheets are clean," he said in answer to my unspoken question.

"Good," I said, unable to stop myself.

Feeling so nervous, I clutched my hands together. I had no idea what to do.

"Relax," he told me as he walked slowly over to me, and I held my breath.

He studied me for another moment.

"Breathe," he instructed with a smile and I remembered to let the breath out.

His hand reached for mine, and he pulled me closer to

him. His free hand went to my hip as my body came into contact with his. I looked up at him. His eyes darkened as he looked down at me. The attraction between the two of us was like an electric spark zapping between us. I wanted to run my hands over his chest, but nervousness kept my hands held tightly together so I wouldn't reach for him.

What the hell was I doing? I was so out of my comfort zone.

"I know this is your first time, and you're nervous," he said. "But you shouldn't be."

It was one thing thinking about losing my virginity and coming up with a plan to lose it. But standing in front of him actually about to do it was a whole different thing. I was too nervous to try and talk, so I kept my eyes on him while I kept silent.

"I'm going to try and make sure it feels as good as possible," he said. His words made my stomach fill with butterflies. I was finally going to experience my first time. I was nervous, excited and turned on.

His eyes flickered from my eyes to my lips and then he leaned closer. I waited with anticipation as his lips touched mine. The kiss was gentle. No longer able to stop myself, I lifted my hands and put them against his chest. As the pressure of his lips against mine increased, I felt the gentle sweep of his tongue against my lips. I opened my mouth and felt his tongue slip in.

My hands bunched his shirt as his tongue stroked mine, and my body came alive and I felt an aching need between my legs. He pulled away for a moment to unbutton my shirt and when he pushed it off my shoulders, I shrugged out of it. It dropped to the floor as his eyes caressed my body. My nipples tightened just at the way he looked at me.

He reached for the hem of his own shirt and pulled it over his head. My eyes drifted over the muscular and ripped chest. He didn't have any tattoos there. I reached out and touched his chest with my hand. His skin was smooth and soft under my fingertips as I trailed them down to his abs. Like I'd previously thought, he had a six-pack.

While I touched him, he'd been silent, watching me as the tip of his tongue flickered against his lip ring. When my eyes lifted to him, his hands settled on my hips, and he pulled me against him. The feel of his skin against mine made my skin tingle with excitement. His hands glided through my hair as his mouth covered mine. This time the kiss was harder and more intense.

The ache between my legs intensified as he sucked gently on my tongue, and I struggled with the new wants he was waking up inside me. Slowly, his hands released my hair, and I felt them move down my sides. Gently, with his hands on my hips, he walked me backward to the bed while he kissed me. I felt the bed against the back of my knees. He broke the kiss long enough to lay me down gently.

He stood for a moment and surveyed me, then he reached for the button of my jeans and released it. He unzipped them, and as he tugged, I lifted my hips to help. Moments later his jeans dropped to the floor. My eyes went to the tent in his boxers, and I couldn't help the nervousness beginning to grow at what was going to be happening next.

His eyes surveyed me for another few moments before he got onto the bed and hovered above me. He kissed me so hard I felt my toes curl. Then his mouth left my lips, and he began to slide his tongue in-between soft kisses down my neck. At a spot at the bottom of my neck, I felt a shiver run through me, and I groaned.

"Do you like that?" he murmured as he repeated the action of kissing me gently. I closed my eyes and allowed the rush of awareness to run through me.

He slowly moved lower to my breasts. He slid his tongue

down my cleavage, and I felt his hands slip under me to unclasp my bra. For a moment, I stiffened.

"It's okay," he murmured to me as he gently eased the straps off my shoulders and took it off.

His eyes took in my naked form.

"You don't have to be shy; you're perfect," he whispered as he leaned down. He took a nipple into his warm mouth and sucked gently. I felt the ache, the need for him grow. The sight of his tattooed arm against my plain pale skin was such a turn on.

"I...." was all I could stutter before his mouth closed over the other nipple. He repeated the action, and I closed my eyes as I gasped. By the time he trailed farther down to my panties, I grasped the sheet beneath my hands. His hands skimmed down my thighs and opened them gently.

"Any time you're not comfortable with something, all you have to do is tell me to stop and I will," he whispered to me. His voice was husky and velvety.

"Okay," I managed to reply when I felt his kiss just above my panty line. I bunched the sheets in my hands as I waited in anticipation.

He placed a kiss on the inside of each thigh before I felt his fingers reach for my panties and slowly eased them off me. I was naked, and I'd never felt more vulnerable. I felt my body tense.

"Relax," he instructed softly. He licked my sensitive core, and I gasped. I felt something building up, and I tried to move, unsure of what I was feeling. He kept me firmly in place as he slid a finger into me.

With his tongue and finger, he had built me up and then I felt myself explode. I bit down on my lip, but I couldn't muffle my gasp as I felt waves of pleasure hit me. I held onto the sheets as I drifted back, dazed and satisfied.

He is good!

I looked up at Sin. He hovered above me. His lips touched mine as he pressed his hard need for me against the apex of my thighs, and I ground against him. Despite the fact that I was still enjoying the after-effects of my first orgasm, I needed him inside of me.

"Are you sure?" he whispered as his eyes held mine.

"Yes," I whispered. I wanted him.

He moved to get a foil packet off the side table and tore it open. He got up and dropped his boxers on the floor. It was the first time I'd ever seen a guy naked and I couldn't help but trail my gaze from top to bottom. He was gorgeous. When my eyes settled on his member, I couldn't help thinking it was bigger than I'd expected, and I felt a little nervous about how it would fit. I tried to ignore the nerves building up inside my stomach as he moved onto the bed above me. He kissed me as he settled between my thighs.

"I'm going to go slow so I don't hurt you too much," he told me softly as I felt his tip nudge at my opening.

Nervously I nodded as his mouth covered mine while I felt him press into me. Inch by inch I felt him move deeper and then he stopped. The fullness I felt was overwhelming.

"Are you sure?" he asked, straining himself. He was giving me one last out. I pressed my lips to his as I felt him push totally into me. My breath hitched when I felt the brief pain.

"Are you okay?" he whispered as he held still.

"It's okay," I assured him. I'd expected the pain.

Slowly he moved out and then he began to enter me again. With the slow movement in and out, the pain began to ease. Then I needed to feel him, so I wrapped my legs around him.

He took my hands in his and held them above my head as he began to move faster into me. The headboard began to bang against the wall, but I didn't care. All that mattered was reaching that peak that would give me the release I needed. The friction built up inside, and I bit my lip to keep from screaming out as I climaxed for the second time.

Sin thrust into me a few more times and then I felt him tremble as he came.

I lay there not wanting to move. I just wanted to enjoy the moment as Sin kissed me one last time and rested his forehead against mine.

"For your first time, you were pretty awesome," he whispered to me.

I smiled at him.

"You weren't too bad yourself," I teased and he laughed as he rolled off me. He disappeared into the bathroom and then when he came back he lay down next to me. He pulled the covers over us. Tired and satisfied, I drifted off to sleep.

Chapter Seven

TAYLOR

When I woke up, it was still dark. I hadn't meant to fall asleep. I wasn't sure if it was okay to spend the night or not. I turned to look at Sin. He lay on his stomach, peacefully asleep. I smiled at the sleeping guy who had given me such an earth-shattering experience. My cheeks blushed at the memories of what we'd done.

I was still a little tender between my legs, but I felt empowered. I had taken control of my life and made the decision to lose my virginity. And now that I had, I felt more confident and sure of myself. Little by little I was building up the person I wanted to be, the person who lived life to the fullest. It was wasted life to hold back because of fear. I believed in the saying, "what doesn't kill you makes you stronger." I was living proof of it. Surviving a horror in my childhood had taught me that.

In the darkness, I slipped out of the bed and began to pick up my clothes. I got dressed as quietly as I could, trying not to wake up Sin. I wanted to be able to slip out without having that awkward moment with him if he woke up. Besides, what did you say to the guy who helped take your virginity? "Thank you" just didn't seem right.

Once I was done, I walked to the side of the bed. For a moment, I looked at Sin still sleeping in the bed. I smiled and let my eyes drift over him. He had been mine for one night, and I savored it for a few more moments.

Our night was over, and he wasn't mine anymore.

Quietly I slipped out of his room and made my way downstairs. The house was dark and quiet. I descended the stairs and walked to the front door.

"Leaving so soon?" I heard Slater's voice. I gasped as my heart slammed into my chest from the fright. I was still clutching my chest when I turned to glare at him. I found the outline of his form sitting in a chair in the living room.

"Do you have to keep doing that to me?" I said as I glared at him.

"Yes," he replied. "It's fun."

"What are you doing sitting in the living room in the dark anyway?" I asked.

"I couldn't sleep so I came down here. I like the dark," he replied lazily. That had been twice that he'd caught me leaving the house at an early hour.

"You don't sleep much, do you?" I asked.

"No," he replied with a sigh. An awkward silence settled between us. He wasn't going to elaborate on why he didn't sleep.

"I'd better go," I said as I turned to leave.

"Do you have a car or are you walking?" he asked.

"I'm walking." It wasn't far from the dorm.

"You can't walk home now," he said, standing up. "It's like four in the morning and it's not safe."

"I'll be fine," I tried to insist. I had a can of mace in my bag. When I'd made my decision to leave home to go to college, Connor had bought it for me. He'd insisted I carry it in my bag as a precaution.

I didn't want still to be in the house when Sin woke up. He might think I was one of those girls who couldn't let go, and I didn't want him to think that. I knew what happened between us was never going to amount to anything more than one night of great sex.

"If you insist on leaving now, I'll have to walk you," he warned in a serious tone.

"Really, I'll be fine," I insisted again, reaching for the door handle. I opened the door and stepped outside. But when I tried to close the door, Slater stopped me. He'd followed me out.

"You really don't have to do this," I said, feeling exasperated that he wouldn't listen to me.

"Yes, I do," he said with a determined voice.

"Fine," I said as I began to walk. He caught up with me and walked beside me. For a few minutes, we walked side by side in silence.

"So, what made you decide to go to college?" he asked conversationally.

I contemplated his question. I shrugged my shoulders.

"It's what most people do when they finish high school. Why did you decide to go?" I turned his question around on him. He was silent for a little while.

"Sin and I wanted to build a better future than our parents had. We grew up living next door to each other," he answered.

I glanced at him for a moment. I didn't have to read people well to see there was a lot more behind that sentence than met the eye. His answer made me want to share more with him.

"I wanted to come to college to experience all the things I never had," I added. He glanced at me.

"I've led a very sheltered life and I always felt I was missing out on those little life experiences kids my own age took for granted," I explained further.

"Sin and I had the opposite. There isn't much we haven't done," he replied. I didn't miss the sad and hard look in his face. I remembered Sin telling me that they weren't good guys, but bad guys didn't watch over a girl they didn't know because she was so out of it, and bad guys didn't walk girls home to keep them safe.

I wanted to ask him more about his childhood, but I knew if he shared more I would have to as well and I wasn't ready. When people found out about my childhood and the horror I'd faced, they treated me differently. I wanted to be treated like a normal college student, not someone who had seen the worst side of humanity and lived through it. We were silent for the rest of the short walk. Outside the dorm building, we turned to face each other.

"Thanks for walking me," I said. It didn't matter that I hadn't wanted him to.

"You're welcome," he replied. "See you around, Tay."

No one but my brother had ever called me that. I smiled at him as he turned to leave. I entered the dorm building and opened the door to the staircase. I was really beginning to get annoyed that the elevators hadn't been fixed yet.

Halfway up the stairs, I heard someone else's footsteps besides my own. I thought it was a little strange so early in the morning. Maybe someone else was also doing the 'walk of shame.' I stopped for a moment and so did the other footsteps. I hesitated for a moment, hoping to hear the footsteps again. Silence.

Strange.

I felt a slither of fear up my spine, and I hastened my steps up the stairs even though I knew I was probably blowing it out of proportion. It could be anyone. The sound of the footsteps again made me climb the stairs faster than before as I began to panic. When I got to my floor, I pushed the door open and hurried down the hallway to my room.

It was only when I got to the door of my room that I turned to look down the hallway. There was no one. I shook my head and let out a deep breath. I was doing it again. I was allowing what happened to me as a child affect me. Feeling angry with myself for reacting the way I had, I opened the door and walked into the dark room.

I kicked my shoes off and climbed into bed, hoping to get a few more hours sleep before Jordan was awake and wanting all the details from my one night with Sin. It took me a while to calm myself down enough to fall asleep. The brief scare in the stairwell had opened the lid to the dark memories I'd buried deep inside of me. And as much as I'd tried to brush it off as an overactive imagination, it had really spooked me.

My dreams turned into nightmares, and I woke up breathing hard, tangled in my sheets, with a concerned Jordan peering over me.

"It was just a dream," she soothed as she hugged my trembling body to hers. She tried to calm me with words, but it didn't work. She didn't know that they weren't just dreams —they were the real life events that I relived in my dreams. It wasn't just a nightmare that would be forgotten about. What had happened had changed my life forever. It didn't matter how much I ran or how deep I buried the memories, they had marked me forever and there was no escaping them.

Jordan peered at me over her coffee with concern as she took a sip. We were sitting in a coffee shop having something to drink. After my nightmare, I'd been trying to avoid talking about it, but she wasn't letting it go. I tucked a stray piece of hair behind my ear while I stirred my sugar into my coffee.

"So are you going to tell me what your nightmare was about?" she asked as she set her coffee cup down on the table. I knew that she thought she was helping by pushing the subject, but she wasn't. I'd been through this with enough shrinks to know that some things could be 'fixed,' but some things were scarred into your soul and there was no fixing that. You just had to learn how to live with it, and I had. Most days I was fine.

People dealt with stressful events differently. What should have crushed me made me stronger, and I promised to make sure every day counted. I'd turned it around and used it to drive me to live life to the fullest. But that didn't mean that I liked to think or talk about the event that had changed my life.

"I don't want to talk about it," I replied firmly as I wrapped my hands around my cup.

"I'm sorry. I didn't mean to push it," she said. "It's just that you're my friend, and I don't want you to hurt."

I reached for her hand and gave it a squeeze.

"I know that. I'm okay," I reassured her. "Most of the time I'm okay, it's just that something yesterday seemed to trigger it again."

"What happened?" she asked as she took another sip of her coffee. I bit my lip for a moment.

"Nothing, forget about it," I said, deciding that it was my overactive imagination working overtime. Her forehead creased slightly as she frowned.

"You sure?" she asked. I nodded my head at her.

"I'm surprised you haven't been at me for details of my night with Sin," I said, effectively changing the subject.

"I hadn't forgotten about that. I want details," she said, happily changing the subject.

"It was..." I paused for effect. "Earth shattering."

Her smile widened at my blushing face when I

remembered how good it had been.

"He just never struck me as the type to do a virgin."

Well, in the beginning he wasn't. I still didn't know what had actually made him change his mind.

"When I first asked him he turned me down," I revealed to her.

"Really," she said, looking at me curiously. "I wonder what made him change his mind."

I shrugged. I had no idea. If I thought back to our conversation, I think it was the fact that he was scared that someone with bad intentions would do what he'd refused to. I didn't know why he'd cared. The main thing was I wasn't a virgin anymore, and the experience had been amazing. My stomach fluttered at the memories.

Later that day, I was doing laundry when I realized a couple of items of my clothes were missing.

"Have you seen my purple underwear and matching bra?" I asked Jordan when I got back to the room. I thought the missing items might have gotten mixed up with her stuff because I remembered wearing them.

"No," she said, shaking her head. She was sitting on her bed with a couple of books open doing some studying.

"You can look through my stuff if you want," she offered.

"No, it's fine. I'm sure I'll find them," I mumbled as I began to look through my clothes. A half an hour search through my stuff still didn't turn up the missing items.

Connor phoned to check up on me, and I forgot about the missing underwear. We had our usual conversation. He asked me about college and my classes, and I asked him about work and his non-existent love life.

"Come on, let's go to movies," Jordan suggested a little later that day. "I can't look at another book and I'm tired of being cooped up in the room."

I was lying on my bed reading a book. I closed it and sat up.

"Sure."

The walk to the theater wasn't far. We were walking side by side when I looked up and saw Sin. The sight of him jolted me unexpectedly. He was standing just outside a popular bar that was just down the street from the movies. It was the first time I'd seen him since we'd had sex. I couldn't stop the flutter of butterflies in my stomach at the sight of him. He was dressed in jeans and a black top that emphasized the tattoo sleeve on his arm.

The fluttering butterflies died a slow and agonizing death when I spotted him chatting to a girl. The girl had long auburn hair that nearly reached her waist. She was beautiful. I didn't know if it would make me feel any better if she weren't. It probably wouldn't. It didn't matter. Pretty or not, he was with another girl.

He was just a one-night stand, and it wasn't supposed to hurt. But against all my logical thinking, it did. I wanted to look away and pretend I never saw it, but I couldn't pull my eyes away from them. Jordan slowed down beside me. Her eyes followed mine to Sin and the girl. I knew what I was getting into when I'd suggested the one-night stand, but I hadn't planned on seeing him move on to another girl the next day. It was hard to watch. He smiled at the girl, and I felt like someone had knocked the wind out of me.

Jordan gave me a sympathetic look. They were directly in our path, and I just wanted to turn around and go back to the dorm room before he saw me. But I stopped myself.

You're not going to turn around and run, I told myself. *You're going to walk past him, and you're going to say hi. And then you are going to walk away with your head held up high.*

"Do you want to go back?" Jordan asked gently, and I shook my head.

I can do this. I swallowed hard, not sure I'd be able to do it without showing how hurt I felt. I took a deep breath and expelled it.

"Okay," I said before I changed my mind and ran.

We started walking again. Sin noticed me first, and he smiled at me. It was a knowing smile, that type of smile that said he knew every inch of my body. And, well, he did. I couldn't help imagining him doing the same with the redhead he was talking to, and I felt like someone had gutted me. I gave him the best smile I could muster. It was a tight one, which never reached my eyes.

"Hi," he greeted us and the girl he'd been talking to turned around to look at us. She was dressed in a short miniskirt and a crop top that showed off her firm midriff. I felt frumpy dressed in a pair of jeans and a loose shirt.

"Hi," I said, trying to keep my voice calm, but I was feeling so much I had no idea if I was actually holding it together.

Jordan never greeted him; instead, she just nodded her head at him. I think if she'd opened her mouth she would have told him off or said something she shouldn't have. I didn't want to make a scene. I was hurt enough, and I didn't want to make a fool of myself on top of that.

"Where are you guys headed?" he asked. I didn't know if he was actually interested or if he was just making conversation.

"To the movies," Jordan said.

"Well, it was nice seeing you again, Taylor," he murmured with his gaze fixed on me.

I gave him a brief nod and pulled my eyes from him. Jordan linked her arm through mine, and we walked away. I'd been through plenty of stuff in my life that had been hard, but that had been one of the most crushing experiences of my life.

Was this a taste of heartbreak? If it was, I hoped I never fell in love to ensure I never had my heart broken. This brief encounter had hurt me and bruised my ego, but I was strong enough to pick myself up and carry on. It wasn't like Sin had done anything wrong. What we shared didn't last longer than one night together. It was my fault for getting too attached to him.

Chapter Eight

TAYLOR

When we got back from the movie, I was quiet and subdued. Jordan eyed me sympathetically, and I waited for her to say something like, 'I told you so,' but she didn't. That night as I lay in my bed staring at the ceiling in the dark, I gave myself a pep talk. I knew what I'd been getting into with Sin, and I needed to put my big-girl panties on and deal with it.

The next morning I woke up feeling emotionally lighter, and I was ready to move on to new experiences. I didn't see Sin around campus for the next couple of days. Wednesday, Caleb and I made plans to go out to the movies. I didn't want to overdress, so I settled for a pair of skinny jeans and a tight pale-blue crop top that matched my eyes. Jordan did my makeup, and I was happy when I surveyed myself in the mirror.

Caleb was waiting for me outside the dorm. He was dressed in dark jeans and white button-up shirt that he rolled up to his elbows. There was no doubt about it— he was a good-looking guy. His eyes took me in, and he smiled.

"You look beautiful," he complimented me.

"Thanks," I replied, feeling excited about our date—my first date. Like a gentleman, he opened the car door for me, and I slid into the passenger seat. I had no idea what type of car it was, but I knew it was expensive. I fidgeted nervously as he closed the door and walked around the car to get into the driver's side.

"What would you like to watch tonight?" he asked as he started up the car. I liked that he asked me that although I really wasn't that fussy.

"Anything," I replied with a shrug.

"Anything?" he questioned mischievously as he gave me a side-glance.

"Yes," I replied as I shot him a suspicious look, wondering what he was up to.

"Even a horror?" he said, lifting his eyebrows.

"Yes, even a horror," I replied, shaking my head at him. Horror movies didn't scare me because I knew they weren't real. And it was hard to get scared at them when I'd lived through real horror.

The ride to the theater was quick—so quick, in fact, we could have walked. Caleb pulled up at the front and got out of the car. It was only when I got out, and Caleb closed the door, that I saw Sin and Slater. They were standing outside the same bar where I'd seen Sin and the girl a few nights before. Was there no getting away from the guy? The bonus was that I was with a hot guy, and he wasn't with a girl. It made me feel more confident this time around.

Slater smiled at me when he saw me and I knew I couldn't just walk away without saying hello. Sin glanced from Caleb to me before giving me a tight smile.

"Hi," I greeted them and turned to introduce Caleb.

"Nice to meet you," said Slater as he shook Caleb's hand. Sin didn't. He just gave a brief nod of his head.

"Where are you guys headed?" Slater asked.

"To the movies," I replied nervously. While Slater was being friendly, Sin was being the exact opposite. I couldn't help but wonder if it annoyed him to see me out with someone else. I didn't let it play on my mind for too long because it didn't matter. I glanced down at my watch.

"We'd better go, otherwise we're going to miss the show," I told them as I reached for Caleb's hand and felt his fingers intertwine with mine. The truth was no matter how much I wanted to say that Sin didn't affect me, no matter how many times I repeated that to myself, I'd taken Caleb's hand hoping to make him a little jealous. I wanted him to feel what I had when I'd seen him with that girl. It was childish, but I couldn't help myself.

"We're having another party on Saturday. Why don't you come? Bring Caleb and your hot friend, Jordan," Slater said as Caleb and I started to walk away.

"I will," I replied as I turned to Slater and gave him a short wave. Sin was staring at me with a look I couldn't decipher, but I ignored him as I turned around. Hand in hand with Caleb, we walked away. When we entered the movie, Caleb turned to me.

"You have history with Sin?" he asked with a questioning look as he let go of my hand. Had it been a bit obvious?

"I don't think it quite qualifies as history," I said with a shrug. It wasn't history; it had been one night. One great night, but there was no way I was going into details with Caleb.

"He looked like he wanted to beat the crap out of me," said Caleb with a smile.

"Really?" I said. He'd been a bit standoffish but I hadn't noticed that. "You don't have to worry. Whatever was going on is finished."

"Good," he said, taking my hand in his. I looked at him.

"You get to choose the movie," he told me. Whatever

had happened hadn't hindered him, and I liked that. He was secure in himself.

I ended up choosing the horror. Caleb insisted on paying for everything, which I found nice. During the movie, he put his arm around me. It had been a nice date and on the walk back to the car there was no sign of Sin or Slater.

"Tell me a bit about you," Caleb said as he walked me to his car while holding my hand.

"I'm not that interesting," I said with a shrug.

"Well, what about your family?"

"My parents are dead and my older brother, Connor, raised me," I answered vaguely, leaving out any finer details. It always came up at some point in conversations, so I decided to get it over and done with quickly.

"I'm sorry," he said softly. I looked at him.

"It's okay. They've been gone for a long time," I replied. It had only been ten years, but they'd been gone for more than half of my life.

"What happened to them?" he asked.

I pressed my lips together. I didn't answer questions about my parents. There was no way I was going to tell him the truth so instead I decided to lie.

"It was an accident," I said with a shrug.

"I'm sorry," he said softly, pulling me to a stop with a gentle tug of my hand.

"It's fine, really," I said and I gave him a reassuring smile as I looked up at him.

"I had a nice time tonight," he said.

"Me too."

Caleb wasn't Sin; he didn't make me feel alive or make me hold on tight as my world spun out of control. But that excitement came with the cost of heartbreak. Caleb was the safer option. He was talkative and interesting. He was attractive, and it had been nice when he'd put his arm around me while we'd watched the movie.

He took me home, and outside the dorm building he stood in front of me. He reached for my hand and tugged me closer. I looked up at him as I took a step closer, and he leaned forward. He was going to kiss me, and I felt a flutter of excitement. His lips touched mine gently, and he pulled away. Caleb's kisses were nice.

"Did you have fun tonight?" he asked and I nodded my head at him.

"I'll meet you here on Saturday and then we can go to the party," he suggested. I'd forgotten about Slater's invitation to his party.

"That sounds good," I replied.

This time when he pressed his lips to mine he threaded his fingers through my hair and kissed me harder. I felt the tentative touch of his tongue on my lips, and I opened my mouth for him. His tongue tangled with mine, and I followed his lead as I held onto his arms. Before the kiss got too intense, he pulled away from me, a little breathless, and he smiled. I smiled back at him. He walked me to the door of the dorm and only turned to leave once I'd entered the building.

I looked at the elevator, hating the fact that it still didn't work. After the other day when I'd got a little spooked when I'd heard the strange footsteps, I felt a shiver of apprehension every time I entered the stairwell. I climbed the stairs two by two as quickly as I could and only felt safe when I reached my dorm room. Jordan was up and waiting for details about the date.

"So, how was it?" she asked eagerly.

"It was nice," I replied as I sat down on my bed and took off my shoes.

"Just nice?" she questioned.

"What's wrong with nice?" I asked.

"Did he at least kiss you?" was her next question.

"Yes," I replied. It had been a nice kiss.

"Did the earth move and did your knees go weak?" she asked expectantly. No, was the answer. I shook my head.

"That's disappointing," she murmured.

"It doesn't always have to feel that way, does it?" I asked her. I liked Caleb, and I wanted to see him again. It wasn't like we were dating or exclusive. I liked the fact that he didn't have heartbreak stamped all over him.

"We bumped into Sin and Slater on the way to the movies," I revealed to her as I began to change into my pajamas.

"And?" she asked. I had her undivided attention.

"It was a little uncomfortable," I told her honestly. "Sin seemed a bit standoffish, but Slater invited all of us to a party at their house on Saturday."

"Yeah, I bet he was. Nothing like him getting a taste of his own medicine. Who is 'all of us'?" she asked as she slipped under the covers of her bed. She was already dressed in her pajamas.

"You, Caleb and me."

Was Jordan right? Had Sin's behavior been because he didn't like seeing me with someone else? I stopped myself from letting it play on my mind. It didn't matter. We'd had a one-night stand and as good as it had been it was never going to be anything more than that. The sooner I put it behind me, the better.

"Can I ask you a question?" Jordan said once we were both settled into our beds, and the lights were off.

"Sure."

"You've been a little jumpy and high strung lately. Is everything okay?" she asked. Her question took me by surprise. She was right. I'd been on guard and nervous the past few days. I didn't want to make a big deal out of something that could just be a figment of my imagination, although I still hadn't found my missing underwear. It was like it had just vanished into thin air.

The constant feeling that I was being watched and the mysterious footsteps in the stairwell had just added to the feeling that something wasn't right. But the problem was I couldn't prove anything. I was scared that if I told her the truth she'd make me go to the cops. And at this stage I had no concrete evidence that there was something going on.

"I haven't been sleeping that well," I said, a little white lie. I told myself that if it escalated then I would tell her. There was no way I would allow the fear to dictate my life. I'd try and be careful, but I wasn't going to allow it to stop me from living my life.

I saw Sin a couple of times around college later that week. It didn't help that every time I saw him I felt a jolt through my body and the inevitable flutter of butterflies. No matter what he wore, he looked good. So I was thankful that each time I'd been walking with Caleb.

I'd briefly greeted him, and he'd returned the greeting a little stiffly. There was definitely something up with him. Then another thought struck me. Maybe it was uncomfortable to see me after having sex with me, and that was his way of keeping his distance from me. It made sense. I began to question if it was a good idea to go to the party Slater had invited us to. I shared my thought with Jordan.

"I really want to go to the party," she said. "Just ignore him. You'll have Caleb to keep you company."

I didn't want to keep her from going to the party. I had a feeling there was something going on between Jordan and Slater. That was another thought. If Jordan and Slater ended up together, I'd be seeing a lot more of Sin, and I had to get used to it. There was no point in trying to avoid him.

"Okay, we'll go," I replied.

We helped each other get ready. I decided to wear a short mini. Jordan looked stunning as usual in a pair of skinny jeans and a crop top that showed off her stomach. Caleb waited for us outside the dorm building. When I'd told him that Jordan and I planned on walking there, he'd insisted on driving us there instead.

"Hi," I greeted him as he dropped a brief kiss on my cheek. I also needed to talk to Caleb about what was going on between us and I was hoping I'd get a chance to talk to him about it at the party. I got the distinct feeling from him that he wanted more out of it than I did. He'd called and texted me. He walked with me when I saw him at college. We hadn't exactly discussed what exactly was happening between us.

I'd just assumed it was seeing each other but in a non-exclusive way. I didn't really want to be in a relationship with anyone at the moment. I was having fun with the dating thing and I didn't want to be restricted.

When we pulled up outside Sin and Slater's house, I felt a little nervous as Caleb opened the car door for me and I got out the car. It was one of the things I really liked about Caleb; he was such a gentleman.

The party was going strong, and there were a couple of people already unsteady on their feet as I entered the house behind Jordan. Caleb followed in behind me. I couldn't help scanning the crowds for Sin as we made our way to the kitchen to get drinks, but I didn't see him. We found Slater in the kitchen pouring drinks.

"You made it," he said as he pulled me into a hug, lifting me off my feet. I hugged him back.

"Yeah, we made it," I replied when he set me down on

my feet again.

"Hi," Jordan greeted him. I felt the nervous energy between the two of them as he smiled at her and said, "Hi."

Was I the only one getting a hug?

"Nice to see you came as well," Slater said to Caleb as he shook hands with him. Slater organized our drinks, and I sipped slowly on my red cup filled with whatever concoction Slater had put together.

While Caleb and I moved into the living room, Jordan remained in the kitchen with Slater. I thought the two of them looked great together. I let my eyes drift over the dancing crowd as I took another sip of my drink. The moment my eyes connected with his, I felt a shiver of awareness.

He was standing on the other side of the room, but this time he wasn't alone. I couldn't believe it still hurt to see him with another girl. Although his eyes were on me, he was listening intently to whatever the girl was saying. You'd think I'd be over it by now, but the truth was I wasn't. It also didn't help the way he looked at me. It was like he was undressing me with his eyes and I felt naked under his gaze.

Suddenly the room started to feel too claustrophobic and I was finding it difficult to breathe. I needed to get some air, and I was thankful when Jordan and Slater joined us.

"I'm going to the bathroom," I whispered to Jordan and I handed her my drink. Without another look in Sin's direction, I headed to the bathroom. Unfortunately the one downstairs was busy so I went upstairs to find another one. The bathroom was empty and I walked inside. As I turned to close the door, someone stopped me. It was Sin. He stepped into the bathroom and closed the door behind him.

I didn't know what to say; instead, I stood there open-mouthed, waiting for him to say something. His features were unreadable as he stepped forward and closed the distance between us. I licked my lips nervously under his gaze.

Then in the next moment his lips were crushing mine and his hands held my body against his. I could have pushed him away, but I didn't. Instead, I kissed him back.

Chapter Nine

TAYLOR

His tongue slipped into my mouth and I felt his hands grip my butt. My arms snaked around his neck as his tongue tangled with mine. The cool touch of his lip ring against my lip made me shiver. The next moment I felt him lift me off my feet and instinctively my legs wrapped around his hips. There were no thoughts and all I could concentrate on was the heat between our bodies and the feel of lips against mine.

He set me down on the bathroom vanity as his tongue stroked mine. His hands moved to frame my face as he kissed me with a hunger that made me shiver in anticipation. I wanted to hold onto him and let him have his way with me, but a prickle at my conscience began to nag at me. The nagging got stronger and stronger until finally I couldn't ignore it anymore and I pulled my lips from his. He rested his forehead against mine as I tried to catch my breath. We were both breathless.

"I can't," I whispered, reinforcing my conscience. I was about to go at it with Sin when Caleb was downstairs, oblivious. It was wrong.

I was going to make sure Caleb knew that we weren't

exclusive, but now I didn't think there was any point trying to date him when I clearly couldn't keep my hands off the bad-boy I'd given my virginity to. He pulled away and looked at me with a slight crease in his forehead. His still stood between my legs and his hands rested on the bathroom vanity on either side of me.

"Why?" he asked as his gaze flickered to my lips and then back to my eyes.

"Caleb," was my answer. His eyes darkened with anger and his jaw clenched as he took another step back. I immediately missed the warmth of his body against mine.

"You can't deny what's between us," he stated confidently as he crossed his arms over his chest.

"I'm not," I replied. I hopped off the counter and he took another step backward, keeping his distance from me.

"It's just—"

"What is it?" he said, cutting me off and sounding a little agitated. "Yeah, don't worry, I get it."

He turned to the door and his hand reached for the handle. I reached for his wrist to stop him from leaving. He turned to face me.

"Don't worry, I get it. You prefer the preppy, rich guys," he said angrily as he pulled his wrist free from my grasp.

I was dumbfounded and speechless as he stormed out of the bathroom. I had no idea how the conversation had gone wrong so quickly. He hadn't even given me a chance to explain. He'd jumped to his own conclusions and judged me. Before I left the bathroom, I splashed some water on my face and dried it with a towel. I was on my way back downstairs to see if I could find Sin to tell him why I'd stopped him.

I was halfway down the stairs when I spotted him kissing some random girl in the corner near the dance floor. It felt like someone had punched me in the stomach. For a few moments I stood rooted to the spot, watching him make out with a girl just minutes after he'd kissed me in the bathroom.

Well, there didn't seem to be any point in trying to explain anything to him now. I descended the rest of the stairs and found my group. By the time I took my drink from Jordan, I had masked my hurt and I took a sip of the alcohol hoping it would numb the pain inside. I tried to keep myself from looking for Sin and the girl he was with, but no matter how hard I tried I found myself watching them. He leaned closer and whispered something in her ear and she beamed up at him. I wanted to throw up.

"Are you okay?" Caleb asked with concern. I looked up at him.

"I'm starting to get a headache." I said the little white lie with ease. I couldn't stand to be there anymore; I needed to get away.

"You want to go home?" he asked as he scanned my features. I nodded my head. I was taking the easy way out.

"What's wrong?" asked Jordan when she overheard Caleb's offer.

"I'm just not feeling very well," I lied again, rubbing my temple a little to make my lie a little more believable. Out of the corner of my eye, I saw Sin kiss the girl again. I needed to leave now. I couldn't watch it anymore.

"I'm going to take her home," Caleb told Jordan as he held me by the elbow. "I'll come back later to take you home."

"Don't worry, I'll get her home safely," Slater stated. Jordan looked at him for a moment before she turned to Caleb.

"Slater will take me home," she confirmed. Caleb nodded briefly at them.

"Are you sure you're going to be okay on your own?" she asked.

"I'll be fine," I assured her.

Caleb walked in front of me and led me through the crowd of drunken people. I couldn't keep myself from looking back at Sin one last time as I walked behind Caleb. His eyes clashed with mine. His eyes flickered to Caleb before they settled back on me. He looked angry. The girl he'd been kissing stood in front of him with her arms around his waist and her head against his chest. Jealousy flared up inside of me, but I pushed it down.

I had no reason to be jealous of her. He wasn't mine, he never had been. I pulled my gaze from his as I followed Caleb out of the house. I was quiet and subdued for the ride back to the dorm. Caleb gave me a few concerned side-glances as he drove. Irrespective of what happened with Sin and me, I still needed to have a talk with Caleb.

When he pulled up in front of the dorm building, he was about to get out of the car and I stopped him.

"I need to talk to you," I began before I could chicken out.

"Okay," he replied as he turned to face me. I clasped my hands together as I suddenly became very nervous.

"You're a really nice guy," I began as I looked at him. He was good-looking and nice. He was everything any girl could want.

"But…" he prompted, obviously having a good idea where this talk was headed.

"I'm sorry. It's just...you're a great guy, you really are...you're just not the guy for me," I told him, feeling horrible that I might be hurting his feelings.

"I have to be honest. It sucks," he said as he let out a sigh. "Thanks for being honest."

I had hurt him. It was evident on his face and it made me feel terrible.

"I'm sorry," I mumbled as I put my hand on his. It sucked that I couldn't choose who I felt things for. He looked at me for a moment and he reached out and tucked a stray piece of hair behind my ear.

"Don't be sorry," he said. "Can we at least try to be friends?"

I smiled at him, my burden of guilt feeling a lot lighter.

"I'd love that," I replied.

"Come on, let's get you inside," he said as he opened his car door and got out. I climbed out the passenger side. He walked me to the door of my dorm building.

"I'll see you in class," he said as he gave me a forced smile.

"Sure," I said and then I entered the building. I turned back to see Caleb walking back to his car. It was better to hurt him now than lead him on and hurt him more.

I let out a sigh. Suddenly I was starting to develop a real headache. It had been an eventful evening and I was feeling drained. I felt nervous and skittish when I entered the stairwell. I climbed the stairs as quickly as I could. When I reached my floor I got out of the stairwell and entered the busy hallway that led to my dorm room.

Once inside my room, I lay on my bed and tried to figure out how things had gone so wrong with Sin. I couldn't stop thinking about him and the girl and why he'd stormed out of the bathroom without giving me a chance to explain anything. It made me angry that he'd just jumped to conclusions and stormed out. Minutes later he'd been stuffing his tongue down another girl's throat. I knew I should just forget about it and put it down to a lesson learned, but I couldn't.

Lying in my bed staring at my ceiling, I wished I'd stayed and talked to Sin. But then if I had stayed I wouldn't have had a chance to talk to Caleb to tell him that I didn't want to date him. I tossed and turned for another thirty minutes before I had a thought. Unlike before, I was free to do what I wanted and I could easily clear up the misunderstanding with Sin.

So what was stopping me? Nothing. I got out of bed and pulled on the clothes I'd been wearing earlier. I put some shoes on quickly and grabbed my purse and phone. It was too late to try and walk even though it wasn't far. I wasn't stupid enough to risk that especially with all the strange things that had been going on lately. I was on the phone calling for a taxi. It was late, but ten minutes later I was in a taxi and on my way to Sin's house. I glanced at the time on my phone. It was eleven. It was the one time I was really thankful that my brother had made me program a couple of taxi company names into my phone. It had been his way of trying to make sure I never got stranded.

The party was still going when the taxi pulled outside the house. I got out and for the first time since I'd made the decision, I began to question myself. Nervousness built up in the pit of my stomach. I had no idea if Sin would even give me a chance to listen to what I had to say. I took a deep breath and expelled it to try and stop myself from chickening out. Life was short and there wasn't time for indecision like this. What was the worst thing that could happen? He could refuse to talk to me and then at least I'd know I'd tried. I didn't want this moment to end up being a 'what if' moment that I would constantly question for the rest of my life.

Determined, I walked up the porch steps past a couple of happy drunk guys. One did try to put his arm around me, but I managed to maneuver out of the way. Inside, the music was still pumping and people were dancing like they didn't have a care in the world. My eyes scanned the faces as I looked for Sin, but I couldn't find him. I didn't come this far to turn around and leave, so that wasn't an option.

There was no sign of Sin and there was no sign of Jordan and Slater either. Someone stumbled against me as I stood at the bottom of the stairs deciding what to do next. I grabbed the railing to keep from falling over.

"Sorry," the guy mumbled as he stumbled toward the bathroom.

If Sin was still in the house there was only one more place he could be. Nerves and fear mingled together as I made up my mind. Before I had a chance to change my mind, I climbed the stairs quickly. The closer I got to my destination, the stronger my nerves and fear grew.

Outside his door, I paused for a moment before I knocked. There was no going back now. I heard movement on the other side of the door as I held my breath. I had no idea if he was alone or not. The door opened and Sin appeared.

"Ah, you're back," he remarked.

"I need to talk to you," I said in a calm voice, hiding the nervousness I felt. He didn't step aside to let me in. I didn't really want to have this conversation in the middle of the hallway.

He cocked his head to the side and studied me for a moment. The tip of his tongue flickered against his lip ring. Then to my surprise he stepped aside and motioned for me to enter his room. I walked inside his room and he closed the door. He turned and leaned against it and surveyed me from head to toe, which sent tingles through me. I stood a couple of feet away from him with my arms crossed over my chest defensively.

"So talk," he instructed firmly. I licked my bottom lip and his eyes fixed on the motion.

"You never gave me a chance to explain why I stopped you," I said. The tip of his tongue flickered against his lip ring again and I couldn't help thinking of what he'd done with that same tongue to make my world shatter into a million pieces. I averted my gaze for a moment to regain my hormones and when I looked up at him, I kept my eyes fixed on his so I wouldn't be distracted. I had expected him to interrupt me, but he didn't. He remained quiet with his features veiled so I had no idea what he was thinking.

"Caleb and I went out a couple of times." He didn't really need to know that it had only been once. "I didn't want to start something with you before I could make it clear to Caleb that I just wanted to be friends and nothing more."

"With me it's not 'something,' it is just sex," he stated. I felt my stomach dip at the word sex. It was what I wanted from him.

"I know," I replied.

I was going into this with my eyes wide open and my fairytale dreams of love and marriage were firmly stuffed in the back of my mind. This thing between us would be purely physical. Sex with him was so hot I couldn't pass it up. It would also give me a chance to gain experience and that was what I wanted. I waited nervously for him to say something, but he remained silent. Then he walked toward me, holding my gaze. The confidence that oozed from him was nearly enough for my panties to melt from anticipation.

"This thing with you… I want more than one night," he said softly as he stopped in front of me.

"Okay," I replied.

Then I remembered him and the girl downstairs earlier on making out. I had one rule that I had to lay down before we started anything.

"This has to be exclusive, though. I don't want you to touch another girl while this is going on between us," I explained firmly. There was no way I was going to share him while we had this arrangement in place. He mulled it over for a few moments.

"Fine. Exclusive fucking," he stated without batting an eyelid. Just what he said made me hot and aware of my own body. My body wanted him and I could feel the ache between my legs at the thought of what was about to take place.

"Any more rules you want to put in place?" he asked.

"No," I said.

"No feelings, just sex, and when it ends we walk away," he said as he took another step closer. He was so close I had to look up to hold his gaze.

"Yes."

He reached for me slowly and I waited anxiously as I felt his hands thread through my hair and I felt the butterflies begin to flutter inside my stomach as I felt his warm breath against my lips.

Then his lips touched mine. I felt his lips move against mine as I reached up and snaked my arms around his neck. His tongue swept against my bottom lip and I opened my mouth. My tongue met his as I felt his hands reach for my waist and lift me off my feet.

I wrapped my legs around his waist as he stroked his tongue against mine. I expected him to lay me down on his bed, but he didn't. Instead he opened the bedroom door and walked down the hallway to the bathroom with me still wrapped around him. Once inside the bathroom, he sat me down on the counter. He pulled his lips from mine so he could close the door and lock it. I felt nervous and unsure. He opened my legs and stepped between them.

"I want to pick up where we left off," he murmured just before he started to kiss me again. I felt his hands ride up my skirt and grip the sides of my panties. He pulled them off and dropped them to the floor.

He reached for my top and took it off, dumping that on the floor on top of my panties. My body came alive under heat of his gaze. His lips slammed against mine and I felt an excitement begin to grow as his kisses became harder and more desperate. He trailed his lips from my mouth to the side of my jaw and I groaned, loving the way that small action sent a shiver through me. This time he didn't bother to take my bra off; instead, he pulled the bra down and flickered his tongue against my nipple. I gasped at the sensation that it sent through me. He smiled as he watched my reaction. I wanted and needed him.

"Are you ready?" he whispered against my mouth as I felt his hand between my legs. He pushed a finger into me and I gasped against his mouth.

"Yes," I gasped as he slid another finger into me. I moved against his fingers, needing the release he could give me.

"Tell me what you want," he said as he pumped his fingers inside of me.

"I... want," I tried to say, but I was unsure of how to say it.

"You want me here," he said as he pressed his finger harder into me.

"Yes," I panted.

I felt disappointed when he pulled his fingers out of me but then realized what he was doing. He undid his jeans and dropped them to the floor. And then he pulled his boxers down. In his hand was a foil packet that he opened with his teeth, and then rolled on the protection that had been inside. I gripped the edge of the counter as he leaned forward and kissed me hard. With his hands, he opened my legs wider and then he stepped between them.

I felt him push against me. I held my breath as he entered me slowly at first. He gripped my butt and pulled me closer to the edge of the counter as he slid totally inside of me. The feeling of him inside of me gave me a sense of fullness.

"I can't take it slow," he murmured in warning as he pulled back and thrust back inside me harder. "I need to fuck you," he rasped as his fingers dug into my hips, holding me in place as he slammed into me harder.

I panted as I held onto the counter when he began to pound against me. But as hard as he was thrusting into me, I needed him to do it harder.

"Harder," I told him, feeling the buildup inside that needed release.

His actions built me up. He brushed his tongue over his bottom lip as he watched me with fascination. Then I exploded and I felt my body shudder against his. His actions became more frenzied and he pushed into me a few more times before I felt him reach his peak. Afterward, I leaned against him for a moment as I struggled to catch my breath.

Chapter Ten

TAYLOR

Sin dispensed with the condom while I got off the counter and grabbed my panties off the floor. I felt nervous as I slid them on again and Sin pulled up his boxers and jeans. It was a little awkward and I wasn't sure what to say.

"It's hard to believe you haven't done this much," he said as he stood before me. I shrugged, unsure of how to respond to that comment.

"I'd better go," I mumbled, feeling nervous and awkward as I reached for the door handle of the bathroom and opened the door.

"It's too late," he said as he stopped me with a hand on my wrist. "Besides, I'm not finished with you yet."

My stomach fluttered at the last comment and I ran my tongue along my bottom lip as my eyes met his. I let him lead me by the hand back to his bedroom. Inside his room, he released my hand and walked over to get his phone from his desk.

"What's your number?" he asked.

I gave him my number and he programmed it into his phone. Once he was done, he put his phone back down on the table.

"Give me your phone," he instructed and I handed it to him. He programmed his number into mine. I wasn't sure how this arrangement between us was supposed to work. Did we call each other when we had an itch to scratch? The only way I was going to know was to ask him the questions.

"So how does this work?" I asked as he handed my phone back to me. His eyes darkened as he looked at me. It was the same way he looked at me when I was naked beneath him and wanting more. It made me feel so aware of my body when he looked at me like that.

"Whenever we need relief, we call each other," he began to explain and I felt myself blush slightly. He smirked at me as he took a step closer. He reached out and caressed my cheek with his knuckles.

"And no hooking up with other people," he said, voicing the rule I'd put into place. "No feelings, just mind-blowing sex. And when we're done, we both walk away."

He leaned forward and kissed me. His tongue pushed into my mouth and tangled with mine. I felt my toes curl. His kiss was hard and seductive. My hands reached out and splayed across his hard chest.

We'd just had sex and I couldn't believe that I felt that ache of need between my legs so fast after the last time. I wanted him again. As he kissed me he walked me backward until my knees felt the bed and he lay me down and covered my body with his.

That night he made me shatter two more times and afterward, sated and tired, I closed my eyes and drifted off to sleep with Sin lying naked beside me.

It was still dark when I woke up. I tried to move and realized something heavy was keeping me in place. Sin was sleeping on his stomach with his arm wrapped around my waist and his leg placed over mine. I wanted to stay there wrapped up nice and warm in his arms, but this wasn't part of our arrangement. Cuddling wasn't part of what we'd decided and if I was going to keep my heart intact, I needed to remember that.

Besides, if I waited till the sun came up and Sin woke up with me still in the bed, I might come across as wanting more than we'd agreed. I slipped out of the bed as quietly as possible without making sudden movements so Sin remained sleeping and oblivious to my departure. I got dressed as quickly as I could and I left without waking him.

Downstairs, I looked for Slater. But unlike the previous two times, he wasn't there. He was probably getting some sleep. I let myself out and called a taxi. It was three in the morning and I waited nervously outside in the dark for about fifteen minutes before the taxi arrived.

Back at the dorms, I entered the stairwell as usual with the fear sitting in the pit of my stomach. At the first sound of the additional echoing of footsteps below me, my heart began to pound in my ears as I rushed quicker up the stairs.

The faster I rushed up the stairs, the faster the mysterious footsteps echoed behind me. It wasn't a part of my imagination—there was someone in the stairwell and they were chasing me up the stairs.

I panicked as I climbed the last step and rushed to the door that would lead me to safety. I opened the door and stepped through just as I heard footsteps behind me. Scared, I ran down the hallway to the door to my room. I didn't look back to see if the person had followed me into the hallway.

I opened the door and entered the room quickly. I closed the door and locked it. Scared and breathless, I leaned against the door. For what felt like forever I listened for the footsteps but there was nothing and after a little while I pushed off the door and switched the lights on.

Jordan's bed was still made, which meant she had slept out. I wondered if that had something to do with Slater. Jordan was a lot more experienced than I was and I hoped that she knew what she was doing. Slater was very much like Sin. They had issues and they weren't the type of guys who made good boyfriend material. I knew what I was getting into with Sin and I hoped she did too.

It was only as I reached for my pajamas that I saw my purple underwear that had been missing neatly spread out on my bed. The bra was placed above the panties. As I took another step closer, I put my hands over my mouth to smother a scream.

Written on the panties and bra in some sort of red marker was the word 'whore.'

Horror and fear shivered down my spine. Someone had been in the room. Then the realization hit me. That person had to have been in my room twice, once to steal the underwear and the second time to put it on my bed.

The fact that someone had been in my personal space twice made me step back and I felt like I was going to throw up. I stepped back until I felt Jordan's bed against the back of my legs. I sank down on the bed, unable to allow what was happening to sink in.

Why would someone do this? I studied the word 'whore.' Why would they write something like that on my underwear? It made no sense. I rubbed my forehead as I tried to figure out why someone would do this to me. Did they somehow know about Sin and me? Is that why they had written 'whore'? Was it possible it was a jealous previous liaison of Sin's who was jealous?

I crept onto Jordan's bed too scared to switch the light

off to try and get some sleep. Most people in the same situation would have called the campus police but I wanted to keep a low profile. I feared they would recognize my name. For hours I sat with my back against the wall, looking at the offending piece of clothing that lay on my bed.

I tried to figure out what I was going to do about it. If I let my brother know, he'd be on the first plane here and he'd try and make me go back home or he'd hire a bodyguard to watch over me. I couldn't let that happen. I wanted to have my own life where I made my own decisions.

If this person had been prepared to break into my room more than once and steal my underwear, would they be prepared to do more? Would they try and hurt me? Maybe I was blowing this out of proportion. Perhaps this was somebody's idea of a joke, as sick as it was. I decided then and there that I wasn't going to allow this to dictate my life. I took a deep breath and released it as I stood up and walked over to the underwear.

I made my decision as I crunched up the underwear in my hand and threw it in the trashcan. I wasn't going to let someone scare me. I was stronger than this. I wasn't going to tell anyone, but I was going to be more careful. No more returning back to the dorms at night or early morning. I had to make sure I always had someone around. With my mind made up, I began to feel better.

"So where have you been all night?" I asked Jordan when she returned a couple of hours later.

"I was with Slater," she replied sheepishly. I knew there was something up with the two of them.

"And did you get lucky?" I teased her, wiggling my eyebrows suggestively. She shook her head at me as she walked over to her bed and lay down.

"No, we just talked."

"You mean to tell me that you spent all night with him and nothing happened? You just talked?" I asked, shocked that things hadn't gone further between the two of them.

"Yes, we just talked," she confirmed and tried to stifle a yawn. Well, that was unexpected. I couldn't stop myself from yawning. I hadn't been able to get any sleep. Despite my logic, I couldn't shake the nervous fear that had settled in my stomach.

"And why are you so tired?" she asked with an arched eyebrow.

"Because I was having mind-blowing sex with Sin," I admitted with a smug smile. I had already decided I wasn't going to tell anyone about finding the underwear on my bed.

"More than once," I added as my smile widened. When I remembered our night together, my stomach fluttered with excitement. She looked at me with confusion.

"But you went home because you weren't feeling well," she argued, trying to figure out how I'd ended up with Sin.

"Yeah, I did. It's a long story. All you need to know is that Caleb and I are just friends and Sin and I are... something."

I couldn't say we were friends with benefits because we weren't friends, so the only way to term it was 'acquaintances with benefits.'

"Really?" she asked, sitting up. I definitely had her attention.

"Yes," I confirmed. "We agreed that while we have this arrangement in place, we won't fool around with anyone else. And when we've both had enough, we walk away and no one gets hurt."

"You really think it's going to work?" she asked. I could see she wasn't convinced that it was a good idea.

"Yes, I do," I replied. I was living my life and I was enjoying every moment of it.

The next couple of days passed quickly. Between classes and studying, I was very busy. It also wasn't helping that I wasn't sleeping well. Despite trying to ignore what happened with the underwear, I couldn't shake the feeling that it was something more than a jealous ex of Sin.

Caleb and I had transitioned back to being friends quickly. Maybe it was because we hadn't really dated for that long. He was funny and easy to be around. I didn't see him much outside of class, but around college I saw him quite often.

One afternoon after class we were walking down the hallway. We stopped for a moment and he told me something that made me laugh and I touched his arm. As I lifted my eyes, they clashed with Sin. Just the sight of him was enough to take my breath away.

Even dressed in a faded pair of jeans and a plain white shirt, he looked smoking hot. He was leaning against the wall. His gaze was dark and brooding as he watched Caleb and me. I gave him a tentative smile, but he didn't smile back. I hadn't seen him since our night together and I wasn't sure how to act around him. I wondered if I should go up to him and greet him, but his lack of response to my smile made me stop myself.

Maybe talking to each other outside of when we met up to have sex was not included in our arrangement. Noticing my distraction, Caleb's eyes followed mine to Sin. Sin was openly staring at me and Caleb looked back to me.

"I know you have history with him, but I think you should stay away from him," Caleb warned and I felt myself bristle at what he said. I tried to calm my irritation down.

I wondered how Caleb would react if he knew exactly how close I'd been with Sin. I had to stop the secret smile from touching my lips. Caleb didn't need to know anything about my personal life. So I kept quiet. I didn't want to make a big deal out of it. I didn't have to explain my actions to anyone. I did what I wanted, what made me happy. That was all that mattered. I wasn't going to allow everyone else's opinions sway my own decisions.

Irrespective of the tattoos and piercing and the 'don't give a fuck' attitude, I believed there was more to him. The fact that he'd watched over me the night someone spiked my drink showed me that there was more to him than the bad-boy that everyone else saw.

I glanced in the direction of Sin to see him push off the wall and walk toward us. This was going to be interesting.

"Hi," Sin greeted me first and gave me that sexy smile of his. Suddenly I felt tongue-tied and shy. It was ridiculous.

"Hi," I managed to reply huskily. Caleb touched my arm and it reminded me that we weren't alone. They gave each other a brief nod of the head while they sized each other up.

"I need to talk to you," said Sin, breaking the awkward silence that had settled between the three of us.

"Sure," I said to him. I turned to Caleb.

"I'll see you tomorrow," I said. Caleb gave me a smile and then turned to glare at Sin. Sin held his gaze and glared back. These two didn't like each other at all and they made no pretense about it.

"I'll see you tomorrow," Caleb echoed to me before he turned and left.

I turned to give Sin my attention, expecting him to say something to me, but he just took my hand in his and began to walk down the hallway in the opposite direction of Caleb.

Once we turned the corner he opened the door to the

janitor's closet and pulled me inside. He closed the door behind us. The room was dimly lit. I was about to ask Sin what he wanted to talk about when he pushed me against the wall and covered my mouth with his.

It took me by surprise. I threaded my fingers through his hair as his hands rested on my waist. He kissed me hard and I groaned. As I opened my lips slightly, he slipped his tongue inside and caressed mine.

The fact that we were in a closet and could be discovered at any moment didn't register with me. There were no thoughts. All that mattered was the feel of his lips against mine.

He lifted me by the waist and my legs wrapped around his hips. His lips trailed from my mouth to my jaw. Then his tongue flickered to the sensitive spot below my ear and I held on to him as I gasped. The ache between my legs intensified. I needed him now.

With his body he kept mine against the wall as his hand slipped between my legs. I was so wet now that my panties were soaked. He ran his finger lightly over the material as I pushed against him, needing more. He moved the material of my panties aside and pushed a finger into me. I gripped his shoulders as I moved against his hand. He slid another finger into me and pumped harder. He kissed me hard as I moved more desperately against his hand. The ache between my legs became unbearable.

"Please," I whispered huskily.

He stopped for a moment and eased his fingers out of me. Slowly, he eased me down onto my legs. I was scared he was going to walk away, but instead he got a foil pack out of the back pocket of his jeans and tore it open. Quickly he unbuttoned his jeans, letting them drop to the floor as he pushed his boxers down and rolled on the protection.

Then he kissed me and lifted me by the butt. My legs

wrapped around his waist again and he leaned me against the wall as I felt him push against me. I gasped as he slid into me in one smooth stroke and he groaned against my lips. I held onto his shoulders as he began to fuck me against the wall. It was hot and hard. His expression was unreadable as he watched me hold on desperately to him as I felt the build up to my orgasm.

I gripped his shoulders and bit down on my lip to stifle a scream as I came. He slammed harder into my body as he began to reach his own release. A few more frantic thrusts and I felt his body tremble against mine.

We were both breathing hard as he eased me down to stand. My legs felt wobbly as I leaned against the wall for a moment. His arms were stretched out on either side of me as he rested his forehead against mine. His lips touched mine again, but this time the kiss was gentle. Then he pulled away and dispensed with the condom. As he pulled up his boxers and jeans, I smoothed down my skirt and tried to tidy my hair.

It was the first time that it registered we'd just been at it in a public place. He didn't look at me again as he buttoned up his jeans. I was unsure of what to say to him so I kept quiet. Then without saying a word to me, he opened the closet door and walked out.

Chapter Eleven

TAYLOR

I touched my slightly swollen lips as I stood alone in the janitor's closest. Sin hadn't said one word to me the entire time. I knew we had an arrangement in place, but I couldn't help feeling taken aback by his behavior. Was this really how this type of arrangement was supposed to work?

The sex had been awesome, but I'd felt the lack of connection between the two of us. It was a good thing my classes were finished for the day because after that I was still feeling a little dazed.

On my way back to my dorm room, I saw my brother leaning against a car with his arms crossed over his chest. Normally he dressed in a suit and tie, but this time he was dressed casually in jeans and button-up blue shirt. His hair was the same color as mine but his eyes were green. My mom had been the one with the blond hair and blue eyes. The green eyes he'd inherited from our dad.

What the hell is he doing here?

I was annoyed. I loved my brother, but sometimes his protectiveness over me was stifling. There was no way I believed he was here on business. He was here to check on me and I resented it. I walked closer. He saw me and smiled. He pushed off the car and walked to meet me as I came to a stop in front of the doors to the dorm.

"Hi," he greeted as he pulled me into a hug. I hugged him back.

"What are you doing here?" was the first question I asked as he released me from the hug.

"A brother can't just drop in to visit his sister?" he asked.

"Visit, yes; check up on, no," I told him, eyeing him suspiciously.

"Isn't it the same thing?" he asked in a teasing tone.

"No, it isn't," I informed him. He glanced down at his super-expensive watch.

"Are you hungry?" he asked.

"Yes," I answered.

"Come on, let's go get something to eat," he suggested. I didn't want to go off campus to eat so I suggested a small coffee shop close to where we were.

"Sounds good," he said as we walked side by side. There were several moments of silence.

"Why don't you see if your roommate is available to join us?" he suggested. I turned to glare at him. I knew exactly what he was up to and I wasn't having it.

"That's what this is about?"

I was fuming.

"You wanted to check my roommate out," I said. I was really angry now. He didn't answer.

"I love you, but I won't tolerate you meddling in my life," I told him.

"Is it so bad that I want to protect you and keep you safe?" he argued back. He was using that parental tone with me and I hated it. He wasn't my parent; he was my brother.

Our parents had died when I was nine and Connor had been eighteen. Overnight he'd been thrust into the role of my guardian and it had been a lot of responsibility for a young adult. My parents had left us some money, but Connor had wanted me to have the best. It had been the driving force behind his success. But it didn't mean he could dictate my life when he felt like it. I understood why he acted the way he did, but he needed to let go of me so I could make my own decisions and live my own life.

"You've probably already done a background check on her. What more would you need to know?" I informed him, crossing my arms over my chest defensively.

He didn't reply so I knew I was right. He pressed his lips together as he held my gaze.

"She is nice and I like her. That's all that counts," I told him. I wasn't trying to be difficult, but my brother was a force to be reckoned with and if he put his mind to something he usually got his way. But this wasn't something I was prepared to give up.

Connor would have a fit if he knew about all the weird stuff that was happening lately. Then I thought about Sin. If my brother knew what I was doing with the bad-boy, he'd have a stroke. I couldn't stop the secret smile that tipped my mouth at what we'd just done in the janitor's closet.

"I just don't want anything to happen to you," he told me in a soft voice. It tugged at my heart. I reached out, taking his hand into mine and I gave it a gentle squeeze.

It wasn't like our parents had just died and all we had to deal with was the grief of their loss. It had been so much more. He'd nearly lost me before and I knew that drove him to be so protective of me.

"Come, let's go and get something to eat," I said as I pulled him gently by the hand.

As I turned to walk to the coffee shop I'd suggested to my brother, I saw Sin standing across the road. The moment my eyes met his, I felt the butterflies flutter in my stomach.

His gaze dropped from my eyes to my hand holding my brother's. I didn't realize what was going through his mind until he shook his head, turned and walked away. Had he got the wrong idea?

"Who was that?" my brother asked, pulling me out of my own little bubble I'd been in. There was no way I wanted my brother to know about Sin.

"No one," I lied easily.

I wanted to go after Sin and explain that he'd gotten the wrong idea, but I couldn't do that with my brother watching so instead I continued walking to the coffee shop with my brother walking beside me, preoccupied. We got some coffees and sandwiches at the coffee shop. I tried to keep the conversation light and talked mainly about my classes. I didn't mention anything about what I did after classes.

"I've got a couple of things I need to do," my brother said as I walked him back to his car. "I'll be back later to say goodbye."

He was getting a flight out again that night.

"Sure," I said as I leaned in to give him a kiss on the cheek. "I'll see you later."

He gave me a brief hug before he got into his car and drove off. I sighed with relief. Being under his scrutinizing gaze had been mentally exhausting.

Sin.

I reached for my phone and searched for his number. He'd put his number into my phone simply under the name Sin. I took a deep, nervous breath as I called him. It rang and finally went to voicemail. I hung up. I tried to keep myself busy so I wouldn't just sit there on the bed with my phone in my hand, wishing Sin would call me.

My brother called at seven that evening to tell me he was outside my dorm. I was starting to feel despondent because I hadn't heard anything from Sin. In my mind I came up with different excuses as to why he hadn't called me back yet, but they had all seemed weak. I walked out of the building to see my brother standing beside his car. My eyes narrowed at the thick brown folder he held in his hand.

"Hi," I said cautiously as I looked at the offending folder in his hand.

"Hi," he said, sounding resigned. He stood up and handed me the folder. "This is for you."

"What is it?" I asked, but I already knew it was a background check.

"It's a background check on Sin Carter," he answered, watching me for a response. I felt my temper spark to life. I didn't even have to ask how my brother had gotten his name. There weren't too many guys on campus who looked like Sin and if he asked around, someone would have given him a name. I knew my brother hadn't believed me when I'd told him I didn't know Sin. Lying had been a waste of time.

"I don't want it," I insisted, shaking my head as I struggled to contain my anger and the blatant invasion into my life.

"You need to read this," he insisted. "He is a bad guy and he isn't someone you should be around."

I remained tight-lipped and silent.

"I know you're old enough to make your own decisions. But make sure you know all the facts before you do," he argued.

I couldn't wait to get rid of my meddling brother so after he handed me the folder and got into his car, I felt relieved. I was determined not to read it. I'd just taken it to get my brother off my back. Back in my room, Jordan arched a questioning eyebrow as I shoved the offending folder in the drawer of my small desk.

"What was that?" she asked.

"Nothing."

It had been a constant battle to get my brother to stop interfering in my life and I wouldn't allow him to now. I couldn't stop him from doing a background check, but I didn't have to look at what he'd had found. The part that Sin played in my life was nobody's business but my own. I wasn't even sure he still wanted to play the part anymore after he'd seen me with my brother.

I think he might have gotten the wrong idea. One of the rules of our arrangement had been that we were exclusive. I picked up my phone and couldn't stop the disappointment I felt when I saw I'd received no calls or text messages from Sin. Sighing, I dropped my phone back on the bed and rubbed my hands over my face.

"You okay?" Jordan asked.

"Yeah, I'm fine."

I was determined not to allow my brother's surprise visit to cause havoc in my life. I loved my brother, but there were times I could happily wring his neck.

That night, I couldn't sleep. I kept picturing Sin's expression when he saw me with my brother. I wanted to pretend nothing had happened and our arrangement was still intact.

The next day, I went about my day feeling tired. I kept looking at my phone wishing it would ring and I had to stop myself a few times from dialing his number again.

"What were you doing last night when you should have been sleeping?" asked Caleb in a teasing tone after our class. I suppressed a yawn as I walked beside him.

"I wish it had been that exciting. Truth is I just couldn't sleep," I admitted with a shrug. There was no way I was going to tell him the truth.

Friday night, Jordan told me we'd both been invited to another party at Slater's house. I had no idea how they could afford to throw a party nearly every single weekend. I wrestled with the fact that I still hadn't heard anything from Sin and I wasn't sure going to a party at his house was such a good idea.

"Come on, you have to go," she tried to persuade me.

If I went to the party and Sin was still trying to avoid me, it would be awkward and weird.

"I can't," I replied, keeping to my decision not to run after Sin. I was sitting on my bed with a book open trying to get some studying in. The truth was I'd been looking at the same page for thirty minutes, but I hadn't been able to concentrate on it. Jordan looked disappointed.

"Did something happen between you and Sin?" she asked. It didn't take a rocket scientist to see I'd been preoccupied for the last couple of days.

"I'm not sure," I replied honestly with a shrug.

"Do you want to talk about it?" she asked.

"Not really," I answered. I didn't know if there was something wrong. It might have been just in my head.

"How are you getting to the party?" I asked as I watched Jordan put the last touches on her makeup.

"When I texted Slater to tell him you wouldn't be coming, he insisted on coming to pick me up," she revealed.

I was relieved that I didn't have to worry about how she was going to get to the party. It wasn't safe to walk alone.

Then I thought about the underwear on my bed. I wasn't even safe in my own room. Most people would probably be too scared to be on their own in a room that had been invaded by a stranger, but I'd experienced far worse than that and it took a lot to scare me. Besides, there were other girls in the dorm so I wasn't exactly alone.

I was determined not to allow it to impede on my life. Twenty minutes later, Jordan said goodbye and hurried downstairs, leaving me on my own. I was dressed in a pair of old tracksuit pants and an oversized shirt that I'd swiped from my brother. It was old and even though it had a couple of holes in it I loved it. It was comfortable.

After another ten minutes of trying to study and getting nowhere, I closed my book. There was no point in trying to study because no matter how hard I tried I couldn't concentrate. I took out my e-reader and began to look for something to read. I loved romance books. I settled on one I'd read countless times before.

I'd just gotten a few pages in when I heard a soft knock against my door. I put my e-reader down beside my bed and went to answer the door. I hadn't been expecting anyone. A nervous feeling settled over me as I walked over to the door. If it were the same person who had broken into my room before, would they knock? I shook my head as I realized how ridiculous I was being.

I opened the door. Sin was standing there with his hands shoved into the front pockets of his jeans. He was dressed in his usual look, faded jeans and a plain shirt. I felt the flutter in my stomach at the sight of him. I hadn't expected to see him. The fact that he hadn't contacted me had spoken volumes. But him coming here put that whole theory up in the air.

"I could have been a rapist or a murderer and you just opened the door without asking who it is," he lectured me with a crease in his forehead.

"If it's my time to go it's my time to go," I replied. He studied me for a moment.

"That is a strange outlook to have," he said.

I shrugged. I wasn't going to explain why I had that outlook. We were exclusively having sex, we weren't seeing each other or dating. For a few awkward moments we stood silently.

"Aren't you going to invite me in?" he asked.

"Are you going to rape or murder me?" I asked in a teasing tone.

"Not tonight," was his comeback. I stepped aside so he could enter and closed the door behind him. Suddenly I felt self-conscious in my comfy clothes. He looked around the room and turned to face me.

"Why are you here?" I asked as I tucked a stray stand of hair behind my ear. His eyes held mine for a moment as I bit down on my bottom lip.

"I was expecting you to come to the party with Jordan," he said. I wasn't going to explain to him why I hadn't gone.

"I wanted to talk to you," he said.

"So when I didn't show, you came here?" I asked.

"Yes," he said as he nodded his head. His tone was serious.

Was what I'd expected for the last few days about to happen? He was going to break our arrangement and move onto someone else.

I'd expected to feel a little hurt and for my confidence to take a slight dent, but I felt way more than that at the realization he was going to end things with me. As much as I'd tried to keep my heart out of this, I cared more than I wanted to admit even to myself and I wasn't ready to let go yet.

"So talk," I instructed him as I crossed my arms. His tongue played with the one lip ring for a few moments as he studied me.

"I wanted to apologize for the other day," he said, taking me by surprise. First off, I didn't see Sin as one to apologize and secondly, I had no idea why.

Chapter Twelve

TAYLOR

I remained quiet, waiting for him to continue.

"I didn't mean to be so rough the other day in the janitor's closet," he began to say. I didn't remember rough sex; I remembered frantic earth-shattering sex. What had hurt me was the fact that he hadn't said a word and then he'd just left.

"I liked it," I responded honestly. His nervous exterior evaporated and in its place was the confident bad-boy I was used to. He smirked at me.

"I'll remember that," he said, sounding a little husky. His eyes dropped to my lips and then he pulled his gaze back to my eyes.

Being under his intense gaze that seemed to pierce right through me, I swallowed hard. The air between us was charged with sexual tension. I wanted him and I knew he wanted me, but I wasn't ready to give in yet. He still had some explaining to do.

"Why did you just leave without saying a word?" I asked. I didn't care if it made me sound like an emotional girl. It had hurt me and I wanted him to explain why he'd done that. He contemplated my question for a few minutes.

"I'm very territorial," he began. "I don't like to see the girl I'm fucking being hit on by another guy."

I had mixed feelings about his explanation. I knew the score and I knew that what we had wasn't based on feelings—it was based on a physical need for each other. But despite the fact that my mind accepted it, my heart hurt a little when he referred to me as the girl he was 'fucking.' That was one of the first signs that our arrangement was starting to mean more to me than it did to him. My mind was telling me to walk away before he had the power to cripple me with the heartbreak that was inevitable, but I just couldn't.

"Caleb wasn't hitting on me," I replied. "He is just a friend."

"Are you sure *he* knows that?" he asked me, looking skeptical.

"Yes," I stated. Caleb would never be more than a friend whether Sin was in the picture or not.

"Who was the other guy you were with?" The question came out of the blue.

"He's my brother," I answered, watching him for a reaction but there wasn't one. "When we put rules in place for this arrangement, we both agreed that we would be exclusive."

"I know, it's just like I said before...I'm territorial," he explained with a shrug of his shoulders. The way he said it made my stomach flutter at his possessiveness. There was something sexy about him feeling that way about me, even if it didn't involve actual feelings.

"When I agreed to being exclusive, I meant it," I assured him. There was no way I would be fooling around with someone when I had Sin to take care of my needs. There would come a time when I'd need more than just sex and then I'd have to move on but, until then, I was going to enjoy what I had with Sin. He remained silent and gave me a brief nod.

"Have you eaten yet?" he asked.

I shook my head.

"Do you want to go and get something to eat?" he asked, shocking me a little. Exclusive sex didn't involve going out and eating together.

"It's just food, not a date," he assured me. My thoughts must have been evident on my face.

"Sure," I agreed. I liked being around him, so why not? "I just need to get some other clothes on."

He ran his eyes over my body.

"You look fine," he replied.

"I need five minutes," I told him, unconvinced that I looked 'fine.'

"Meet me downstairs when you're ready," he instructed as he turned and left. I let out a nervous sigh as the door closed behind him. The room felt empty without his presence. I got dressed into a pair of jeans and a shirt. I slipped on a pair of sandals and ran a brush through my hair. There was no time to bother with makeup so I just put some lip-gloss on.

Despite what he said about it not being a date, I couldn't help but feel nervous as I took the stairs. He was leaning against a smart-looking car when I exited the building. The car was some sort of expensive Jeep. I wasn't sure what type of model it was, but I knew it was expensive. I wondered where he got the money for it because he didn't seem like the typical rich kid. He opened the passenger side for me and I slid inside the car. The car smelled like leather inside.

"I know a little place close by that makes killer burgers,"

he said as he got into the car.

"Sounds good," I replied, fidgeting with my hands.

Being with him made me feel nervous and aware of the effect that he had on me. I ran my tongue over my bottom lip as I remembered what he'd done to me in the janitor's closet. The car ride was fairly quiet and before I knew it he was pulling up in front of some old burger joint I'd never been to before. It looked a little run down. The sign above it looked like it had seen better days and only half of the name lit up. It was small inside with only a few tables and chairs.

"It might not look like much, but they make the best burgers," he assured me as he helped me out of the passenger side by taking my hand. The small gesture made the butterflies in my stomach flutter with excitement.

We walked in and gave our orders at the counter and Sin paid for the food. I hadn't expected that. Just before I'd left, I'd stuffed my phone and money into my back pocket. Sin held our drinks and straws in his hand as he walked to an empty table. It wasn't like the place was really busy. There were only two other people sitting at another table eating their burgers. I had to admit the burgers did look good.

"So why did you decide to go to college?" he asked as we sat down at a table and he handed me my soda and opened up his.

"It just seemed to be the next logical step," I said with a shrug. "What made *you* decide to go to college?"

"I wanted to prove I could do it," he answered.

"Who are you proving it to?" I asked the personal question not sure he would answer me.

"Myself."

"Why?" I asked the next logical question. He pressed his lips together for a moment.

"It's a long story," he replied. In other words, he didn't

want to talk about it. "I want to know more about you," he prompted, trying to steer the conversation back onto the subject of me.

"What do you want to know?" I asked with a shrug. His question had made me a little apprehensive. It was the same feeling I got when people were prodding too close to the past that I didn't want to reveal.

"Tell me about your family," he suggested as he fidgeted with the straw. I wanted to be able to tell him enough to keep his curiosity satisfied but not enough for me to be scared that he would look at me differently.

"My parents are dead," I said without emotion. His eyes looked at me sympathetically.

"That sucks," he said.

"Yeah, it does," I agreed. "My brother Connor looked after me."

That was about as much as I wanted to reveal.

"How did your parents die?" He asked the question I'd been dreading. I didn't want to tell him the truth so my only alternative was to lie.

"They died in a car accident," I lied effortlessly.

"My father died," he stated out of the blue as his eyes dropped from mine to the straw he was still fidgeting with.

"I'm sorry," I said automatically. It was what you said to people when they told you something like that.

"It's okay—he was an asshole," he informed me as he met my gaze. There was a story behind that statement and I wasn't sure if he was ready to tell me yet. Sin seemed to tense once he'd mentioned his father.

"So how long have you and Slater been friends?" I asked, trying to change the subject to lift his mood. At the mention of Slater, his mood changed and he smiled.

"We used to live next door to each other and we've been

friends from the time we could walk," he told me. I hadn't known them for that long, but I could see the type of friendship they had went deeper than a conventional friendship. It was like they were family.

"Do you have any siblings?" was my next question.

"No, I'm an only child," he replied. My life would have been very different if I'd been an only child. As annoyed as I got with Connor's overprotective nature, I was glad I had him. Our burgers arrived and we began to eat.

"Mmm," I sighed as I took a bite of the food. He was right, it was so good.

"I told you," he said with a smile. Most of the time he was intense, but for those brief few minutes he was relaxed and easy-going. I liked to see this new side to him.

He didn't seem to be the type to open up so the fact that he'd told me a few things about himself made me feel just a little bit closer to him. He seemed to be less the 'hard bad-boy' persona and more just a boy who had problems like everyone else.

After we finished our burgers we walked back to his car. It had been a nice and unexpected evening. By the time we got back to the dorm, it was really late. He got out of his car and walked me to my dorm building. I was nervous because I wasn't sure what happened next. I turned to face him.

"Thank you, that was nice," I said, thanking him for the non-date.

"You're welcome," he said. The relaxed and easy-going Sin was gone. The intense bad-boy was back. I could see it in his eyes. I didn't want him to leave. I wanted him to stay.

"Do you want...to come in?" I asked, nervously brushing my hair from my face. He stepped forward, putting his body so close to mine. I lifted my eyes up to his. His hand cupped the back of my head as he leaned forward and touched his lips to mine. My hands flattened against his chest as his tongue twirled against mine. He pulled away.

"If I come in, we won't be talking," he murmured against my lips.

"I know," I replied, wanting him just as much as he wanted me. I had no way of knowing if Jordan was still out or if she would be coming back to the dorm tonight.

"I need to get something from my car."

"I'll meet you upstairs," I said, feeling the flutter of butterflies. I was glad I'd have a few minutes to send Jordan a text message to let her know I was having company. He went back to his car as I entered the building.

I was busy on my phone as I entered the stairwell. It was darker than usual and I wondered if the light had broken. I'd just sent a message to Jordan as I began to climb the stairs. Excitement and anticipation made me smile to myself as I hurried up the stairs and I shoved my phone into the back pocket of my jeans. I was nearly halfway up the stairs and I'd just reached a landing when I heard a door open behind me.

I didn't turn around to see who had entered the stairwell. I should have taken more notice, but I was lost in my thoughts when I felt hands grab my arms and lift me off the step I was on. A hand covered my mouth before I could scream. Panic began to build up inside of me at the realization of what was happening. I struggled, but my assailant was stronger and I couldn't move.

My stomach sank when I realized I had no way of defending myself. Warm breath against my ear made me press my eyes closed tightly and I felt a shudder of fear as he pinned me against the wall. I got a whiff of an overpowering cologne that made me want to gag.

"You're my whore, not his," a guy's voice whispered against my ear as I felt him press his body suggestively against mine. Tears began to slide down my cheeks at the fear and revulsion at what he was doing to me.

I heard a door open from below us. My assailant stiffened and when he realized we weren't alone, he pushed me hard against the wall. I lost my balance and fell onto the floor. He made an escape back out the door. I rubbed my side hip that had taken the brunt of my fall as I sat up.

"Taylor?" I heard Sin question from a few steps below. His eyes widened in surprise when my eyes met his. A sob tore from me at the concern on his face. Tears began to stream unchecked down my face.

He rushed up the last couple of steps as I tried to stand up. I winced when the pain in my side throbbed. Concern was etched into his features as he took my hysterical state in.

"What happened?" he asked as his hands reached for me and he scanned my features. I was shaking so badly that I could feel my teeth rattle. I don't know if it was shock or fear that kept me silent. I struggled to process what had just happened.

You're my whore, not his, echoed through my mind and I felt my fear take hold and I trembled as I cried. I couldn't think about what he would have done to me if Sin hadn't been there.

"Shh," Sin soothed as he pulled me into his arms and held me. After a few minutes of being held in Sin's protective hug, my tears began to ease. He pulled away slightly and looked at me. He brushed the remaining tears from my face as he scanned my features.

I was still trembling slightly when he put his arm around me and helped me climb the remaining stairs. I'd never feel safe again. Sin got me back to my room and sat me down on bed. I sank down onto my bed and let my gaze drop to the floor. I had so many thoughts racing through my mind. Sin's finger lifted my chin so my gaze met his. He was kneeling in front of me on one knee.

"What happened, Tay?" he asked softly.

I pressed my lips together for a moment to stop myself from letting my emotions turn me into a sobbing mess. The sting of tears made me brush the unshed tears from my eyes as I tried to pull myself together.

"You have to tell me what happened," he said gently as his eyes held mine.

"Someone...a-attacked me," I stuttered as my throat thickened with emotion. His jaw tensed and he pressed his lips together.

"Did you see who it was?" he asked calmly. I shook my head.

"He came up behind me and I couldn't..." was all I managed to say before I put my hand over my mouth.

"I need to call the cops," he explained as he reached for his phone. I nodded my head.

There was no ignoring what had been happening now. This wasn't just some jealous girl who was trying to be spiteful; it was worse than that. Sin stood up and began to pace the small room as he called the police. He ran a hand through his hair while he talked. I clasped my hands together as I thought about all the strange events that had led up to this.

First someone had spiked my drink. Was it just a coincidence or had it been the same guy? Then I thought about the incident when I'd heard the sound of footsteps chasing me in the stairwell. At the time, I'd brushed it off as my imagination, but after what had just happened I knew it hadn't been.

Then there was the incident with my underwear. It had to be the same guy. He'd broken into my room and invaded my privacy twice: once to steal the underwear and once to put it back with the message written on it.

This wasn't just an attack that had happened because I was in the wrong place at the wrong time. It was like I had a stalker. I shuddered when I thought about what would have happened to me if Sin hadn't come back.

Sin finished the call and sat down beside me. He put his arm around me and pulled me close. I rested my head against his shoulder.

"They're on their way."

Chapter Thirteen

TAYLOR

The cops arrived quickly and a flurry of activity followed. While an officer who introduced himself as Officer Johnson questioned me, a couple of officers searched the building for the attacker. I didn't miss the look that the officer gave Sin as he began to question me.

"What's your name?" he asked as he gave me a kind smile.

"Taylor Price."

"Taylor Price," the officer murmured to himself as he wrote it down in his notebook. "Your name sounds familiar. Have you had any run-ins with the law?"

Oh no!

I swallowed hard. This couldn't be happening. I remained as calm as possible and shook my head. I hadn't had any run-ins with the law, but there was only one reason why my name might have sounded familiar.

Please don't let him remember why he knows my name, I thought to myself as I waited anxiously to see if he was going to question me further about it.

"What happened?" Officer Johnson asked me as he shot Sin a questioning look. Sin remained indifferent. It was like he was used to it. I felt relieved that he had moved on and wasn't going to ask any more questions about the fact that my name sounded familiar to him. I relayed the events best as I could. I couldn't stop myself from trembling in fear when I told him about the attack itself. An arm wrapped around my shoulders and I glanced to see Sin standing beside me.

"Did he say anything during the attack?"

I hesitated for a moment.

"He said that I was his whore," I said. I felt the heat of Sin's eyes on me. I left out the other part because it would be too embarrassing to say in front of Sin. It was like everything happening around us was making our arrangement out to be more than it was.

"Did you get a look at him?" the officer asked with his hand holding the pen to the small notepad.

"No."

I wrapped my arms around my body as I remembered the feel of his body pushing against mine. I wanted to throw up. He'd held me so hard I couldn't turn to look at him.

"Was there anything you noticed that would help us identify the attacker?" he asked.

I shook my head, feeling disheartened. The truth was I could walk past this guy at any time and have no idea who he really was. It was scary. The officer looked at me for a moment and then dropped his gaze to a notepad where he scribbled something down.

"Have there been any other incidents that you think might be related to this?"

"Yes," I answered. Sin stiffened beside me. It was time to lay it all out.

"There have been a few weird incidents," I began to explain as I rubbed my forehead. I was starting to get a headache and it was hard to concentrate.

"Take your time and start from the beginning," the officer suggested. I told him about all the incidents. When I got to the underwear incident, I felt Sin's arm tighten around my shoulders, but I didn't look at him.

"Why didn't you report your drink being spiked?" he questioned.

"I couldn't prove it," I replied. At the time, I'd thought it was an isolated incident. There was no way I could have known it was going to be so much worse.

"Did you keep the underwear?"

I shook my head, feeling stupid that I'd thrown away evidence that might have been able to lead the police to my attacker. At the time, I had just wanted to get rid of it so I could forget about the incident.

"Do you have somewhere to stay in the meantime?" Officer Johnson asked me. The truth was, I didn't. I'd have to try and find a hotel nearby. But I knew that once Connor found out what had happened, he'd be on the first flight here and he'd be packing my things for me. I rubbed my forehead as I tried to sort through my thoughts and decide what I was going to do.

"Ma'am?" the officer said.

"Yes, she does." I turned to face Sin, who was standing beside me. What was he talking about?

"She'll be staying with me," he told the cop.

The officer eyed him for a few moments before he gave a brief nod. It was only after the police left that I had a chance to talk to Sin.

"I can stay in a hotel," I said as he watched me pack some of my clothes in a bag. I didn't want to impose myself on him and besides it wasn't like we were dating or anything like that. He didn't need to play the concerned boyfriend. He was a guy I was screwing and that was it. Staying with him went way beyond what we'd agreed.

"You've got some crazy nut after you and you want to go and stay in a hotel where he might find you?" he argued with a frown.

I hesitated.

"We both know what would've happened if I hadn't come back and frightened him off," he said, driving the point home. He was trying to make me face the reality of my situation.

I paled at the reminder. I tried to swallow my fear as my eyes stung with tears. It was all I could think about when the officers had questioned me. I'd been so lucky. A tear escaped and slid down my cheek despite my attempts to keep it together.

"I'm sorry," he said softly as he reached for me and pulled me into his arms. Another tear slid down my cheek as I pressed my cheek against his chest.

"I didn't mean to make you cry," he whispered as he held me. He pulled away gently to brush the tears from my cheek as I bit my lip. He held me for a few minutes while I pulled myself together.

"I'm sorry," I mumbled as I pulled away from him. I felt fragile and exposed because I'd cried in front of him.

He remained quiet.

"What about your roommates?" I asked. I wasn't sure how many guys lived in the house.

"It will be fine," he assured me.

I debated for a few minutes before I relented. It wouldn't be for long because I had to call Connor to tell him what happened, and when he found out he would insist I move back home.

"Okay."

I packed up some of my stuff. Sin took the bag from me and carried it for me as I followed behind him. At the door to the stairwell, I hesitated for a moment. The cops had searched the building and they hadn't found the guy who had attacked me, but I was still scared to go back inside the stairwell where I'd been attacked.

Sin turned to me in the doorway and extended his hand. I took a deep breath and put my hand in his. Side by side, he walked me down the stairs with my hand in his.

I was subdued as he drove us back to his house. I felt his gaze on me a few times during the drive. The party was still going when we arrived. I'd completely forgotten about it. We got more than a few curious looks as Sin got my bag out of his car and walked me into the house.

"Hey, man, where have you been?" asked Slater as we entered the house. His eyes moved from Sin to me.

"I didn't think you were coming tonight," said Slater to me. I gave him a weak smile.

"What's up?" Slater asked Sin when he noticed my bag in his friend's hand.

"Taylor is staying with us for a couple of nights," Sin informed his friend. Slater looked a little surprised as his gaze moved to me.

"Sure, no problem. Do you want me to close up the party?" he asked. Sin gave a slight nod of his head.

"Tay," Jordan squealed when she saw me.

"Hi," I greeted her, fastening a smile to my lips as I hugged her. I could smell alcohol on her and she was a little unsteady on her feet.

"Were you planning on taking Jordan back to the dorm room?" Sin asked Slater as Slater put an arm around Jordan's waist to make sure she didn't stumble.

"No," he answered, giving his friend a questioning look.

"Good," replied Sin as he reached for my hand and led me up the stairs. I turned back to see Slater press a kiss to Jordan's head as she leaned against his chest. They looked so good together.

I didn't have a chance to call Jordan and tell her about the attack so I was glad that she wasn't going anywhere near the dorm room tonight. In the morning, I would tell her everything.

As we got to the top of the stairs, I wondered if they had a spare couch that I could use. I was surprised when he opened the door to his room and held it open for me. Nervously, I stepped inside as he switched the bedroom light on and he closed the door behind him.

He put my bag down beside the bed and then he turned to face me as he ran a hand through his hair. His tongue flicked against the one lip ring as he studied me for a moment.

The events that night had left me nervous and jittery. I knew I was safe with Sin, but I couldn't help feeling that deep-rooted fear that had been put there by the attack earlier. He walked up to me.

"How are you doing?" he asked softly as he cupped my face.

"I'm okay," I lied outright. I was anything but okay. I wasn't sure if I would ever feel safe again.

"Do you need to shower?" he asked as his hands dropped from my face to settle on my hips.

"Yes," I answered. It was hard to concentrate on my thoughts when he was so close to me.

"Get what you need together and I'll put a clean towel in the bathroom for you," he said as he released me and stepped back.

"Okay," I said as I walked over to my bag.

I heard the door open and then close. I was alone. I sat down on the bed for a moment and rubbed my hands over my face, trying to get it together. I didn't want to be an emotional mess that Sin would have to deal with.

After I got my stuff out of my bag, I went to the bathroom. There was a clean, dark blue towel neatly folded beside the sink. I stripped down and climbed into the shower. Once I'd started up the shower and adjusted the temperature, I leaned my head against the tiles.

Some bruises had started to develop where my attacker had grabbed me. A shiver of fear ran through my body at the physical evidence left by the horrifying encounter.

At the sight of the bruises, I showered quickly and got out. I dried off in record time and began to pull my clothes on. I began to feel better now that the bruises were hidden from my sight by my clothes.

When I stepped out of the bathroom, I noticed the party had stopped. It was quiet except for some voices. The party was over. I went back to Sin's room expecting him to be there, but he wasn't.

I knew I had to call Connor, but I really wasn't looking forward to it. I grabbed my phone from my discarded clothes and I sat down on the bed while I tried to contemplate how I was going to tell my brother what had happened tonight. There was no use delaying it, and it didn't matter how I told Connor, he was going to freak.

"Hi," I heard Connor answer my call.

"Hi," I replied.

"What's wrong?" he asked. I could hear the nervous fear in his voice. A phone call this late at night was never for good news.

"I don't want you to freak out," I said.

"Tell me what happened," he instructed firmly, but I could hear the rising panic in his voice.

"I was attacked tonight," I revealed softly as I closed my eyes and prepared for his reaction.

"What happened? Are you okay? Have you reported it to the police?" He screeched one question after the other. He was flipping out.

"Calm down," I instructed.

"How the fuck do you expect me to calm down!" he yelled. I bit down on my lip to keep from snapping back at him. I remained silent as I let what I said sink in.

"Tell me what happened," he requested tightly once he'd managed to calm himself down enough to talk further.

"I'd just gone out to get something to eat with a friend," I began to explain. There was no way I could tell him I'd gone out with the guy I'm casually screwing.

"I was in the stairwell of the dorm building when someone came up behind me and pushed me against the wall," I said. While I was talking, I was already sifting through the finer details, deciding what to tell him and what to leave out.

"Someone scared him off when they entered the stairwell," I said, leaving out what the attacker had said to me, and the fact that it had been Sin who had scared off my attacker. He would go ballistic if he knew the guy he'd warned me off and given me a folder full of reasons to stay away from him was the guy I'd gone out with. He didn't need to know everything.

"Are you okay?" was Connor's next question.

"Yes, I'm fine." I was a little shaken, but physically I was fine.

"I'll get the first flight in the morning," he said. If it hadn't been so late I know he'd been on the first flight to get to me as soon as he could. I wasn't surprised. I knew he would come out as soon as I told him.

"Where are you?" he asked.

"At a friend's place," I replied vaguely.

"What's the address?" he asked. I gave him the address.

"I'll meet you there as soon as my flight lands," he told me.

"Okay," I replied, not sure how I was going to be able to keep Sin a secret now that I'd given my brother his address. Feeling overwhelmed, I decided I would sort it out tomorrow. It was one of the reasons I hated lying. Lies always had a way of coming out.

"I'm so glad you're okay," my brother said, sounding a little hoarse. He was emotional and I couldn't blame him. Tonight had reminded him about the time he'd nearly lost me.

"Travel safe and I'll see you in the morning," I replied, trying to keep my emotions from bubbling over.

"I love you," my brother said.

The last time I'd spoken to him before the night that had changed our lives, he'd forgotten to tell me he loved me. So now every time I spoke to him—brief or not—he would always say those three little words to me. It was like he was scared if he didn't say them that something bad would happen to me.

"I love you too."

The call ended and I sat for a while after just staring down at my phone. I rubbed my forehead as I tried to think of a way to make sure Connor didn't see Sin. I let out a sigh when I realized that I couldn't let my brother control my life. I was old enough to make my own decisions and even if he didn't like the decisions I made, they were mine to make.

Feeling tired, I lay down on the bed as I waited for Sin to return. I curled up in a ball and held my phone to my chest as I let myself relax for the first time since the attack. I must have fallen asleep because the next time I opened my eyes, it was dark. The darkness reminded me of the darkness in the stairwell. I felt something touch me and I shot up in the bed.

The memories from my attack assaulted me and I found myself trembling as I remembered my assailant pushing me against the wall. The fear I'd felt at that moment returned.

My heart pounded so fast I put my hand to my chest.

"Hey, it's just me," Sin said to me as he sat up beside me.

I put my hand to my head as I tried to breathe through my panic. Gently, Sin put an arm around me and pulled me against his bare chest.

One minute ticked into two. I began to relax and my heart began to slow down. It was the warmth from his embrace and the steady beating of his heart under my ear that soothed me. The fear began to disappear as I shoved the memory of the attack into the back of my mind.

"I'm sorry," I mumbled, feeling like an emotional mess.

"It's okay," he soothed gently as he stroked my hair. I pulled back slightly and looked at him. The moonlight lit the room enough to see the outline of his features.

His fingers reached out and tucked my hair behind my ear. I ran my tongue across my bottom lip as I felt the soft touch of his fingers against my skin. Something sparked to life inside of me. Without even questioning it, I leaned forward and kissed him.

Chapter Fourteen

TAYLOR

He kissed me back but not with the same fierce intent he normally did. It was like he was holding back. I pulled away from him, feeling vulnerable and confused at his actions.

"What's wrong?" he asked when I shifted away from him slightly.

"Don't you want me?" I blurted out, feeling embarrassed at the rejection.

He pressed his lips together for a moment. That little hope that it had been my imagination vanished. There was something wrong.

"I'm not sure if this is really what you need right now," he said. His eyes held mine as I clasped my hands together. "You were attacked tonight. You've been through so much, it has been an emotional roller coaster."

I didn't need to be reminded of what had happened. Every time I thought about it I wanted to be sick. The way his body had pressed up against mine had made me feel dirty. I understood why he was so hesitant to let things go further, but he didn't understand why I needed this so much.

"When he attacked me, he pushed his body...against

mine," I tried to put my need into words. "I need you...to wipe that memory from my mind."

"I don't think that's going to help you deal," he told me.

"Please."

He studied me for a few silent moments.

"Come here," he said softly in the darkness.

I moved closer and he leaned forward. His lips touched mine gently. His kisses were usually fierce and demanding, leading to physical gratification, but this was different. He moved his lips against mine softly as he cupped my face and pulled me closer. Maybe it was because he wanted to be careful with me because of the attack. I ran my tongue lightly over his bottom lip and against his lip ring. I heard a sharp intake of breath as he opened his mouth and touched his tongue to mine.

A flutter of excitement ignited in me when his tongue swept into my mouth. I covered his hands cradling my face and closed my eyes as I felt the sensation of need sweep through me. Moments of the attack flitted through my mind, but I pushed them back. I was determined to erase the violating memories with this new memory of what Sin was doing to me. As if sensing my inner turmoil, he pulled his lips from mine and gently pushed me down onto the bed. I bit my lip as I felt my nervousness increase as I felt his body cover mine. For a moment I stiffened as the memory of my attacker pressing his body against mine came back through my mind.

"It's okay, it's me," Sin murmured softly as he held himself up with his hands on either side of me. I relaxed and opened my legs and he settled between them as he kissed me again.

He kissed me thoroughly and trailed kisses down my jaw. I was breathing hard by the time he lifted himself off me. I lifted my hips as he tugged my pajama shorts off along with my panties. In the darkness, he tugged off his clothes. He got a foil packet out of the drawer beside his bed and put the protection on. The bed dipped as he got onto the bed and helped me remove my top. He kissed me as he pressed his naked body against mine.

Usually he would ask me what I needed and sometimes he'd talk dirty, but this time he was quiet as he began to kiss his way down my body. There was a tenderness in his kisses that had never been there before. He moved above me and I wrapped my legs around his waist as I felt a need to have him inside me. His lips pressed against mine as he gripped my hips and thrust inside me with one stroke. I hitched my breath at the fullness I felt. He began to move in and out of me with a steady rhythm and I held onto his shoulders as I felt my orgasm begin to build.

Sweat mingled as our bodies moved together toward the release we both craved. With soft touches and kisses, he erased the horrible memories. There were no more dark memories; all that mattered was the tattooed boy who made me spin out of control.

I shattered into a million pieces and moments later he pushed inside me one last time as he came. Breathing hard and sweating, he leaned his forehead against mine for a moment and I hugged his body to mine. That was the exact moment I realized that there was no way I would be able to walk away from him without feeling the heartbreak that I'd been determined to avoid.

He pressed a soft kiss to my cheek and then he shifted off me. While he went to dispose of the protection, I lay in the bed with a sheet covering my nakedness wondering how I could have let myself care about him. I knew falling for a bad-boy wasn't a good idea. It was only going to bring me heartache. But the problem was any logical reasoning went out the window when I felt the warmth of feeling in my heart at the sight of him. I was pretty sure I was falling for him.

When he returned, he got into the bed and lay down beside me. We didn't touch; we just both lay on our backs looking at the ceiling in the darkness.

"Is Sin your real name?" I asked. I wanted to know more about this guy whom I'd fallen for.

"Yes," he answered. It was hard to believe that someone would name their son that.

"It's unusual. What made your mom choose that?" I asked, not quite sure if I was crossing a line by asking him so many personal questions. A few minutes of silence settled between the two of us and I was convinced he wasn't going to answer my question.

"My mom had an affair with a married guy," he revealed. "She was young and from the wrong side of the tracks when she met a rich, married guy who swept her off her feet. They started having an affair. He kept telling her he was going to leave his wife, but he never did...then she got pregnant with me."

Oh, wow!

"The day she told him she was pregnant with me was the last time she saw him," he explained. "She named me Sin so she would always remember how I came into this world."

"That's horrible," I said as I shifted onto my side to look at him. I couldn't believe a mother would do that to her son. It hadn't been his fault; it had been her mistake. I wanted to hug him, but I stayed still.

"It's okay. I like the name," he said as he turned to face me in the darkness. "The girls love it."

The girls loved him, but it had nothing to do with his name. I wasn't sure if he was serious about his last remark or if it was an attempt to cover up the hurt.

"It's also a reminder to me that people are human and they make mistakes. My mom made a mistake believing my father's lies."

A heavy silence descended. It was a depressing way to view people. It was like meeting a person for the first time and already taking for granted that they were going to fuck something up.

"Did you ever meet your father?" I asked tentatively. I knew it was a really personal question and I wasn't sure if he was going to be prepared to answer it. He seemed to consider my question for a moment.

"No," he answered. "He wasn't really a father in the true sense of the word. He was just a sperm donor."

He shifted to lie on his back with his hands behind his head.

"Did he ever try to contact you?" I kept probing, unable to believe someone would turn their back on their child.

"No, and then he died a couple of years ago."

I remembered him telling me that his father had died when I'd told him about my parents' death. It was a finality that was hard to face. He'd never met his father—or, sperm donor—and the fact that he was dead meant he never would. My heart hurt for the fact that his father had never shown him any interest and he had no idea how it felt to have a father who loved you. I knew that feeling. I hadn't felt that in a long time, but at least I'd felt it.

I swallowed the emotion that bubbled to the surface. My parents had loved me. But then one dark night they had been taken away from me. I closed my eyes for a moment to keep myself together as a brief memory from that night passed through my mind.

The loss that I'd felt had been like a piece of me had died along with them and there was no recovering from it. All I could do was try to ignore it and carry on. The easy option would have been to allow it to crush me and take away my will to live. But I persevered because my parents had given up their lives to protect me and simply giving up was taking their sacrifice and throwing it away.

That was the thing—no matter how crushing the loss of someone close to you was, life kept moving along. Maybe it was a good thing so you couldn't just fall apart and never put yourself back together. Perhaps it was life's way of pushing you along until you started living again. I let out an emotional sigh. Some days it was hard to carry on without them and then there were days when it was impossible.

"I'm sorry," he said softly as he reached for my hand and held it in his. "I didn't mean to remind you about your parents."

He was so sweet. Little did he know it was the horrors from their death that made it harder to handle.

"It's okay."

"How old were you when they died?" he prodded further.

"I was nine."

There were times I'd wished I'd been younger so the memories of my parents' death would have been forgotten. But I'd been old enough to remember everything clearly.

"Do you still see your mom?" I asked, redirecting the conversation to him.

He was silent for a few minutes.

"Yeah, I check up on her every week. She doesn't live far from here," he said as he shifted on his side. I lay on my side, facing him.

"She never quite recovered from the rejection from my father. From then on, she tried to find solace in the form of alcohol," he revealed further. My heart tightened at the realization that his childhood had been hard. Maybe even as hard as mine. It was difficult to think that he didn't have a father and that his mother was an alcoholic who could barely look after him.

"Who took care of you?" I asked the question, already knowing the answer.

"I did," he stated as a fact.

"I'm sorry," I said, knowing it was inadequate. But what did you say to someone who'd told you that no one had loved him enough to put him first?

"Don't feel sorry for me. I had Slater and he had me," he said. I had to keep myself from letting the sadness of his words wash over me; otherwise, I would have started to cry.

I also knew they were close, but now I was getting a little insight into their deeply formed friendship. Had Slater grown up with no one to look after him either? My heart broke at the image of two young boys growing up with no one to love and care for them. It made me angry that people would have children that they didn't want. The lack of love and affection was detrimental to a child who was unwanted. I was thankful I'd been loved even if that love had been taken away from me at such a young age. At least I remembered the love that my parents had felt for me. It was the type of love that had saved my life.

"Does Slater have any siblings?" I asked as I looked at the outline of the guy who meant more to me than he should. He would walk away and it would break my heart. Walking away now was pointless; it wouldn't ease the heartache that was to come. With the lack of love from his childhood, I wasn't surprised that he was the way he was. How could you expect him to love someone when he didn't know how?

"He had a sister," he revealed softly. Had. My inquisitiveness grew.

"What happened?" I asked, unable to stop myself.

"It isn't my story to tell."

My heart broke a little more for Slater. The next time he hugged me I would hug a little tighter.

"Did you tell Jordan about all the strange stuff that had

been happening?" he asked, changing the subject. I rolled onto my back and let out a sigh.

"No."

"Even after the incident with your underwear?" he asked. I could hear the shock mixed with anger in his voice.

I remained silent, knowing he was getting angry. How could I explain that I hadn't thought it would lead to me being attacked? Never once before today's attack did I think it would escalate.

"Why didn't you tell anyone?" he asked, trying to figure out why I'd kept quiet.

"Because at the time I didn't think it was a big deal." It was a weak explanation, but it was all I had.

"Did you think ignoring it would make it go away?" he asked, sitting up. I could tell by the tone of his voice that he was angry and agitated.

"Hey, I've had a rough day and I don't need you lecturing me on top of everything else," I bit back, sitting up as well. I kept the sheet against my chest with both hands to cover my nakedness as I rubbed my forehead.

"I'm sorry," he apologized. "It's just that there is a naivety about you that I've never seen in a person before."

I couldn't tell him why I was the way I was.

"So naive that I keep worrying that something really bad is going to happen to you," he said. I had mixed feelings about that statement. I should be happy with the fact that he cared about me, but the way he said it hurt. It was like he didn't want to be burdened with worrying about me.

"Like not taking drinks from strangers."

He was right. If I'd been a normal teenager growing up, I would have known that, but I hadn't.

"It's like you haven't experienced anything that most teenagers have and I can't figure out why."

He was starting to figure everything out and I could feel

myself start to panic. Even though it was dark and he wouldn't be able to read my expression, I dropped my gaze in an attempt to hide my secret. The cop earlier this evening had recognized my name for a reason and I was just lucky he couldn't remember why it had seemed familiar to him.

"You're not going to tell me, are you?" he said softly. The moonlight illuminated him as he crossed his arms over his chest.

My silence answered his question. I couldn't tell him.

"You're not going to tell me anything, are you?" he asked tightly. "I bared a part of my soul to you, but that doesn't make any difference."

Guilt made my heart suddenly feel very heavy in my chest and I swallowed hard. If I told him, it would ruin everything. Was it asking too much to want to start over somewhere where no one knew what had happened? I wouldn't have to see those sympathetic looks that reminded me daily of what I'd been through. I pulled my knees to my chest as I lifted my eyes to Sin. He moved off the bed and he picked something up off the floor. He pulled his jeans up and then he turned to face me.

"I should've known better," was all he said before he walked out of his room.

I rested my forehead against my knees as I felt the sting of tears. I'd really messed things up. Just when I was getting to know him a little better, he'd pulled away from me completely. And could I blame him? No, I couldn't. He was right. He'd opened up to me and in turn I'd refused to let him in.

I felt my heart crack a little. I'd done it to myself and I wasn't sure if there was any way to fix the damage I'd done. Sin didn't strike me as the type to blab about his childhood so he'd trusted me enough to talk to me about it. I had my reasons for not wanting to tell him about my past and none of them had anything to do with trust, because I trusted him with my life.

A few quiet tears slid down my face and I wiped them away. I'd really messed things up and I was pretty sure our arrangement was over. I doubted that Sin believed in second chances so even if I revealed my secret to him, it still wouldn't fix things between us. I lay down in his bed and hugged a pillow as I buried my tear-streaked face in it. I inhaled him and held onto the precious memories he'd given me.

Chapter Fifteen

TAYLOR

Sin never returned and I didn't go looking for him. He was angry and it was best to give him space until he cooled down. Somehow I drifted off into a restless sleep. When I woke up, I was tangled in the sheets and the sun was streaming through a gap in the curtain. I felt exhausted even though I'd slept a little.

I sat up and stretched. The sight of the bruises on my arms reminded me of the events from the previous night. I dropped my head into my hands when I remembered my heated conversation with Sin before he'd left. As much as I wanted to hide away from him and the world, I needed to face my problems. Hiding would only give me a temporary reprieve, but it wouldn't solve anything. I checked my watch and saw that it was seven. I didn't waste any time. I got up and got dressed. Out of habit, I made the bed before I went across the hall into the bathroom and brushed my teeth. The house was quiet and I doubted that anyone else was awake.

Quietly, I packed all my stuff into a bag and made my way downstairs. I hesitated on the last step as I saw Sin sprawled on the couch, sleeping. He looked so peaceful while he slept, lying on his back with his one arm flung over his eyes. I felt a pang of guilt at the fact that he'd opened up to me and I'd refused to tell him about my past.

I placed my bag gently by the front door, trying not to wake Sin up. He needed the sleep. My heart was still fragile and I knew that after last night things between us were probably over. I was staving off the inevitable heartache that was to come. I went into the kitchen to get some water. As quietly as I could, I got a glass and filled it halfway with some water out of the tap. I took a couple of sips as I began to think about what I was going to tell my brother.

In my mind I was already formulating my argument to him. He would try and make me go home, but I wasn't going to allow him to dictate my life, even if he meant well.

At the sound of a noise behind me, I spun around and nearly dropped the glass of water.

"Sorry, I didn't mean to scare you," the guy said. I think his name was Eric. He was one of Sin's roommates. I'd seen him around although I'd never actually spoken to him.

Unlike Sin and Slater, he didn't have any visible tattoos or piercings. He had short blond hair and green eyes. He wasn't bad-looking, but he didn't have the special something that both Sin and Slater possessed that pulled the girls in. From the little interaction I'd seen, I knew Sin wasn't as close to his other roommates as he was with Slater.

"It's okay," I replied, setting the glass down on the counter as I tried to calm my heart that was still beating too fast.

"You guys have a fight?" he asked as he walked over to the fridge and opened it.

The sight of Sin sleeping on the couch was a sure sign that everything wasn't going well between the two of us. But we weren't dating, and after last night I wasn't sure we were anything.

"Something like that," I answered with a slight shrug of my shoulders.

Eric got some orange juice out of the fridge and walked over to where I was standing. He reached past me and got a glass out of the cupboard beside me.

"I wouldn't stress about it too much," he told me as he put the orange juice back in the fridge. "Girls never last long with him."

I shrugged again as I took another sip of the water. There was no way I was going to talk about what was or wasn't happening between Sin and I with someone I barely knew.

"Although I've never seen him sleep on the couch before," he added.

I took another sip of water.

A slight noise made me look to the doorway of the kitchen to see Sin standing, watching us. Suddenly I felt nervous. His hair was rumpled and sexy. It was wrong that someone could look so hot first thing in the morning. He scratched his chest as he walked into the kitchen.

Eric grabbed his glass of juice and gave me a slight nod as he left the kitchen, leaving me alone with Sin. Sin watched him leave with an annoyed look on his face and then he turned to face me. I set the glass of water I held in my hands down on the counter.

"You sleep okay?" he asked as he stood a couple of feet away from me.

I nodded my head.

He stepped forward and took my one arm into his hands. His fingers brushed gently over the bruises left by my attacker. The touch tingled right through me. Then he dropped my arm and took a step back as if he needed space from me.

An awkward silence descended as I held his gaze. I didn't know what to say, I wasn't even sure if there was anything that I could say that would fix the rift between us. No, I was wrong—the only way to fix it would be to tell him about what happened and I just couldn't. My stomach twisted into knots. Any hope I'd had that last night wouldn't be as bad as I thought dissolved. My inability to open up had damaged what we had and there was no going back.

The doorbell rang.

Sin looked at me one last time before he turned and walked out of the kitchen. Being able to read minds would have come in really handy. I pushed off the counter and followed him out. Sin had just reached the front door, and I knew who it was without having to look.

"I think he's here for you," Sin said. As he opened the door more, I saw my brother standing with a thunderous look on his face. I wasn't surprised. I knew my brother would be mad when he saw who I'd slept over with.

"Get your stuff," my brother ordered me without entering the house. My brother was angry.

Sin threw him a glare but my brother ignored it while he waited for me with his arms crossed over his chest. More often than not, Connor acted like a father and not a brother. I let out a sigh and walked over to collect my bag nearby the door. Once I picked it up, I looked at Sin. He couldn't even look me in the eye. I felt myself tremble for a moment before I took a deep breath and buried my heartache down deep to deal with later when I was alone.

"Don't let Jordan go back to the dorm. Tell her I will call her a little later," I told him.

He nodded his head as he still held the door handle.

"Thanks for everything," I said softly as I hesitated in the doorway for a moment. I wanted him to say something.

"See you around," he said as his eyes held mine. There was no emotion in them and it sounded like he couldn't wait to get rid of me. With that final sentence, he made it abundantly clear that we were over and I felt a pain in my chest.

It hurt like I knew it would. I will never know how I managed keep myself together as I turned and walked out of the house to my brother. The door closed behind me as my brother pulled me into a hug. I felt the sting of tears as my brother pulled back slightly to scan my face.

"I'm so glad you're okay," he said, sounding relieved as I struggled to fight my tears of heartache. My brother mistook my tears for something else entirely and pulled me into another hug.

"It's okay," he soothed as he hugged me tighter.

For the moment, I wasn't okay. I was experiencing my first heartbreak. When I'd started things with Sin, I knew there was a possibility it would end up the way it had. But the reality of the heartache was much worse than I'd ever anticipated. My brother pulled away from me and ushered me into a waiting car. I brushed my tears off my cheeks as I stared unseeing at the scenery that passed as we drove to the hotel where my brother was staying.

I was sitting in my brother's hotel suite while he was pacing up and down, trying to talk me into going back home with him. The suite was big, with a sofa facing a flat-screen TV. It had two adjoining rooms. It was hard to concentrate on my brother's lecturing voice when all I wanted to do was climb into a bed and pull the covers over my head to ignore the outside world while I tried to figure out how I was going to deal with my broken heart.

"It's not safe here," he stated. He'd already said that thirty times in the last hour.

"I'm not going to live in fear because someone is stalking

me," I said, refusing to budge. This was my life to live and I wasn't going to let a stalker or my overprotective brother stop me from living it how I wanted. I wasn't stupid—I knew I had to be careful—but I wasn't going to allow the stalker to scare me.

"I told you to hire a bodyguard and I will stay in a rented apartment instead of the dorm," I tried, renegotiating with my brother. He stood with hands on his hips, glaring at me. It was at times like this that he felt more like my father than my brother.

"Fine," he said, throwing his hands up in the air with frustration. "I'll get a place big enough for you, Jordan and the bodyguard."

"And the bodyguard?" I questioned.

"The bodyguard will stay with the two of you in the apartment to keep you safe," he explained.

I saw that determined look in his face and I just nodded my head. I didn't have the energy for more fighting. I'd won the battle but not the war. I was going to stick out like a sore thumb with a bulky bodyguard following me around school, but it would keep my brother happy and it would keep me safe. He ran an agitated hand through his hair as I stood up and walked over to him.

"I'm not trying to be difficult," I told him as I reached for his hands. He was so stressed and I felt guilty that it was because of me.

"I just want to be able to live my life," I added. His expression softened slightly as he pulled me into a hug.

"I love you and I just don't want anything to happen to you," he reminded me. "When I thought I'd lost you before, I..."

He pulled away and looked down at me.

"I never want to feel that again," he said hoarsely. It was hard to keep my own emotions in check at the visible emotion on his face.

"I'll be fine," I assured him and I swallowed hard. They were just words because there was no way to guarantee I'd be safe, even with a bodyguard. I could cross the road and get hit by a bus. I was determined to ensure that the life I had, no matter how long I had, was mine to live as I wanted.

"Did you read the folder I gave you on your friend?" was my brother's next question. I was hoping he wouldn't bring it up, but I'd been wrong. I pulled away from him and took a step back.

"Sin is none of your business," I stated with determination to keep my brother out of my private life. I crossed my arms and glared at my meddling brother.

He gave me a look of disbelief.

"You've got to be kidding me," he said as he rubbed his hands over his face. I pressed my lips together. I was going to stand my ground. It didn't matter that whatever arrangement we'd had was gone and the likelihood was I wouldn't see much of him again. The thought made my chest hurt.

"It's my life and my choice."

We had a stare down for a few seconds before my brother stalked off. I sat down on the sofa and let out a sigh. I rested my head back against the sofa as I closed my eyes. All I could see was the indifferent look Sin gave me before he told me he would see me around. My chest hurt; it sucked. I just needed to hold it together until later when I was alone. Then I could cry and try to heal my bruised heart.

Connor and I were looking on the Internet at apartments to rent when my phone began to ring about an hour later. My brother had managed to calm down from our previous argument. I looked down and felt my heart sink when I saw it was Jordan. I had been hoping that it would be Sin.

"Hey," I answered as I put my phone to my ear. I stood up.

"Are you okay?" she asked, sounding concerned. She'd been told about last night.

"Yeah, I'm fine," I assured her as I held on tightly to the phone and walked over to the window of the hotel room. Connor remained at the table, looking at his laptop.

"Sin told me about the attack and all the other stuff," she told me. I could hear the bewilderment in her voice.

She paused.

"Why didn't you tell me?" she asked softly. I felt bad that I hadn't confided in her.

"I didn't think they were that serious until the attack," I replied as I peered out of the window. "Until the underwear, I thought it had been my imagination."

"You should have told me," she said, sounding a little upset.

"I'm sorry. You're right, I should have," I apologized.

"I heard that your brother came to pick you up," she informed me. Slater and Sin had brought her up to speed on everything she'd missed.

"Yes," I sighed. "He was worried and he got the first flight in this morning."

"Is he going to make you go home?" she asked. She knew how protective my brother was.

"He wants to, but I'm not going anywhere," I told her. "I've agreed to a bodyguard and a rented apartment instead of staying at the dorm. It will be big enough for the both of us."

"Both of us?" she questioned, unsure of what I was saying.

"They've tightened up security on campus, but I don't think staying in the dorm will be safe, at least not until they catch this guy," I reasoned.

"Okay," she agreed.

A few moments of silence settled between us.

"He is only doing it because he cares," she said

unexpectedly.

I paused for a moment. I knew that, but it didn't make his protective ways any less annoying.

"I know." I turned and Connor walked up to me. He signaled that he wanted to say something.

"Hold on for a sec," I told her.

"Okay," she said. I held the phone away from my ear as I looked at my brother.

"Tell her I'll send a car around to pick her up. He'll take her to the dorm and go with her to get some of her stuff," he whispered. I nodded my head at him.

"My brother says he'll send a car to pick you up," I informed her.

"Okay. See you soon," she said as she ended the call. I told my brother she was also at Sin's house and he called his driver.

In the time it took for the car to leave and pick up Jordan, my brother had already organized a fully furnished apartment close to the college. He was on the phone in the process of organizing me another bodyguard when Jordan walked into the suite.

"Hey," she said as she dropped her duffel bag and pulled me into a hug.

"Hi," I replied as I hugged her back.

"I can't believe he has organized bodyguards already," she said as she glanced back at the door. She was talking about the two bodyguards who were already standing guard outside the hotel room.

"Yeah, he's not taking any chances. He is still trying to get a younger bodyguard to be able to blend in better at college."

"Do you have any idea who it could have been?" she said as she pulled back and scanned my face.

"No." I had no idea who would want to attack me.

"Connor has organized us a place that is fully furnished for the rest of the year," I told her as we walked over to the sofa to sit down. Connor nodded his head briefly at Jordan to greet her as he spoke on his phone.

"That's cool," she said with a shrug.

"I'm going to have to get used to someone following me around all the time," I muttered to my friend. She reached for my hand and gave it an affectionate squeeze.

"Maybe he will be hot," she said as she wiggled her eyebrows. For the first time since my fight with Sin, I smiled. Jordan had that way of easing stressful situations.

"I hope so."

But I knew that my heart was still hung up on a tattooed bad-boy who wasn't interested in seeing me again.

Chapter Sixteen

TAYLOR

Oh my!

Hot didn't even begin to describe my new bodyguard who'd just arrived at the new place we'd just moved into. It had been a couple of days since my brother had showed up at Sin's house to pick me up.

"Matthew Weiss, this is my sister, Taylor," my brother introduced. "And this is Jordan."

I was still trying to recover from the shock so I gave him a brief nod instead of trying to greet him with words that I couldn't seem to find. He wasn't what I'd expected. Jordan, who'd been sitting down on the sofa watching TV, stood up.

"Hi," she greeted.

Matthew gave her a brief nod and a smile. I swear I saw her swoon. I'd been expecting someone big and bulky, and, well...mean looking. The type of guy who could kill with one evil look or the type of guy you wouldn't want to meet alone in a dark alley. The only thing that this guy could do with one look was make panties disappear.

He didn't look like the lethal bodyguard my brother had assured me he was, but I knew that there was no way my brother would leave me without the best protection he could buy. He was tall and lean. His hair reached past his ears. It was a sandy brown color with streaks of blond. His eyes were a beautiful dark green. Long, dark eyelashes emphasized his striking eyes.

"Hi," he greeted us with a relaxed smile, which spread wider and showed off his dimples.

More bloody dimples.

He was dressed in black trousers and a plain button-up white shirt. The collar was undone and the sleeves were rolled up to his elbows. He set his luggage down where he stood.

"Here is a folder that has all the information that you'll need," Connor told him as he handed him a blue folder. My brother and his stupid folders. Matthew opened the folder briefly and his eyes scanned a couple of the pages before closing it again.

"If you need any more information, call me," my brother instructed.

"I will," he assured Connor. The easy smile was gone and he was all business. It was the first glimpse I got of Matthew the Bodyguard.

My brother turned to face me.

"I need to get back for a very important meeting," Connor said. He looked anxious even though he knew that he was leaving me in very capable hands.

"I'll be fine," I assured him as I embraced him and gave him a squeeze.

"I love you," he whispered to me softly as he kissed my cheek. He gave me one last squeeze before he released me.

"I love you too," I said softly.

"I'll call you when I get to the airport," he said, picking up his suitcase.

"Sure," I said as I walked him to the door. I loved my brother, but I was glad he was going. He'd been suffocating me the last couple of days while he'd sorted out the rental and bodyguard. The perks were that the apartment was nicer than staying at the dorm.

Connor gave me one last quick hug before he left.

"Which room is mine?" asked Matthew, looking at me expectedly.

I pointed at the only empty room left that was next to mine. The other room, which was occupied by Jordan, was on the opposite side. When it had come time for Jordan and me to choose rooms, my brother had insisted that the bodyguard sleep in the room next to mine. I'd asked why and he'd said he would feel better knowing the bodyguard was close to me. I shook my head at the memory. If you looked up the word overprotective in the dictionary, I swear there would be a picture of my brother under the description.

"I'm just going to unpack my stuff," he told us and then he disappeared into the bedroom with his luggage.

Jordan's eyes met mine.

"See, I told you he'd be hot," she whispered to me as she wiggled her eyebrows suggestively. There was no disputing it, he was. I shook my head at her as I smiled.

It didn't matter how hot he was, I wanted Sin. I hadn't heard from him since my brother had arrived. I rubbed my forehead as a slight headache began to develop. It wasn't like I'd expected him to call, but the fact that he hadn't even sent me a text message did hurt. It shouldn't surprise me because he'd made it very clear when I'd left that what we had was over.

"I'm going to lie down," I said, wanting some space so I could wallow in my hurt without having to pretend I was fine. Her eyes narrowed at me for a moment before she said, "Okay."

There was no pretending with her. I'd told her what happened with Sin and me. She'd been sympathetic and supportive. I was glad she hadn't told me 'I told you so.' Let's face it, everything that had happened with him she'd warned me about and I hadn't listened. But as crappy as I felt emotionally, I still couldn't bring myself to wish I'd ever met him or experienced the few moments he'd given me.

It was early evening and tomorrow would be my first day back at school since the attack. I was nervous, but having Matthew around would make me feel safer. It had taken my brother two days to get the best bodyguard who was young enough to pass for a college student. My brother had insisted that the bodyguard blend in with students so it wasn't too obvious who he was. He thought it would help the bodyguard protect me better if he was in all the same classes as me, which made sense. Connor had organized it with the college. The police had no leads on who my attacker was. The college had tightened up security and everyone—especially the girls—was told to be careful.

The fact that the bodyguard was going to be around me so much, my brother said it would be easier to tell people he was a friend of the family's then to try to explain who he really was. Jordan had also agreed not to reveal who Matthew really was. I'd agreed to it. I wasn't going to fight my brother on any of it. After our initial heated argument, he'd agreed to stop fighting with me about staying as long as I agreed to the measures he put into place to keep me safe. One was the new flat, two was the bodyguard and three was the daily phone calls that he would be making to make sure I was okay.

I went into my room. I lay down on my bed and stared at the ceiling. Every time I closed my eyes, all I could see was Sin's face the last time I saw him. He'd been so indifferent that it had hurt. It was like the connection we'd made by being physically closer was gone. I didn't feel anger toward him. He'd been clear when we'd started the arrangement that when we were finished we walked away without any feelings and carried on.

The problem was I'd developed feelings. I still felt badly that he'd opened up to me and I hadn't been able to do the same. Even now, given a second chance, I still wouldn't tell him anything.

My headache got worse so I got up and went looking for headache tablets in the kitchen. The aroma that hit me when I stepped out of my room made my stomach grumble. I hadn't been eating much, but at that moment I was ravenous.

Jordan was talking to Matthew while he cooked.

"Was that part of the requirement?" I asked as I joined them. Matthew turned to flash that deadly smile at me as he switched off the stove.

"No, it's a perk," he quipped then he turned to place the steaks on three plates.

"Good, because the two of us are pretty useless in the kitchen," Jordan said as she began to dish up a salad onto the plates.

"Then I'll be the one cooking," he stated. Some people would say it was relaxing and that they enjoyed it, but I hated it so it wasn't surprising I couldn't cook much.

"It smells good," I said as I reached in the cupboard for the headache tablets.

"I promise it will taste better," he assured me.

I'd had my reservations about the bodyguard staying in the apartment with us, but Matthew seemed to fit in well.

The next morning my mouth dropped open when I bumped into Matthew in the kitchen. Gone was the formal suit and in its place were faded jeans and some heavy metal band brand on a black shirt. The transformation in Matthew was astounding. He looked like a laid-back surfer guy and all that was missing was the surfboard. His long hair and deep tan added to the look.

"So what do you think?" he asked with a mischievous sparkle in his eyes.

"You undercover?" I asked as a grin spread across my face. He was just so easy to be around and most of the time he was funny. He was so different from Sin.

Sin. I still felt that pain in my chest and got short of breath when I thought of him. It felt like someone had sucker-punched me and I hated the physical effect he had on me. It had been four days since the last time I'd seen him.

"Yes," he replied indignantly. "So, do you think I'll blend in?"

"Yes," I said, still smiling.

"Good," he said. "The last thing I want to do is stand out."

He would still stick out because he was going to turn heads wherever he went. I was going to have to put up with a lot of jealous looks.

"Come on, surfer dude," I told him as I picked up my bag and walked to the front door.

I'd always imagined that having a bodyguard entailed a bulky guy who looked something like the secret service following closely behind me. I'd never imagined a hot, laid-back guy who looked like he couldn't tackle a tree. I was apprehensive by the time we made it to college. It had been just a ten-minute walk from the flat. Connor had made sure the apartment was close to college.

I was feeling fearful and apprehensive at the same time. My eyes scanned the features of every male student who walked past me. I couldn't help studying them briefly, trying to figure out if I recognized anything.

A hand briefly touched my lower back.

"I won't let anything happen to you," Matthew

whispered to me. I glanced at him and he gave me a reassuring smile. There was no hiding the fear that I felt and he'd seen it.

"Thanks," I whispered as I tried to calm myself down. I'd fought so hard against a bodyguard, but in that moment I was so thankful that I had Matthew walking beside me. I took a deep breath and put one foot in front of the other with a determination not to allow the attack to scare me from doing what I wanted.

Matthew stuck to me like glue. Wherever I went, he went. He intrigued Caleb when I introduced them after class. Caleb seemed to buy the story that Matthew was a friend of the family.

"You still hanging out with Sin?" Caleb asked me out of the blue. I stopped and turned to him as I felt Matthew's gaze on me. I was annoyed that he thought that Sin wasn't someone I should be hanging out with.

"You are my friend, but it's none of your business," I informed him firmly. It might have sounded a bit harsh, but I was tired of everyone giving their opinion on Sin whether I wanted it or not. It wasn't like everyone I knew got to vote on whether I got to hang out with him or not. It was only my vote that counted.

"Sorry. I shouldn't have said anything," Caleb apologized as he reached out and touched my arm. I felt Matthew tense slightly beside me. It was like he was ready to pounce if needed.

"It's fine," I said, brushing it off.

"I'd better go, otherwise I'm going to be late for my next class. I'll see you tomorrow," he said as he turned and walked down the opposite side of the hallway.

"You know, he is right," said Matthew as he watched the retreating figure of Caleb. Why did everyone think they could tell me what to do? I bit my tongue when I turned to face the next jury member.

"Look, I've read the file on Sin and let's put it this way, on paper, he isn't someone you want to get involved with," he told me.

He was right, I'd never read all the stuff that my brother had managed to collect on Sin, but I'd seen a side to him that had convinced me that there was more to him than some bad stuff he might have done. The brown folder had been moved to the apartment with the rest of my things. I still hadn't opened it. I'd stuffed it into the table beside my bed. It hadn't even crossed my mind to open the folder.

"It isn't any of your business, either," I stated to him as firmly as I had with Caleb. He crossed his arms over his chest and studied me for a moment.

"Unfortunately, who you hang out with is my business. Remember, I'm here to protect you," he explained. It made sense even though I didn't like it. I bit my lip to stop myself from snapping back at him. There was no point in trying to fight it.

"Fine," I relented. "Let's go."

I turned and began to walk down the hallway. My classes were finished for the day so we were going back to the flat.

"Speak of the devil," I heard Matthew whisper behind me.

The moment my eyes landed on him, I felt a flutter of awareness inside of me. Sin was standing on the other side of the hall. I felt relieved that he didn't have his tongue shoved down some girl's throat.

Our eyes met and I felt an awareness run through me. I was feeling so many things at the same time. I felt nervous, scared, hurt and plenty more. It was hard to pretend I was fine on the outside when I wasn't on the inside. I stopped walking as I watched Sin walk determinedly to me. The nervous knot that had started in my stomach grew. His eyes looked past me to Matthew and his step faltered slightly.

His lips pressed into a line and he closed the distance between us quickly. Matthew stood beside me and I really wished at that moment that he wasn't there. I wanted to be alone with Sin. Sin shot one more intense look at Matthew before he shifted his gaze onto me.

"Who is he?" he asked directly. I couldn't help hoping that he was a little jealous.

"Matthew, Sin, Sin, Matthew," I introduced even though Matthew was well aware of who Sin was. I could have told him that Matthew was my bodyguard, but for that little hope that he might be jealous I left that detail out.

They didn't shake hands; instead, they seemed to size each other up for a moment. Guys were so weird.

"I want to talk to you," said Sin when he pulled his gaze from Matthew.

It was good to see him, but seeing him had made the feeling of hurt more intense. I'd been waiting four days for him to talk to me and he hadn't bothered to contact me. I remembered the hurt I'd felt at his indifferent brush-off four days earlier and decided not to make it easy for him.

"I'm not sure I want to talk to you," I told him. His eyes searched mine and he reached to take my hand in his. Matthew watched the interaction carefully.

"Please." He undid me with that one word.

"Fine," I replied, looking at him expectantly.

"Where are you staying?" he asked as he flickered a glance in Matthew's direction.

"In an apartment nearby," I answered, wondering why he was asking.

"Could I come by tonight to talk?" he asked.

For a few moments I mulled over his request. There was no way I was going to say no, but I thought I'd let him sweat it out a little. His eyes held mine. He looked a little nervous as he waited for me to answer him. Confident and arrogant, Sin was hot, but there was something about the vulnerable side to him that pulled at my heartstrings.

"Fine," I answered and he gave a slight nod as he shoved his hands into the front pockets of his jeans.

I gave him the address.

"I'll be there at seven," he told me. I gave him a nod and watched as he shot Matthew a glare before he walked off.

"That one is trouble," said Matthew.

He was right, but I didn't care.

Chapter Seventeen

TAYLOR

At seven o'clock sharp there was a knock on the door. I was a bundle of nerves as I opened it.

"Hey," Sin greeted with a tentative smile when I stepped back and allowed him into the flat.

"Hi," I greeted, feeling the flutter inside my stomach at the sight of him. Those damn butterflies.

He followed me into the apartment and turned to see his reaction when he saw Matthew sitting on the sofa watching TV.

"He's living with you?" he asked in disbelief as he turned to me. He looked angry and shocked.

"Yes," I answered calmly, although I felt nervous on the inside. I could have offered him more information than that. I could have told him that he was my bodyguard and that was the reason he was living with me, but I didn't. Some part of me wanted to hurt Sin like he'd hurt me.

"Who is he?" he asked fiercely. I took a deep breath as Matthew turned around to look at us.

"No need to talk like I'm not here," he said sarcastically. He held Sin's glare.

"You came here to talk...so talk," I instructed firmly as I crossed my arms over my chest.

I felt so much for this tattooed guy in front of me, but I wouldn't allow anyone to treat me like a doormat. He'd hurt me and he needed to work hard to soothe over those hurt feelings. It hadn't been totally his fault. I'd refused to open up when he had bared his soul, but there had been no need to shut me out like he had. He pressed his lips together for a moment and threw a deadly side-glance at Matthew who was still watching us intently.

"I want to talk to you alone," he insisted as he shoved his hands into the pockets of his jeans, ignoring the heat of Matt's gaze on him. It was a fair request.

"Fine," I said in a clipped tone and walked into my bedroom. Sin followed quietly behind me and once inside my room he turned to close the door. For a few moments his eyes held mine as I stood with my arms crossed, waiting for him to say what he needed to.

"Your brother came to see me," he revealed to me.

I hadn't expected that. My brother meddled in my life all the time, but he'd never gone that far. Anger flared up inside of me at the thought that my brother had gone behind my back despite the fact that I'd told him I was old enough to make my own decisions.

"What did he say?" I asked, still reeling from his revelation. This wasn't going to be good, I could just tell.

"He told me to stay away from you," he stated as he took a step closer, but I took a step back, keeping my distance from him. To keep a clear mind, I couldn't be too close to him.

"He told me you'd been through enough," he explained as his eyes held mine. It was like he was trying to see deep into my soul. "He said that I'd just end up hurting you and you wouldn't be able to deal with that."

I wanted to hide I felt so mortified that my brother had gone to talk to Sin behind my back and had told him that. He'd no right to do that. I was going to kill him.

"He wouldn't tell me anything about your past," he added like it was some sort of consolation, but it wasn't.

I closed my eyes and pressed my hand to my forehead as I tried to comprehend the lengths that my brother had gone to. I was so angry that he'd done this to me. Betrayal mixed in with my anger. When I opened my eyes, Sin was standing just a foot away from me. I lifted my eyes to his. I recognized that look.

Oh. My. God.

The air locked in my lungs. His eyes looked at me with the sympathy that had followed me for most of my life from the time my parents had died. It was that same look I'd been running from and I'd fought so hard to get away from.

It wasn't possible.

"I'm sorry," he whispered softly as he tried to reach for me. I wrenched away from him as the first sob tore from my chest.

"Don't touch me," I spat at him as I put out a hand to keep him from me.

He knew. Somehow he knew.

"How much do you know?" I whispered as I felt the emotion welling up inside of me.

"Everything."

I swore I felt my heart crack. I could feel myself being crushed by the pressure of the realization that he knew everything that I'd been trying so hard to hide. I pressed my hands to my mouth to suppress my horror. He ran a hand through his hair. How had he found out? He'd said Connor hadn't told him.

"I'm sorry," he repeated as he tried to take a step closer, but I maneuvered out of his reach.

"Stay away from me," I instructed as I tried to hold myself together. The new life I'd been trying to build was slipping from my grasp. Sorry wasn't good enough. It didn't erase the information from his mind and take us back to the place where he didn't know about the horrors of my past. There was no going back.

"Get out," I said firmly, my voice thick with the emotion of my hurt that he'd gone behind my back to find out about my past even though I'd made it clear it I didn't want him to know about it.

"Don't do this, Tay," he said, reaching for me.

"I didn't want you to know," I said, my voice beginning to rise in anger that he'd ruined everything. "But that didn't stop you."

I closed my eyes for a moment to ride the wave of betrayal that hit me.

"I'm sorry," he repeated. It was a word that meant nothing to me.

"Get out!" I shouted at him. My eyes holding his started to blur as the tears began to stream down my cheeks. A gut-wrenching heartache ripped through me at the realization that whatever we had, even if it had meant more to me than him, was damaged. Possibly beyond repair.

The door to my bedroom crashed open as Matthew filled the doorway. It took him only seconds to take in the emotion on my face and the tears.

"What happened?" Matthew asked me as he stepped into the room and between us, like he was protecting me.

"This has nothing to do with you," Sin said in a determined voice as he took a menacing step toward Matthew, but Matthew didn't look intimidated and held his ground.

"If it has anything to do with Taylor, then it has something to do with me," he stated firmly as he crossed his arms.

"Just go," I said to Sin with my gaze fixed on the floor. I couldn't look at him in case seeing him made me waver. He'd done something I wasn't sure I would ever be able to forgive him for.

"Tay, just let me explain," he pleaded as he tried to step forward and Matthew blocked his advance.

"There is nothing you can say," I said, shaking my head. Matthew turned to face Sin with a hand to his chest.

"You need to leave," he instructed fiercely.

Sin glared at him for a moment before his eyes moved to mine. His eyes softened for a moment.

"I don't want to upset you more, so I'll leave," he told me.

I clasped my trembling hands together as I felt a pain in my chest where I was pretty sure my heart was breaking.

"But this isn't over," he promised me softly.

With one last glare at Matthew, he left the room. A few moments later I heard the front door slam closed.

"What happened?" Matthew asked as he stood in front of me, scanning my features. I brushed the tears from my face as I tried to pull myself together.

"I don't want to talk about it," I said as I tried to push down the emotions overwhelming me from the inside. He studied me for a moment with concern and then he released my arms.

"He will be back," he told me in a serious tone.

SIN

Initially I'd been angry and disappointed when I'd shared snippets of my past with her and she hadn't trusted me enough to share any of hers with me. I don't even know why I'd opened up to her. Maybe it was because I rarely felt calm, but I did when I was with her.

My life had always been a rush of activity and noise. Maybe it was because in those moments of quiet I had time to think of all the things I'd done wrong in my life and, trust me, I could spend a lot of time on that.

Taylor.

When I thought back to the first time I'd met her, I couldn't help the affectionate smile that tugged at my lips. She'd been a breath of fresh air the moment I'd laid my eyes on her. She was beautiful—there was no denying that. But a lot of girls were beautiful. Taylor's beauty went deeper than just the surface of her skin. She was like an enigma that I couldn't figure out. It was obvious from the start that she wasn't like other girls her age. There was an innocence about her that had nothing to do with the fact that she'd been a virgin. It was more than that.

Her brother seemed to be the overprotective type, but why was he that way? Had it been the result of her parents' car accident that her brother had become overprotective over her? Plenty of people lost their parents, so it didn't explain the extreme naivety in Taylor. It was like I was sitting with more questions than answers.

"Sin!" I heard Slater call from downstairs. If my bedroom door hadn't been open then, I probably wouldn't have heard him.

I stood up and rubbed my hands over my face. I was tired. Since I'd told Taylor 'I'd see her around' I'd been agitated and nervous. I had no idea what was wrong with me.

I made my way down the hall and then down the stairs. I hesitated for a split second when I saw the person standing beside Slater waiting for me. For a moment I'd hoped it might be Taylor, but it was her brother studying me with a reserved expression.

I knew how this talk was going to go before we even got started. He was going to tell me to stay away from his sister. When he'd come to collect his sister the day before, I hadn't missed the looks. He didn't think I was good enough for her and he was probably right. I'd spent my life not being good enough. For my sperm donor, I hadn't been good enough to be a son he could love, and even my own mother struggled to love the reminder of her bad judgment. It didn't matter what I did now or what I had, nothing would change that.

The only person I was good enough for was Slater. I was good enough to be his friend. Maybe it was because he'd grown up in a similar situation to me that had bonded us in friendship and had pulled us through a lot of dark times.

As I reached the bottom step, Slater gave me a questioning look that Connor didn't see because his eyes were fixed on me. I shook my head at him and he reluctantly left us alone.

"What do you want?" I asked him in a clipped tone as I held his gaze. It didn't matter that I already knew the answer. We stared at each other, neither of us wanting to look away first.

"I wanted to talk to you about Taylor, my sister," he began. And there it was. I crossed my arms over my chest and waited for him.

"Whatever is going on between the two of you needs to end," he stated firmly and I laughed in his face. He looked a little taken aback. He hadn't expected my reaction.

"And why would I listen to you?" I scoffed. I hated being told what to do by people I knew so I didn't take it very well from someone I was meeting for the second time. It didn't matter that I'd pretty much ended things with her. I'd meant it when I'd told her 'I'd see her around'.

With that one sentence, I'd closed the door on our arrangement and made it clear from then on I would only consider her an acquaintance that I would see when we passed in the hallways.

He studied me for a moment.

"I know what type of guy you are," he said. "You'll have your fun and then at some point you'll get bored and then you'll walk away."

I remained silent. He pretty much summed me up. The only difference was that, with Taylor, it had been more than one night and I'd formed a connection with her. I didn't want to admit it, but when she'd been attacked in the stairwell, it had scared me. It was then that I'd realized then that I cared about her. It wasn't like I wanted to date her or anything like that. I just didn't want anything bad to happen to her—it was hard to explain.

"Look, man, I don't know how any of this is any of your business," I retorted, feeling my anger at his outright meddling in his sister's life. She was an adult and she could make her own decisions about her life. There was no need to be difficult, but I couldn't help myself. I wasn't going to let him think that he could control me.

"She isn't like other girls," he tried to explain. I knew that already, but the way he said it piqued my curiosity. There was a somber sadness in his voice that was matched in his eyes.

She'd been so adamant that she didn't want to share her past with me, but I knew that the knowledge of what happened to her would help me understand her better. I didn't know what made me want to understand her. I'd never wanted to know anything about the girls I fucked. There were a few times I wondered whether the fact I'd been her first had made me feel more protective over her.

The fact that she was so naive worried me. It left her more susceptible to something bad happening to her. It shouldn't be my problem, but somehow it was.

"Why isn't she like other girls?" I asked, hoping that he would tell me what I wanted to know.

"Something really bad happened to her...I don't want to go into details, but she had a very protected childhood."

That was all he revealed. I could tell he wasn't going to tell me any more.

"You are going to hurt her and she might not be able to recover from it," he added. That was really weird to say. Girls had their hearts broken all the time and they got over it, though some took longer than others.

I held his gaze for several moments.

"What happens between your sister and me is our business. Stay out of it," I warned. I could be intimidating when I wanted to be, but I didn't feel the need to be. He gave me one last look before he turned and left, slamming the door behind him.

"You okay?" I heard Slater ask as I turned to walk up the stairs.

"Yeah."

My curiosity got the better of me in that moment and I climbed the stairs on a mission to uncover what Taylor was hiding. I wasn't trying to go against her wishes, but I felt that knowing everything would help me understand her and help keep her safe. She'd been drugged and if it hadn't been for me, God knows what would have happened. As soon as I got to my laptop, I started searching the web. I searched her name and it didn't take me long to find the news articles.

My blood ran cold and I felt the horror come alive inside of me as I read the details of her parents' death. After nearly half an hour, I knew enough and closed my laptop. She'd lied about her parents dying in a car accident. It also explained why the cop had recognized her name. I rubbed my hands over my face as I contemplated what to do next. There was a pain in my chest at the thought of what she'd been through and I knew I had to see her.

She'd probably be mad when I told her what I knew, but there was no way I would be able to look at her without thinking about it. It would come out eventually.

Chapter Eighteen

TAYLOR

I moped around the apartment for the rest of the evening. Matthew gave me a couple of concerned looks, but he didn't ask any questions. Maybe it was because he knew I wasn't going to tell him anything.

Later, when Jordan got back, it was clear that I wasn't myself. She asked what was wrong.

"Sin came over to talk and it didn't go well," I'd summarized for her. She didn't need to know the details and I didn't want to talk about how it.

"If you need someone to talk to, you know where I am," she'd offered.

Just after eating I'd gone to my room and closed my door. The emptiness inside of me was hard to deal with. I was sitting on my bed with my head resting in my knees. The whole scene with Sin replayed in my mind. I still couldn't believe my brother had gone to talk to him behind my back. If he hadn't gone to meddle in my personal life, Sin wouldn't have been pushed to search about my past.

It wasn't completely Connor's fault. Sin could have respected my privacy. How we got to this point didn't really matter, what mattered was how I was going to handle it. There was no rewind button. I let out a sigh as I looked up and stared unseeing at the white wall in front of me. It was hard to think about what happened without seeing the blood and the bodies of my parents. I could still remember the smell of death. I closed my eyes for a moment to try and push the horrific images from my mind.

Bringing up the past only dragged me down into an abyss of nothingness that was nearly impossible to escape. The fear that I'd felt that night returned and I began to shake. Most people had fears. Some had fears worse than others. What happened that night had been so much worse than my worst fear.

There was a knock on my door and I got up to open it.

"Your brother wants to talk to you," Matthew said, offering me the phone. After my heated discussion with Sin, I'd turned off my phone because I didn't want to talk to my brother. I was still so angry at him.

I refused to take the phone.

"Tell him I don't want to speak to him," I said with determination as I closed my bedroom door. Matthew had probably told him that Sin had come by and he would know why I was angry with him.

I'd told him countless times that I could make my own decisions. The fact was that he kept trying to undermine the little independence I'd been able to build and I wasn't going to allow it. He'd forced my hand. Shutting him out was going to hurt him, but he'd left me no choice.

That night I woke up screaming, with Matthew trying to calm me down. I'd relived the memory of my parents' death in my dreams. I was shaking, and breathing erratically.

"It's okay," Matthew soothed as he hugged my trembling form.

I leaned against him as I tried to sort through what had been real and what had been a dream. After a few minutes, I calmed down and I pulled away from him.

"I'm sorry," I mumbled as I brushed the remains of my tears from my face. "I bet your job description didn't include this."

He brushed a stray piece of hair out of my face.

"Does this happen often?" he asked as his eyes softened.

"No, not really. It was just a very emotional day," I answered with a shrug. I didn't like the fact that Matthew was seeing me like this. He studied me for a few moments.

"Are you going to be able to sleep?" he asked with concern.

"Yes," I lied as I nodded my head.

"Are you sure? I can make a bed on the floor if it will help," he offered.

"Thanks, but I'll be okay," I assured him.

"Look, I'd feel better if I stayed in your room. I'll just sit here until you go back to sleep," he insisted.

It touched me that he cared and I felt myself nod. He got up and switched off the light as I lay down in my bed and pulled my covers up to my chin. Even though Matthew stayed with me for the rest of the evening, I didn't sleep—although I kept my eyes closed, wishing for it. I heard Matthew leave my room early in the morning. I was exhausted when it was time to get up for classes.

"You look tired," Matthew remarked when I entered the kitchen still dressed in my pajamas. I gave him a slight shrug as I poured some coffee into my cup.

"Your brother phoned this morning to check up on you," he revealed to me. I ignored him. I'd made it clear the night before that I wasn't talking to my brother. The fact that my phone was still off should have given my brother the clear message that I still didn't want to talk to him.

"I still don't want to talk to him," I reminded him even though I knew at some point I would have to switch on my phone and go through all the messages from Connor. I felt an ache in my chest when I wondered if Sin had tried to call me. I tried to push the thought from my mind.

"Morning," Jordan muttered as she entered the small kitchen was well.

"You guys are like little dwarves this morning," Matthew said as he leaned against the kitchen counter and took a sip of his coffee.

Jordan and I shared a questioning look before looking expectantly at him.

"You know, the seven dwarves," he added.

"You're Grumpy," he said while looking at Jordan and then his eyes shifted to me. "And you're definitely Sleepy."

Our only responses were to glare at him and he quickly moved out of the kitchen to the living room a safe distance away from us.

"He is far too chirpy in the morning," mumbled Jordan as she got a cup and poured coffee.

"He is a morning person," was all I said.

"So are you going to sort things out with Sin?" she asked, watching me for my reaction. She didn't know the whole story. She'd probably assumed it was just a disagreement that could be easily fixed, but it wasn't that simple.

"I don't think it can be sorted."

I was tired and feeling a little raw. I really hoped I wasn't going to bump into him at college today.

"I know that I warned you off him," she started. "And trust me, I never in a million years thought I'd be saying this, but he is different with you."

I dropped my gaze to the floor, unable to look her in the

eye.

"Don't sweat the small things."

I looked up at her. She had no idea last night hadn't been about something small—well, at least it wasn't small for me. Normally I kept most things to myself, but I had a need to share some of the weight on my shoulders and she might not be as sympathetic to Sin when she found out what he'd done.

"He told me a little bit about his past and he wanted to know about my past," I began to explain, "but I didn't want to tell him."

I let out a sigh. She knew how I was about my past.

"He pretty much told me that we were done when I wouldn't open up to him."

"That's a bit harsh," she said, frowning.

"Then my brother went to go and see him," I revealed and she looked a little shocked.

"What did your brother say to him?" she asked.

"He told Sin to stay away from me," I revealed with a shrug.

"That's out of line," she said frowning.

"You're right, it was out of line. My brother's little visit made Sin look into my past and he found out...everything," I said with a little emotional hoarseness in my voice.

A few moments of silence turned into a minute.

"I'm not one to defend Sin, but maybe he did it because he cares about you."

I bit my lip, contemplating what she said.

"When someone cares about you they want to know things about you. And if you're dealing with stuff, they want to share in the burden of it."

There was more to her words than what was going on with Sin and me.

"Is there something up with you and Slater?" I asked.

"There is no Slater and me," she revealed. "He said he wasn't interested in dating."

Her lip trembled as a tear slid down her face and I put my coffee down. I hugged her as more tears ran down her cheeks.

"It will be okay," I soothed as I held her. Matthew appeared in the doorway and gave me a questioning look.

"Guys suck," I told him.

I promised myself I wouldn't look for him, but my eyes swept across the sea of students looking for him anyway. The need to catch a glimpse of him was stronger than my anger.

After I'd switched my phone back on, I had countless voicemails from my brother, but I was still too angry to even consider talking to him. He needed to realize that he couldn't control my life anymore and I felt if I gave in too easily he wouldn't learn. He'd called every couple of hours and got updates from Matthew.

I hadn't received any voicemails or messages from Sin and despite how angry I was I felt disappointed that he hadn't tried to contact me. Jordan's words kept echoing in my mind. *Maybe he did it because he cares about you.*

I'd been so angry when I'd discovered he'd found out my past. I'd been so confused with betrayal that I hadn't even considered that maybe he'd done it because he cared. I considered the thought. But if he cared so much, why hadn't he tried to contact me?

"You're thinking too hard," Matthew said, pulling me out of my deep thoughts. I glanced at him and he arched an eyebrow at me.

"I can smell roasted peanuts," he added with a teasing smile and I couldn't help but smile back.

"Really funny," I threw back at him as I shook my head.

Matthew had a way of easing stressful situations with his jokes and easy-going attitude. I really liked having him around.

He'd even promised Jordan he'd get us ice cream so we could eat ourselves into a sugar frenzy to forget about our heartache. I still didn't see how sugar was going to help, but I was going to try anyway.

It scared me that I'd gotten so attached to Sin in such a short space of time. He was such an intense person and the feelings I had for him matched that intensity. When I thought about him not being around, I felt short of breath like my lungs didn't have enough air to breathe.

I never caught a glimpse of Sin for the entire day and by the time Matthew and I were walking back to the apartment, I was feeling deflated. On the way home we stopped by the shop and Matthew bought two tubs of ice cream. Apparently the one was for me and the other was for Jordan.

"That is way too much ice cream," I told him as we left the shop.

"I've seen heartbroken girls eat way more ice cream than this," he informed me with a teasing smile. I still wasn't convinced that ice cream was going to ease the hole that had settled in my chest.

A little later that evening, Jordan and I were sitting side by side on the couch covered in blankets each with a tub of ice cream and a spoon. Somehow the sugar was making me feel a little better. Jordan seemed as heartbroken as I was, and she was staring unseeing at the TV like her mind was somewhere else. I set the ice cream down on the table, unable to eat any more.

"You feeling better?" Matthew asked from the single chair to the side of us.

"A little," I replied. He was like a big brother doing his

best to try and mend our broken hearts.

"Why are you so good at this?" I had to ask. Most guys wouldn't have a clue.

He smiled.

"I have two younger sisters," he revealed. Then I understood how he slipped into the big brother role so easily, he was a big brother to two sisters. It made so much more sense.

"I'm going to go and get ready for bed," I said. Matthew gave me a smile and I glanced to Jordan who gave me a weak smile.

I went into my bedroom and closed the door. I leaned against it for a moment and let out a sigh. This whole heartbreak thing sucked and I hated the feeling that my heart was missing and in its place was an empty hole. It was like an ache where my heart should be. I walked over to my dresser and checked my phone. There was that feeling of disappointment that Sin had still not tried to contact me. He'd said it wasn't finished, but I couldn't help feeling that he'd given up on me.

Could I blame him? The answer was no. I hadn't given him a chance to explain anything, I'd just told him to leave. I put my phone back down and went into the bathroom. In the shower I let some of my sadness spill out in tears that streamed down with the water. I was feeling emotionally exhausted by the time I got out of the shower and got dressed.

My phone beeped. I'd received a message. Subconsciously I held my breath as I walked over to pick up my phone. I was so used to the feeling of disappointment that I was momentarily shocked that it was a message from Sin.

I'm sorry.

Two simple words that gave me hope. For several moments I took the words in and then they spurred me into action. I got dressed as fast as I could and shoved my phone into my jeans. Matthew was still watching the girlie movie in the living room with Jordan who was still trying to get to the bottom of the tub of ice cream.

"I need to go," I said to him.

"You're not going anywhere without me," he told me as he stood up. "Can't it wait till tomorrow?"

I shook my head. I'd wasted enough time and I wasn't going to waste any more. My decision was made and I just hoped that I wasn't too late.

"Will you be okay here on your own?" I asked Jordan.

"I'll be fine. I have enough ice cream and I have TV," she said, trying to make light of her heartbreak.

"So where are we off to?" Matthew asked as we walked to the car.

"I need to talk to Sin," I said as he opened the passenger side for me. He studied me for a moment before he shrugged.

"Okay."

Maybe it was the determined look that told him there was no talking me out of what I'd set out to do. I knew how precious life was and wasting any time was wrong.

Nervously, I fidgeted as Matthew made the short trip to Sin's house. I didn't ask how he knew where Sin lived. I assumed my brother had given him the same folder he'd given me on Sin. I was unsure of how Sin was going to react to my sudden visit and I felt the nervous knot in my stomach twist as I got out of the car. Matthew got out of the driver's side.

"No," I said to him as firmly as I could. "I need to do this without you."

"It's my job to keep you safe," he reminded me in a serious tone.

"I'll be safe with Sin," I assured him. "I will call you if I need you."

He looked to the house and then back to me.

"No," he stated. "I can't stay out here while you go

inside."

We had a stare down for a few seconds before I threw my hands up in the air in frustration.

"Fine," I bit out.

I needed to talk to Sin, but I was scared that he would close up if he saw Matthew. I had no choice. Matthew followed me up the stairs and he stood beside me as I rang the doorbell.

I bit my lip as I felt the nervous knot in my stomach tighten at Sin's reaction to seeing me and Matthew. His reaction to Matthew when he'd seen him in the apartment hadn't been good and I had a feeling he wouldn't react well to seeing him with me now. I just hoped he would let me explain who Matthew was and why he had to go where I went.

I heard some noise behind the door and then the door opened.

Chapter Nineteen

TAYLOR

Sin looked slightly surprised to see me when he opened the door. His eyes brightened and he smiled when he saw me. He looked happy and relieved to see me and I felt the flutter of awareness that I felt when I was around him. There was something about this guy that made me come alive when he was near. I'd never felt it with anyone before and I had to admit I loved the feeling.

When his gaze moved to Matthew, his eyes hardened and his lips thinned. He wasn't so happy to see Matthew.

"What the fuck is he doing here?" he asked angrily as he glared at me. All the softness he'd been looking at me with was gone.

"Calm down. Don't jump to conclusions," I said to him, holding my hands up to him. "Just let us in and I'll explain everything."

He studied me for a moment before he stepped back and allowed me to enter. Matthew followed behind me. He seemed unfazed by the glare he was getting from Sin. He was his normal easy-going self even though Sin looked like he wanted to hit him.

"I need to talk to him alone," I said to Matthew. He gave me a brief nod of his head.

"I'll stay here," he said as he sat down on the sofa and made himself at home.

Sin had been watching the two of us with his arms crossed. I looked to him. He dropped his arms to his side and walked up the stairs to his bedroom. I followed him into his room. He closed the door and leaned against it.

"Where's everyone else?" I asked. Normally where Sin was, Slater was as well.

"They're out," he said in a clipped tone.

"So are you going to explain the tag-a-long?" he asked as he crossed his arms and fixed his gaze on me. There was no warmth in his eyes for me, his features closed off.

"You've met my overprotective brother," I began to explain. He gave a brief nod.

"Well, that overprotective brother hired a bodyguard," I explained as I clasped my hands together, waiting for his reaction. I should have just told him from the beginning who Matthew was.

"And I thought that overprotective brother of yours was stupid," he remarked. His hard features softened and he dropped his arms.

The jury was still out on that as far as I was concerned. I knew that my brother did things that he thought were in my best interest even if I didn't agree.

"He doesn't look like a typical bodyguard," he said as he cocked his head to the side. I was glad to hear I wasn't the only one who thought that.

"I know, it's probably why he is so good at his job," I replied with a shrug.

"And here I thought he was my replacement," he added as he straightened up but didn't close the distance between us.

My eyes lifted to his. I didn't want anyone but him. To

me there was no replacement for Sin. He'd hurt me by looking my past up, but that didn't mean that I didn't care about him or still want him. He was the one who had brought an end to our arrangement. For a few moments our eyes connected. There was so much between us that needed to be talked through. He'd shut me out when I wouldn't open up and I was still upset with the fact he'd found out about my past.

Deep in his gaze was still the look I'd been running from. It was a look of sadness. There was also that part that looked at me, not quite knowing what to expect. It was finally time to talk about my past. I had shut him down before, but now I was willing to listen to what he had to say.

"I'm sorry for shutting you out," I murmured, dropping my gaze to the carpet. I hated talking about my past. Talking about it gave it life to haunt me. It kind of felt like no matter what I did, I couldn't escape what had happened.

"I'm sorry too. I shouldn't have taken things into my own hands. You didn't want me to know, but I went searching anyway," he said, rubbing his hands over his face and into his hair. "But no matter how mad you are and how sorry I am, it doesn't change the fact that I know."

He dropped his hands. His hair was messy and I had to fight the urge to walk up to him and run my hands through his hair.

"I was upset after I'd told you stuff about me and you refused to open up," he began to explain. "I was angry so I tried to shut you out."

I remembered the heartbreaking moment when he'd told me he'd see me around.

"Then your brother came to see me," he said, running an agitated hand through his hair. I couldn't help but roll my eyes at the mention of my brother who I still wasn't talking to because of that visit.

"He told me to stay away from you. He said that you wouldn't recover if I hurt you," he said softly, watching for some sort of reaction to his words.

And there it was, that look again.

"I know that you didn't want to tell me about your past, but after your brother came to see me I couldn't stop myself," he reasoned softly. I bit down on my lip.

"There were so many things about you that just simply didn't add up. Your naivety and lack of knowledge."

I swallowed hard as he paused for a moment.

"Then your brother came to see me and told me to stay away from you. That just pushed me over the edge and I had to know. I tried asking your brother, but he wouldn't tell me so I did the only thing I could think of, I googled your name."

It hadn't been hard for him to find out. A simple Internet search would have brought everything up I'd been trying to hide. He took a step closer as his eyes held mine.

"I've been through some rough shit, but I don't know how you survived what happened to you," he offered softly.

I swallowed hard to keep the emotions from bubbling over to the outside. I closed my eyes for a moment and took a deep breath to keep the tears at bay. When I opened my eyes again, Sin was standing closer, but he didn't touch me. He stood only two feet away as he watched me while I struggled to rein in my emotions.

"I don't like it," he said softly to me. I wasn't sure what he was talking about so I gave him a questioning look.

"What?" I asked.

"I don't like seeing you upset," he answered and I felt my heart melt a little. He had the power to make me feel alive and he had the power to make me feel like I couldn't go on.

Just thinking about what happened was enough to evoke a whole array of emotions. Talking about it was worse, which was one of the reasons I didn't like talking about it. It was just too emotionally draining. I'd been to endless shrinks and I'd talked about it so much, but no amount of talking would erase the events of that day or bring my parents back. All talking did was remind me of that horrific day.

"You don't have to talk about it," he said as he reached out and caressed my cheek with his hand.

He'd told me he knew everything so anything I told him wouldn't be anything that he hadn't already read about, but I felt that I had to tell him the story in my own words. Everything he'd read would have been correct with the facts of what had happened, but I was the only who was able to relay the events with the human emotion because I'd lived it.

"I've been trying to forget that day for as long as I can remember," I began. He reached for my hand and held it in his.

"I was nine." I swallowed hard. "It was a Friday night and Connor went out to a party. He was eighteen at the time and he'd planned on sleeping over at his friend's house."

That night had started off as a normal evening. I'd pouted a little when he'd left. I loved my older brother and at that age I'd worshipped the ground he walked on. In my eyes he could do no wrong and he loved me just as much. He loved to do things with me and didn't mind me tagging along with him most of the time.

"I spent the evening watching a movie with my mom and dad. They liked to do that with me so I wouldn't miss Connor too much when he was out," I told him, smiling at the fond memory I had of them.

My mom laughed and my father wrapped his arm around me and gave me a hug. I'd been so loved. At that time it had been so normal and I'd give anything to go back to that. I swallowed the emotion down as I tried to continue.

"Sit," Sin instructed as he pushed me down to sit on his

bed. I rubbed my forehead and I tried to get my thoughts together as he sat down next to me, still holding my hand.

"I'm not sure what time they tucked me into bed and read me a story. My mom gave me a kiss on the forehead and told me to have sweet dreams. My father came to kiss me goodnight and told me he loved me. It was our usual routine for bedtime."

It was strange that some memories were blurry as you got older and it was harder to remember them, but there were just some memories that didn't dull with time and that night was one of them. I could recall everything, the good and the bad. Sin squeezed my hand for reassurance that I wasn't alone and I gave him a weak smile in return.

"I'd been going through a stage of having nightmares and that night I woke up scared. I held my favorite teddy, Mr. Cuddles, tightly in my hands and went to my parents' bedroom to ask my mom if I could sleep in the bed. Still half asleep, my mom opened her covers and I climbed into the bed bedside her."

I paused for a moment and took a deep breath and expelled it.

"I was jolted awake by my mom. She was scared and shaking. My dad wasn't in the room. She'd told me to remain calm and to hide in the closet. Confused and still half asleep, I asked her what was wrong. She whispered to me that there was someone in the house and told me I needed to be quiet. I didn't understand what was happening, but I did what she told me. Once I was safe inside the closet she closed the doors. There was enough of a gap to be able to see my mother walk to the door."

I dropped my eyes to the floor for a moment as I built the courage to continue. It was hard talking about those events and remembering the last memories that I had of my parents.

"You don't have to," Sin said as he took my other hand in his. I looked at him.

"You know everything, but I need you to understand why it was something that was so hard to carry around with me. What you read would have given you all the grim details, but I want you to understand why I am the way I am," I tried to explain.

As hard as it was, I carried on.

"There was some noise inside the house and I heard my father shout. My mom looked frantic and scared. I'll never forget that fear that I saw on her face. She hurried back to the closet and got me out and then she led me to the window. She opened it up as quietly as she could. I wanted to stay with her, but she begged me to be a good girl and to climb through the window."

I fought the tears that gathered in my eyes and as they overflowed I brushed them from my face.

"I whimpered as I climbed through the window. She told me to go and hide in the back yard. I had no idea what was happening, but it was the desperation in her voice that made me run through the darkness to the back of the house. Our property was quite large with a tall boundary wall so I ran as fast as I could still holding onto my teddy bear. I tripped a couple of times... I don't know if it was the adrenaline that kept me from feeling the pain."

More tears silently slid down my face and as fast as I brushed them away, new tears replaced them. I felt a gentle touch to my cheek and Sin brushed my tears gently with his hands.

"I don't like it when you cry," he said softly, his voice hoarse. As much as he didn't like seeing me cry, I didn't like feeling this open and exposed.

"I hid in some thick bushes against the wall. I huddled holding Mr. Cuddles, too scared to move."

I'd lost track of time and with the fear that I'd felt, every minute felt like ten so what had only been an hour had felt like forever.

"It was only when the sun came up that I came out of hiding. In the daytime, everything seemed less scary."

He nodded.

"The house was quiet and the front door was wide open. The house had been ransacked and I crept as quietly as I could. I was scared that the intruders were still in the house. The first place I went to was my parents' bedroom."

I closed my eyes for a moment, riding out the emotions that overwhelmed me at the next stage of my memory. Sin squeezed both of my hands and kept them in his.

"While I'd been hiding in the dark, I'd imagined all sorts of scenarios, but nothing prepared me for what I found. There was so much blood. My father was lying on his stomach with a knife sticking out of his back. I rushed over to him, but he didn't respond. I'd never seen death before, but I saw it in his eyes. I heard a slight noise and realized my mom was still alive."

I put my hands to my mouth as a sob tore from me. The next part had been the hardest.

"Crying... and becoming more hysterical, I rushed over to her. She was lying in a pool of her own blood. She had a couple of stab wounds...honestly, I don't know how she'd survived that long. I wanted to go and get help, but my mom held my wrist and...told me to stay with her."

I gulped down my emotion.

"She knew she wouldn't make it and she didn't want to die alone. I held my mother's hand as she struggled to breathe. I told her I loved her just before her chest stopped moving and I couldn't hear her breathe anymore. It was the hardest thing I've ever had to do."

"I'm so sorry," murmured Sin as he let go of my hands

and wrapped his arms around me. He hugged me as I leaned my head against his chest. After a few minutes, I pulled away from him and stood up. I needed to finish and I felt if I didn't do it now, I would clam up again.

"I kind of shut down after that. It was like I was in a bubble. I knew exactly what was going on around me, but I couldn't interact. I lost track of time."

I rubbed my forehead as I tried to remember what happened after that.

"The next thing I remember was when Connor came home and discovered what happened. It's hard to remember exactly what happened after that because I had some sort of breakdown. I just couldn't cope with everything."

My eyes met his and I saw that look again.

"I wasn't crazy," I stated as I began to feel emotional as well as agitated. Afterward, people looked at me with sympathy, but hidden in those looks was the wariness that I was unstable.

"You weren't crazy, you just lost your parents and you couldn't cope. It's understandable," he explained as he stood up and walked to me.

The newspapers hadn't just covered the brutal murder of my parents in an apparent robbery gone wrong, they'd also covered my downward spiral into oblivion that had landed me in a psychiatric ward.

"You look at me the same way they did," I murmured as I took a step back. I knew this would happen when people started to discover my secret past. It had been the main reason I'd tried to keep it from coming out.

"That's not how I see you," he argued as he took a step closer.

Chapter Twenty

TAYLOR

I wanted to believe him, but I didn't.

"How do you see me?" I asked, wanting him to convince me that he didn't see me like everyone else did when they found out about my past.

He took another step closer and I held my breath. Being so close to him was enough to have a physical effect on my body and I looked up at him.

"When I look at you, I see someone who is strong and fearless," he whispered to me as his intense gaze held mine. "There aren't many girls who see what they want and go for it."

He smiled at me and I felt my heart flutter.

"No one has ever asked me to take advantage of them like you did," he revealed with his smile widening. I let my gaze drop from his as I took a deep breath. His fingers lifted my chin so I'd look at him.

"I see a beautiful girl who is just as beautiful on the inside," he added, all smiles gone. "Finding out about your past has made me understand you better, but it hasn't changed the fact that I wanted you then and I still want you now."

That was the moment that I fell head over heels for my tattooed bad-boy. There was no going back; he had my heart and there was nothing I could do to change that.

His eyes flickered down to my lips and back to my eyes.

"Show me," I whispered as I ran my tongue along my bottom lip.

He'd hurt me badly when he'd brushed me off, but despite that and the fact that he was probably going to break my heart, I needed this. There would be no forever with him, but I wanted every little moment I could still have with him. I needed him to look at me like I was the beautiful girl he wanted so badly, not the crazy chick who had landed in the loony bin after witnessing the horror of her parents' murder.

He leaned closer and I felt his breath against my cheek. I closed my eyes for a moment and savored the way it made me feel.

When I opened my eyes, he was staring at me with an intensity I'd never seen before and for the first time since he'd found out about my past, he didn't look at me the way that reminded me about my parents' murder and my time when I'd been battling against my own mind. His hands settled on my hips and I held my breath in anticipation.

"You are so beautiful," he whispered just before his lips touched mine. The touch was so gentle, but it still made my stomach flip and I gripped his arms.

The fact that Matthew was waiting downstairs should have pulled me away, but it didn't. His lips moved against mine gently as my hands ran along his arms and wrapped around his neck.

I felt the light touch of his tongue against my bottom lip and I groaned. My lips opened slightly and it was enough of an invitation for his tongue to slip inside my mouth and tangle with mine. His arms wrapped around my waist and he held me closer and deepened the kiss. I felt my toes curl as he assaulted my senses and his tongue caressed mine.

Slowly, he walked me back until I felt his bed against the back of my knees. Gently, like I was a precious package that he didn't want to break, he laid me down on his bed. For a few moments, he stood letting his gaze caress me. The look of want was unmistakable in his eyes.

I reached for him as he knelt down on the bed and then covered my body with his. I wrapped my legs around his waist as he settled between my open legs. He kissed me hard and he ground his hips against mine. His need for me was evident. I kissed him back as he continued to rock against me. The ache between my legs grew as I breathed hard. He kissed me hard one last time before he pulled free and, for a moment, I felt disappointed that he was putting a stop to it. But with relief I realized he was pulling his shirt over his head.

My eyes feasted over his perfectly defined body and he knelt on a knee beside me. I sat up and he reached for the hem of my shirt and pulled it over my head. The discarded piece of clothing hit the floor as he stood and began to unbutton his jeans, his gaze promising me what I wanted and needed. His jeans dropped and he kicked them off. I lay back as he unzipped my jeans and I lifted my hips to help him pull them off me. Only our underwear was left as a barrier between us while the warmth of his body covered mine. I cupped his face as he pressed his body against mine.

For a moment his eyes held mine, and in that moment it was just about the two of us, and what we were sharing. Slowly I lifted my lips to his and gently kissed him. Our soft and tender kiss became more heated as our bodies ground together. He pulled away and he gripped my panties and pulled them off. I lifted up just slightly so his fingers could work the clasp of my bra. He pulled it off me and I lay back.

He discarded his boxers.

His eyes drifted over my nakedness and I didn't want to cover up. I didn't feel shy. He made me feel beautiful. He kissed me hard and then trailed his lips along my jaw, nipping and licking gently. I gasped as he drove me to the edge, keeping me there. My nipples pebbled as I waited in anticipation. He didn't keep me waiting. His mouth closed over one nipple as his fingers gently tweaked the other. Feeling more confident, I pushed him down onto his back and he smiled at me. I trailed kisses down his body.

Sin lay back and put his hands under his head. I started with gentle touches of my tongue and Sin tensed beneath me. I took him into my mouth and I felt his hand thread through my hair. It took me a few tries and the tensing of his body beneath me told me when I was doing it right.

"I can't take much more," he told me hoarsely as he pushed me back onto my back.

He reached for a foil packet and tore it with his teeth. Once the protection was on, he kissed me as he settled in between my legs. His hand trailed down my thigh as my leg wrapped around his waist again. He kissed me as he pushed into me. I held onto his shoulder as he began to move inside of me. The tempo was slow and deliberate.

I gasped as the tempo increased and he covered my mouth with his. He pushed against my body, trying to bury as much as he could inside of me. The ache inside me built up until he thrust inside of me and I exploded. The waves of the orgasm were still convulsing through me when I felt him push into me and stiffen.

For me it hadn't been just gratifying sex, it had been more than that. It had been sharing something special with the guy I'd fallen in love with. Afterward, he leaned his forehead against mine, both of us still breathing hard. He kissed me before he got up and went into the bathroom.

When he came back into the room, he lay down on the bed and I snuggled up beside him.

He held me in his arms and pressed a kiss to my forehead. I lay my head against his chest and I wrapped my arm around his waist. There had been a few times in the past few days that I thought I'd never feel the warmth of his body against mine again and I was content to just enjoy it even though I knew it wasn't going to last. I ignored the pain in my heart when I thought I was losing him.

"What are you thinking about?" he asked softly.

There was no way I could tell him what I was thinking. Sin didn't want to hear that I'd just fallen in love with him and that I wanted more than he was ever going to be able to give me.

"Not much." I let the little white lie roll off my tongue.

Sin squeezed me closer for a moment before he moved so he could lay on his side, facing me.

"Thank you for telling me your story," he whispered as he trailed his fingers along my cheek.

"I needed you to understand why I didn't want anyone to find out about it," I explained. "It was bad enough going through what I did but doing it under the watchful eye of the press was traumatic. It didn't just affect me. I put Connor through hell. Not only did he lose both of our parents, he lost me for a while and he fought hard to get me back."

It was the reason why I let him get away with so much when it came to meddling in my life, but I'd drawn the line when it had come to Sin.

"My parents had left us some money, but my brother worked hard to make sure he had the money to send me to the best shrinks and get me the best help money could buy."

It was still hard to talk about that time in my life. Sometimes I wished I could wipe it from my memory, but life didn't work that way.

"When most people had given up, my brother refused to. And then one day about a year after it happened, I started to improve a little. It took a long time, but I recovered."

"Now I understand why your brother is so protective of you."

A few minutes of silence settled between us.

"But at least they caught the guys who murdered your parents," he murmured to me.

It should be a consolation, but it wasn't. Nothing would bring my parents back, although I was glad that I wouldn't have to constantly wonder about the identity of the two guys that had murdered my parents in cold blood.

"Yeah, they both got life sentences without the chance of parole even though they'd argued they'd been high on drugs," I said. He'd probably read about it on the web.

Sometimes I wondered whether if circumstances had been different and if they hadn't been high on drugs my parents would still be alive. I got a physical pain in my chest when I thought about the loss that I would carry for the rest of my life. The pain of the loss eased a little as time went by, but it would never go away.

There would still be so many important days in my life that the loss of my parents would be harder to bear. I squeezed my eyes closed when I thought about my father and the fact that he wouldn't be able to walk me down the aisle when I got married one day. It was difficult to think about the day when I had children of my own. Two young criminals who'd been high had taken so much from me. Their mistake had cost me, and I'd be paying every day for the rest of my life.

Sin pressed a kiss to my forehead and hugged me tighter.

I allowed myself to lay for a few more moments before I pulled away. I was confused. Before, we'd had an arrangement with clear rules, but now I wasn't sure what this was between us. I could have asked him to clarify what we were now, but I didn't want to be one of those girls trying to put a label on everything. Maybe another reason I didn't ask was because I was too scared of what the answer would be.

"Where are you going?" Sin asked me as he watched me gather up my clothes and start getting ready.

"I have to go," I told him as I pulled my panties on. "Matthew is still waiting downstairs."

"Ah, Matthew. I forgot about him," mumbled Sin as he sat up. I smiled at him as I pulled my shirt over my head.

I wanted to ask him when I would see him again. I so desperately wanted the surety that this wasn't just a one-night thing but I couldn't bring myself to ask the question. Instead I smiled at him as I slipped into my jeans and zipped them up. I didn't want him to think I was desperate so I plastered the fake smile to my face and acted like this was normal. He slipped out of the bed and pulled his jeans on as I shoved my feet into my shoes.

"I'll walk you out," he told me as he opened the door to his bedroom for me.

I felt my heart squeeze at his casual words. This was going to be it. What we'd shared didn't make us anything more than what we'd been before. I couldn't help the hurt I felt as I walked down the stairs with Sin following behind me.

Matthew was sitting watching something on TV when he turned to see me. He switched the TV off as he stood up and walked over to us. Sin was shirtless and I felt myself blush at the realization that it looked like we'd been doing more than talking in his room. Even though Sin knew that Matthew was my bodyguard, he seemed to size him up for a minute. Matthew kept his cool under Sin's intense gaze. Sin broke his gaze away from Matthew and fixed it on me.

"At least I know you'll be safe," he said as he walked me to the door. Matthew opened the door and left us alone as he walked to the car.

"Yes, he is the best my brother could find," I assured him. It was nice to know that Sin cared.

"He'd better be."

I wasn't sure what he meant by that. Did it make Sin worry about me less, knowing that I had one of the best bodyguards money could buy? While standing there nervously and with my insecurities flitting like questions through my mind, he leaned forward and kissed my cheek.

My thoughts disappeared as I touched my cheek where he'd kissed me. A noise outside made me look back to see Matthew leaning against the car, watching us.

"I need to go," I said as I turned to leave.

"Bye, Tay," he said as he watched me walk to the car. Matthew opened the door and I got into the passenger side. He was still watching from the doorway as Matthew got into the driver's side and started the engine. I watched Sin as Matthew reversed the car. My body was still humming from my tumble with Sin, but the sinking feeling in my stomach grew stronger as Matthew pulled away and I lost sight of him.

Did this mean that despite everything we'd shared we were going to go back to being strangers?

Matthew was quiet for the drive back to the apartment, leaving me alone with my thoughts. I should have been happy and smiling after what had happened between Sin and I, but I wasn't. Convinced that because he hadn't said anything about seeing each other again meant that he wasn't interested in taking things further with me made my chest hurt.

It wasn't like he'd made any promises. I'd known the score and I'd known the rules. The fact that I'd still fallen hopelessly in love with him lay squarely on my shoulders.

The apartment was dark and quiet when we returned. I checked on Jordan. She was fast asleep in her bed. When I walked back into the living room, Matthew was leaning against the wall, watching me.

"So you and lover-boy all made up?" he asked.

I shrugged, not wanting to admit anything out loud before I had the time to process it.

"Have you read his file yet?" he asked. I knew exactly where this was going and I wasn't going to stand for it. I was tired of everyone telling me how to live my life. I got that they loved and cared for me, but enough was enough.

"No, I haven't. Actually, the next time I get a chance, I'm going to toss it out," I snapped, feeling my temper rise. "Or burn it."

He held up his hands.

"I just wanted to make sure you know what you're getting yourself into."

Little did he know I wasn't getting into anything and it sucked.

"You're nearly as bad as my brother," I said, getting annoyed. It was bad enough to having one overprotective brother. Matthew pressed his lips together as he studied me for a moment.

"Okay, no more lectures from me. You're a big girl and you can make up your own mind," he said.

"Thanks."

I appreciated the fact that he was going to back off on the subject of Sin and whether he was good enough for me, because to me he was.

It was really late when I finally got dressed for bed and crawled under the covers, but the heaviness in my heart made it difficult for me to relax and go to sleep. I was staring up to the ceiling, waiting for sleep to claim me when I heard my phone receive a text message. Who would be texting me so late? I reached for my phone and looked at the screen. It was a text message from Sin.

Sweet dreams Tay.

Three little words that instantly lifted my heart and I smiled. He was thinking of me.

Night Sin, I texted him.

Did this mean we were going to be more than just strangers passing each other in the hallways? I couldn't help but take it as a sign for something more. There was that nagging in the background of my mind that I could be setting myself up for more heartbreak.

After that, I drifted off to sleep and woke up feeling refreshed the next day. Jordan tried to appear happy, but I could see past it to the real hurt she still felt over Slater.

We all had breakfast and coffee quickly before leaving for class. Matthew opened the door and noticed a note pinned to the front of it. His face was stone-like as he read the message.

"What is it?" I asked as I stepped forward to reach for the message.

"Don't touch it," he instructed, stopping me by taking hold of my wrist. "It's a note from your stalker."

Oh. My. God. The stalker knew where I was living?

I needed to see the note for myself. I stepped around Matthew and looked at the note.

I know where you live, whore. You can't hide from me. You're my whore not his.

Chapter Twenty-One

SIN

I smiled when I spotted Taylor walking to class with Matthew following closely beside her. I'd just seen her last night, but it had felt longer.

She'd surprised me when she'd finally opened up and told me about her past. It didn't matter that I'd already read all of it off the web. Hearing it in her own words had made it more real and more heart-breaking. She'd forgiven me for finding out about her past, but I still felt a pang of guilt when I thought about it.

It had been my concern for her safety that had pushed me to search her name on the Internet. Just thinking about what happened to her made me sad and angry at the same time. It was different having parents who couldn't give a shit. I couldn't miss something I'd never had. I couldn't imagine losing the unconditional love from a parent after experiencing it.

Something was off. Matthew was watching his surroundings like a hawk. It wasn't like he was being obvious, I think the only reason I picked up on it was because I knew he was a bodyguard. Taylor seemed a little jumpy and nervous. It wasn't like her. I frowned as I reached her. Matthew swung his gaze at me and his features seemed to relax when he recognized me. Taylor gave me a weak smile.

"You okay?" I asked, letting my gaze move between the two of them.

"Everything's fine," she tried to reassure me with a weak smile but I could see past the front she was trying to put on.

I gave Matthew a questioning look.

"The stalker left a note on the door of the apartment," he told me. Taylor glared at him for revealing the information.

"What did it say?"

My question was directed at Taylor, but she hesitated. My unease grew.

" 'I know where you live, whore. You can't hide from me. You're my whore not his,' " Matthew told me and something in my gut twisted.

You're my whore not his echoed through my mind. I stepped closer to Taylor and scanned her features. It explained her nervousness and I took her hand in mine. The thought that the crazy guy who had tried to attack her was stalking her made me angry. After everything else, she didn't deserve this. She bit on her lip nervously as she held my gaze. I wanted to make her feel better and I wanted her to know I wasn't going to let this guy get anywhere near her. I leaned closer and kissed her. I pulled back in time to see her lip tremble and I hugged her for a moment. I forgot about Matthew as I held her.

"I'm okay," she assured me as she pulled away, but I knew she wasn't okay.

"Are you sure?" I asked, watching her carefully. She nodded her head at me, but I could still see the fear in her eyes.

"It's okay if you're not," I tried to tell her. No one expected her to be brave in the situation she was in.

"I'm fine," she insisted with determination.

In that moment, I glimpsed the part of Taylor who had survived the horrific deaths of her parents and the downward mental spiral afterward. It was the part of her that wouldn't just lie down and let it consume her. I understood that part of her. My life hadn't been good and I also had that same part in me that part that fought for survival. We were different people with different circumstances, but we both had that survival part that had kept us going through the tougher times.

"Are the cops any closer to catching the guy?" I asked Matthew. He shook his head.

“No,” he revealed.

I looked to Taylor again and felt a pang of something in my chest. I didn't want anything to happen to her.

"Why did you come to school? Don't you think it would be safer to stay at home?" I asked softly.

She shook her head.

"I tried to tell her that it might be a good idea to stay at the apartment today," Matthew added.

"I won't allow this to make me too scared to do the things that I want to," she told me.

I understood that she didn't want what was happening to dictate her life so I tried to keep myself from bundling her up and taking her home. She'd fought to lead the normal life she was and I could see it was difficult to give that up because some crazy guy had a fixation on her.

"Come on, I'll walk you to class," I offered as I took her hand in mine. She smiled at me as we walked to her class with Matthew still watching the surrounding crowd.

At the doorway of her classroom, I gave her a brief kiss and watched as she entered the classroom with Matthew. There were no clues and the cops had no suspects. My eyes scanned the room, lingering for a moment on each guy in her class. I couldn't help wonder if it was someone sitting in her classroom. My eyes went to Matthew who was sitting beside her. I didn't trust a lot of people and it was hard to trust Matthew to keep her safe. Taylor had told me that he was the best that her brother could find who was young enough to pass off as a college student, but that didn't make it any easier to walk away from her classroom.

I noticed Caleb, the preppy boy that she'd briefly dated and my eyes narrowed. He was sitting at the desk beside her on the opposite side to Matthew. I would be late for my class, but I couldn't pull myself away. Caleb leaned over to say something to Taylor and I felt a pull of possessiveness inside of me. Fisting my hands, I stopped myself from walking over to him and beating the crap out of him. She was mine. The brightening in his eyes as he talked to her told me volumes. Despite Taylor telling him she only wanted to be friends, I could see he felt more.

I wondered if he could be the stalker.

You're my whore not his.

It sounded like something that someone would say because they were jealous. Was it Caleb, who clearly still had a thing for her? Was he jealous of the fact that she'd been spending time with me?

It wasn't like we were dating or anything like that. As much as I wanted to stay there to watch Caleb around Taylor, I turned and walked away from the classroom before I did something I would regret. I rubbed my hands over my face, trying to get my thoughts together. There had to be another way to see if my suspicions for Caleb were correct. I pulled my phone out of the front pocket of my jeans. It didn't take me long to find the contact I was looking for. I dialed the number and waited for him to answer.

"What's up?" a male's voice asked as soon as he picked up.

"I need you to do something for me," I told the guy.

I didn't question why I had such a need to protect Taylor. Maybe it was because I was scared to face the reason why I felt the way I did. I wanted to believe it stemmed from the fact that she'd had a hard life and I wanted to make sure nothing bad happened to her again. She'd fought hard to overcome her mental breakdown and it worried me that if something horrible happened she wouldn't be able to recover from it.

But the truth was, even if I didn't want to admit it, I cared about her. More than I should. She'd been the first girl that I'd screwed more than once. Usually if there was any sight of any drama, I'd have been the first one to walk away, but despite Taylor's past and the whole stalker thing, I was still around. I didn't want to analyze why; instead, I was going to make it my mission to keep her safe.

TAYLOR

It had been a long and nervous day at school. I wouldn't admit it to anyone, but I'd been scared. Keeping up the brave facade had been exhausting and I was glad to be back inside the apartment where—despite the fact that the stalker had left a note on the door—I still felt safe.

I glanced at Matthew. He was also the reason I felt safer. He never stopped scanning the crowds of students passing by us today.

"Thanks," I said to him out of the blue.

"What for?" he asked as he took his eyes off the TV and glanced at me.

"For everything."

"You're welcome. I'm just doing my job," he replied.

I didn't know how he could do the job he did. Putting your own life on the line for someone else wasn't easy so I had the utmost respect for him and what he was trying to do for me. I made a mental note to try and do as he told me and not to be difficult.

Jordan was still dealing with her heartbreak. She'd tried to hide her it, but I'd seen right through it. The moment we'd gotten back from college she'd disappeared into her bedroom. I wanted to comfort her, but I didn't really know what to say. Maybe she needed to deal with it on her own.

There was an unexpected knock on the door and my eyes shot to Matthew.

"The stalker wouldn't knock," Matthew said in a teasing tone as he shook his head at me.

He was right of course, but I couldn't help that nervous edge of fear that shot through me. He went to the door and opened it while I remained seated with my hands digging into the arms of the chair.

"It's for you," he yelled at me.

I hadn't been expecting anyone and as I got closer to the door, I was surprised to see Sin standing outside the front door waiting for me. I smiled at him and he smiled back at me as our eyes met. It was a nice surprise and my nervousness evaporated.

"Hi," he said as I invited him in.

"Hi," I greeted back, feeling so happy to see him.

Matthew was seated in front of the TV again, flicking through the channels and he turned to watch us. It was like having an older brother around and he was making it a little awkward for me so I reached for Sin's hand and led him to my room. I heard Matthew laugh as I closed the door.

"Sorry about that—the disadvantages to having a bodyguard," I joked as my eyes met his.

"The advantages are he won't let anything happen to you," Sin shot back, but there was no teasing in his face.

He was right—Matthew was all I had standing in the way of some crazy stalker trying to get me. I had no idea what the stalker would do to me if he got me and it scared me.

Sin's gaze caressed my face as he stepped closer and I held my breath. I could feel my skin tingle under his intense gaze as he leaned closer and I felt his warm breath on my face. My hands reached up and I put them against his chest as his lips lightly touched mine. No matter how many times he touched me, it always felt like the first time and I felt the rush of desire to be as close to him as humanly possible.

His tongue stroked my bottom lip gently and I opened my lips. His tongue pushed into my mouth as my hands crept up and wrapped around his neck, pulling him closer. I needed more. What started out soft and gentle grew more fierce and insistent as his hands pulled me closer, closing the slight gap between us.

He broke the kiss, his chest rising and falling rapidly as his gaze held mine. I couldn't pull my eyes from his as my fingers touched my bruised lips. I wasn't sure why he stopped so abruptly, but before I could ask him, he reached for me again and pushed me firmly against the wall as his mouth slammed against mine. I didn't think; all I wanted to do was feel what he was doing to me.

He lifted the hem of my shirt and pulled his lips from mine long enough to get my top off. It was a good thing I was wearing a skirt because I felt his fingers reach underneath it, hitching it up as he pulled my panties off. He reached for a condom in the back pocket of his jeans and tore the foil packet open with his teeth. He unbuttoned his jeans and let them drop. Once the protection was on, his mouth was on mine again as I felt him press up against me.

This time the sex was different. The last time we'd been

together it had been soft and gentle, but this time it was nothing like that. He turned me to face the wall and I put my hands against the wall to steady myself. His hand reached for my breasts that were still covered by my bra and pulled the bra down. I felt his fingers tweak my nipples as he pushed into me and my breath hitched as he began to move inside of me.

I moaned and placed my hands against the wall, trying to steady myself as he began to move inside of me. At first he moved slowly, but as he began to push into me with more force, it became more difficult to take. His hands were holding onto my hips so hard I was sure they would leave bruises, just so he could penetrate me deeper. I gasped as he reached a new angle and began to pant as he worked me closer to my release.

I felt the graze of his teeth against my shoulder and I closed my eyes and savored it. Just when I didn't think I could take any more new sensations, I felt his fingers move to the front and begin to stroke the front of my core. Moments later, I felt my whole body tense and then I exploded. The orgasm pulsed through me as I felt him push into me harder, trying to find his own release. His body tensed and he groaned against my neck as he came inside of me.

For a few moments, we stayed that way—me leaning against the wall and him breathing hard against my neck, still inside of me. He pulled out of me and pulled up his jeans. I turned and leaned against the wall as I pulled my skirt down. Sin went into my bathroom and came back out after a few minutes. I'd put my panties and top back on. I was just running a hand through my hair when Sin looked at me.

There was something going on in his mind and I wished I knew what it was. The sex had been great—don't get me wrong—but it was like he was trying to prove something to himself. It was like he was trying to make it all about sex and nothing else. I swallowed hard as I held his gaze, feeling vulnerable.

"I'm sorry if I was a little rough," he apologized as he ran a hand through his hair, making it untidy and disheveled, which just made him sexier.

"You weren't," I said with a shrug.

I loved this guy even though there was no guarantee that this, whatever it was, would last. He didn't date and I didn't know how long I could do this without wanting more. Eventually it would come to a head and then it would fall apart.

I sat down on my bed and Sin sat beside me. I loved being so close to him. A calmness that eluded me when I wasn't with him settled over me as he took my hand into his and gave it a squeeze. We started to talk about anything that wasn't related to the stalker. I wondered if it was his way of taking my mind off it. We were both lying down on my bed, talking, when I realized I needed to go to the bathroom. I went to the bathroom and closed the door.

"Have you got any headache tablets?" I heard Sin ask through the door.

"Yeah, in the drawer by my bed," I answered. Once I finished up, I walked into my room.

Oh. My. God.

Sin was sitting on my bed next to my side table. The small drawer was open and in his hands was the folder that my brother had given me. His face was tense as he paged through the folder and I felt my heart sink as dread crept into the pit of my stomach.

"I can explain," I said nervously as I walked over to him, but he closed the folder and stood up.

He refused to look at me as his lips pressed together and I watched his jaw tighten. He was trying to rein in his temper. He had every right to be upset, but I could explain everything.

"I don't think you can explain this," he said in a level voice that was waiting to explode. "I think it speaks for itself, doesn't it?"

His eyes lifted to mine. And the look he gave me made me flinch and take a step backward. My heart sank at the hatred in his eyes.

Chapter Twenty-Two

TAYLOR

"You need to let me explain," I began to plead with him. I stood between him and his only means of escape. I had to explain before he left. He shook his head at me and I felt the fear of losing him spark inside of me and start to engulf me.

"I don't have to do anything for you," he said angrily as he glared at me.

He'd never used this tone with me before and I was momentarily stunned. He didn't have all the facts so he had every right to be angry, but the least he could do was let me explain. In just seconds he'd gone from caring to hating me and I was still trying to catch up to the mess I was in.

"I didn't read it," I tried to explain, but I could see him close himself off from me. He'd already made up his mind and there was no amount of explaining that was going to change it. I was wasting my time.

"Connor gave it to me, but I never read it," I insisted, my eyes pleading with his. He had to believe me.

"Why?" he asked, looking at me suspiciously.

"I told you he was overprotective. This is him taking the over protectiveness a step too far," I tried to reason with him.

"Yeah, I get it. One look at me and he knew I was no good," he said and my heart squeezed.

"You are good—"

"I trusted you," he admitted, letting his gaze fall to the floor as he cut me off. He couldn't even look at me. "I opened up to you and told you things I don't tell a lot of people."

The tone of his voice changed. He sounded hoarse and emotional. The normal confident and strong Sin was gone and in his place was a vulnerable boy who'd spent most of his life unloved. It pulled directly at the strings to my heart and I stepped forward to comfort him, but he took a step back, putting himself out of my reach. He couldn't stand the sight of me and he didn't want me to touch him. It was a hard blow. I wrapped my arms around my waist to keep myself from reaching for him. His eyes shot to mine and the anger was back, and so was the hardened Sin with the protective shell.

"If you wanted to know so badly, all you had to do was ask," he added. "If you'd asked...I would have told you."

His voice broke slightly on the last sentence and I bit down on my lip as I felt the sting of tears. I was losing him—I could feel it.

"There are a lot of things I've done that I'm not proud of," he said as he ran a hand through his hair. "I did them for survival."

I swallowed hard, wanting to hold him and tell him I didn't care what he'd done. From the little he'd told me about his childhood, I'd understood that he hadn't been brought up the way I had been and I wasn't going to judge him on what he'd had to do to survive the childhood he'd been stuck in.

He hadn't judged me and I wouldn't judge him. The horror of my parents' murder had sent me straight into a white, padded room and that would have sent most guys running in the opposite direction, but Sin had stayed.

"After I found out about your past, I didn't want you to find out about some of the stuff from my past. I was scared about how you would handle it."

I fought the emotional torrent that wanted to break free from me as his eyes held mine. What could he have done that make him scared of how I'd handle it? My curiosity was piqued. Although he was still angry, his eyes held a little sadness that made me feel guilty just for having the folder in my drawer.

"But it doesn't matter anymore."

It was the tone and how he looked at me that made my heart crack because I knew what was coming. To him, I didn't matter anymore. There was no way to stop it—all I could do was stand there with what little self-respect I had. Somewhere deep down inside, I hoped that he just needed some time to cool off. I'd reacted the same when I'd discovered he'd uncovered my past and it had taken a few days for me to be able to talk to him again. He needed time.

"We're done," he stated in a defeated tone.

I could beg and plead, but it wouldn't change his mind. I stood still as he stepped past me and opened my bedroom door. My eyes watered and I felt the first sob escape me as I pressed my hand to my mouth when the front door slammed closed.

"What happened?" Matthew asked from the doorway of my bedroom moments later, looking confused.

I tried to take a breath, but another sob tore from me. Worry etched Matthew's features as he walked to me and pulled me into a hug. The emotion I'd bottled up began to break free and I closed my eyes and cried.

He held me as I released all my heartache in the tears that streamed down my face and wet his shirt.

"It will be okay," he soothed as he held me.

He was saying it to make me feel better because there was no way he could know that for sure. I wanted to hope that there was still a chance that it could be fixed, but I was scared to face up to the fact that it was unfixable.

The pain in my chest was hard to comprehend.

He just needs some time, I kept repeating to myself to keep it together. If I thought for one moment that this was truly the end, I didn't think I could cope. Going back to the dark place I'd fought so hard to break free from wasn't an option; I had to keep a handle on things. I'd been so driven to experience all life had to offer, but this pain and the hollowness inside me was unbearable.

Loving someone was so exciting, and the feeling that person created inside you every time you were with that person was addictive, like a drug. It was thrilling, but with the good comes the bad. To love a person left you vulnerable to them and the pain that they could cause was like crashing into a dark pit of despair.

Matthew continued to hold me as my tears finally dried up and I took a deep breath. He pulled away from me slightly to scan my features. He pulled me into one more hug before he led me into the living room and sat me down. I brushed my tears from my face as I took another shaky breath.

"I'll make you some tea," Matthew offered as he disappeared into the kitchen.

I nodded absentmindedly, feeling numb. It was like the heartbreak was too much to bear so my body shut out the pain and in its place was a nothing. A few minutes later, Matthew walked back into the living room with a steaming cup of tea and he set it down in front of me.

"Tell me what happened," he said as he sat down on the sofa beside me.

"He said it's over," I said and Matthew reached for my hand and gave it a squeeze. I was looking straight in front of me, not seeing anything.

"It can't be that bad," he tried to console me.

I wanted to believe his words and I wanted to hope that he was right, but I knew that deep down inside, this might not be able to be sorted out. I rubbed my head as I tried to block out the thoughts that began to cycle through my mind. I wasn't ready to contemplate a life without Sin in it, I just couldn't. I closed my eyes for a moment and took a deep breath to ease the pain building up inside of me.

We hadn't known each other for long, but there was no denying that in that short time I had fallen in love with him. I could handle him not being able to love me back, I could even handle the weird togetherness we had where there had been no labels, but I couldn't handle the fact that he didn't want me anymore.

Matthew tried his best to try and cheer me up, but even a tub of ice cream couldn't make me feel any better. I didn't sleep much that night, my mind too busy reliving my argument with Sin, trying to figure out how it had all gone wrong.

A tear slid down my cheek when I remembered how he'd told me we were done. It had hurt then and it still hurt now. I just hoped that after giving him some space, he would come around.

That night I tossed and turned. Finally, when I heard the birds chirping outside my window, I decided there was no point in trying to sleep anymore so I got up to make some coffee. I would need a lot of caffeine to keep myself awake.

I rubbed my eyes as I wandered into the kitchen. Once I had a steaming cup of coffee in my hands, I sat down on the sofa. It was quiet and easy to get lost in my thoughts of Sin. It was strange that when a person was happy, everything seemed brighter, and now that my heart was broken, everything had lost that extra color. Everything seemed darker and sadder. In the back of my mind, I had the constant worry that I would slip back into my old habit of blocking everything out. I didn't want to go back to that dark place that my parents' murder has sent me to.

I took a sip of the coffee and savored the taste. It would be so easy to hold on to the hurt and let it control me, but I wasn't a nine-year-old girl anymore. I was older and I believed I was stronger. I was up for an hour before I heard someone's bedroom door open. Jordan was the first one up.

"Good morning," she mumbled as she walked into the kitchen.

"Hey," I replied, following her into the kitchen.

She made herself some coffee and then turned to face me as she took a couple of tentative sips.

"How are you feeling?" I asked, taking in her still slightly puffy eyes.

"I'll be okay," she said as she gave me a weak smile. "I'm tired of feeling like I'm missing something."

I knew the feeling. It meant that she didn't just care for Slater, there was a good chance that she'd fallen in love with him.

"No more tears," she said with a determination I hadn't seen in her since Slater had broken her heart. "I'm done moping in heartbreak land."

"Good," I said, nodding my head, hoping that the determination would be enough to pull her out of the heartbreak she'd been moping around in.

"How are things going with you and Sin?" She asked like she genuinely wanted to know.

I hesitated for a moment.

"We're over," I admitted, feeling my eyes sting with tears.

"What exactly does that mean?" she asked, her forehead creasing with confusion.

"When Connor first met Sin, he got a background check done on him," I began to tell her.

"Really?" she gasped.

"Yes," I answered. "You have met my overprotective brother."

"Overprotective is one thing, but getting a background check on someone is something else," she said as she set her coffee down on the counter.

I shrugged. I'd gotten so used to it and until Sin, I'd allowed my brother to be overprotective, but I put my foot down. I still hadn't spoken to him since my first fight with Sin. He'd kept phoning to talk to me, but I wasn't ready to forgive him; and now that his actions had caused another fight, it was even harder for me to want to forgive him. But it had been my own fault as well. I could have thrown the folder away, but I hadn't.

"I kept the folder, but I never read it," I explained. "To me it didn't matter what he'd done in his past; what mattered to me was the person he was now."

"What happened?" she asked.

"He found the folder," I admitted as I tried to keep my emotions from bubbling over into the surface.

"And he didn't take it well," she stated. It wasn't a question. "Sin and Slater grew up together and they are both very reluctant to talk about their pasts."

"I know." I nodded.

"Besides, you have to admit finding a background check on yourself isn't going to go down well for anyone."

She was right. He had a right to be upset.

"Give him a few days to deal with it and he will come around," she suggested.

"You think so?" I asked, feeling hopeful that he just needed some time to work through his anger.

"Yes, I do," she assured me. "I see the way he looks at

you. He cares."

Taking my friend's advice, I decided to leave Sin alone for the next few days. It still didn't stop me from checking my phone constantly, hoping that he would call or text me. Not surprisingly, I never heard from him or saw him at school. I wanted to give him the space he needed, but as each day passed without a word from him, it made me fear that he wasn't going to be able to forgive me. Jordan stopped moping around and got back to her usual self. Every now and then I would still see the sadness in her eyes, but most of the time she kept it well hidden.

Finally, after nearly a week, I decided I'd waited long enough, so I tried to call him, but he never answered. Then I messaged him, but he never responded. I decided it was time to go around to his house to speak to him. My mind had gone crazy with reasons why he hadn't called or messaged me. The more time that passed without contact made me think that he may have already moved on with another girl and that was going to be hard to deal with.

I was nervous as I stood outside his front door.

Please don't let him be with another girl, I prayed silently before I stepped forward and rang the doorbell before I could decide I'd rather not know why he hadn't phoned. Slater answered the door.

"Hi," he greeted with a friendly smile.

"Hi," I greeted him back, trying to hide my nervousness.

"He isn't here," he informed me and I felt my heart sink a little. I'd really hoped that by having the courage to see him in person, it would heal the rift between us.

"Do you know when he will be back?" I asked, hoping that I would be able to come to talk to him.

Slater studied me for a moment and then let out a heavy sigh.

"I'm not sure," he informed me. "He packed a bag and

left. He didn't say why he was leaving or when he would be back."

He'd left. It felt like the earth had shifted under my feet.

"Where did he go?" I asked hoarsely as my emotions began to react to the news that he'd actually left me.

It hadn't been like we were dating, but it still felt like he'd left me. I didn't think it would feel worse than when he wouldn't answer my calls or message me back but it was crushing.

"Honestly, I'm not sure," he admitted. "I haven't heard from him, but I'm sure he will be in contact soon."

"When did he leave?" I asked, not sure why I needed to know that.

"A few days ago," he said.

I'd been oblivious and still hoped that we would be able to sort things out, but I'd been so wrong. Feeling the sting of tears, I wanted to get out of there before I started bawling in front of Slater.

"Thanks," I mumbled hoarsely as I turned to leave.

"I'm sorry," Slater said, taking a step through the doorway and I turned to look at him. "I'm sorry he hurt you."

I shrugged, not wanting him to know how badly I'd been hurt.

"I'll be okay," I said, not believing one word I'd just said.

I knew I was never going to be okay. I managed to leave before my tears broke free and tumbled down my face. Matthew got out of the car and hugged me as I cried.

Chapter Twenty-Three

TAYLOR

One day passed slowly into another and time seemed to drag on. I tried to pick myself up and move on, but it was so hard when I couldn't stop thinking about him. I replayed our last fight over and over in my mind to figure out how I'd made him so angry that he'd packed his stuff and left.

I'd hoped that just a few days of cooling off was all he'd needed, but apparently I'd been wrong. There would be no cooling off. He'd closed the door on what we'd had. He'd shut the door with a bang and left.

There was a knock on my bedroom door.

"Come on, you can't stay in there forever," Matthew said through the door.

I begged to differ. I could stay in my room for as long as I wanted, or at least until the hole in my chest closed up, but I doubted it would ever heal completely. I lay on my bed looking up at my white ceiling, happy to be by myself. If I was around people, it was harder, since I had to put a smile on my face and pretend everything was fine. It was exhausting.

In my room, I didn't have to pretend. People say that

you never forget your first love, but in my case I wasn't sure if I would ever stop loving him despite how quickly he'd cut ties. Each time I thought about him packing up his stuff and leaving me, the pain in my chest worsened. It felt like betrayal. The least he could have done was listen to what I had to say, but instead he'd disappeared the first chance he'd gotten.

I hoped if I ignored Matthew, he would leave me in peace.

"It's a Friday night. Why don't I take you to see a movie?" he suggested.

I kept tightlipped, hoping that he would just leave me alone. He was trying to help and I understood that, but I just wanted time to deal with my heartbreak. I had to figure out a way to carry on.

"Taylor, you have to come out," he instructed and then he let out a sigh.

Silence ensued.

"I'll stand here all day if I have to," he threatened. I pressed my lips together, feeling annoyed.

He would stand there and keep talking until I came out. I let out a frustrated sigh and then got off my bed.

"Fine," I relented when I opened the door and faced him. "But I'm choosing the movie."

It would have to be a comedy or an action because there was no way I could make it through a romance movie.

"You get to choose the movie," he agreed with an eye roll.

"Is Jordan going to come with us?" I asked as I peered past him into the living room.

"I don't think so. She's getting all dressed up to go out," he informed me.

I was happy that she seemed to be getting back to normal and going out on dates with guys. It wasn't a step I was ready to take yet. Jordan had nearly her entire wardrobe laid out on her bed when I entered her room.

"I can't decide what to wear," she said as eyed out the different items of clothing.

"I can see that," I commented as I stood beside her. "Where are you going?"

"Steven asked me to out to dinner," she said with a smile and I mirrored it. She'd mentioned Steven was a cute guy in one of her classes.

"That sounds great," I replied, trying to keep my voice cheerful and light.

I wanted to know if she'd seen Slater, but he'd become that person whose name we never mentioned out loud in the flat. It had been another week and there was still no sign of Sin. I'd hoped he would have been back soon or at least have been in contact, but I'd received nothing from him. No messages or calls.

There also hadn't been any more incidents with the stalker, either, which was a good thing. I still wasn't talking to my brother. He still phoned regularly and spoke to Matthew. I wouldn't stay angry with him forever; at some point I would forgive him. There had been a few times that I'd wanted to contact Sin, but I'd stopped myself. The fact that he wasn't responding to my messages or calls spoke volumes and I didn't want to be some desperate chick who couldn't let go.

Jordan managed to find something to wear and she hurried out the door when Steven arrived for their date. He seemed like a nice guy and I told her to have fun.

Matthew walked me down to the car and opened the passenger door for me and I got in. Maybe Matthew was right, maybe spending a little time outside the apartment would be good for me. At least it would take my mind off my heartbreak for a couple of hours.

The street Matthew took to the theater was quiet and I

stared out of the window as we drove in silence.

Suddenly, I heard the slight scrape of metal against metal. The car swung and the force of the movement pressed me painfully against my seatbelt that dug across my chest and waist.

"Fuck!" Matthew swore as he began to frantically fight with the direction of the car by pulling hard on the steering wheel in the opposite direction. I remember my brother telling me that advanced driving courses were a necessity for any bodyguard, but when I looked and saw the panic in Matthew's face and I knew we were in trouble.

I held on to the seatbelt as the force swung us across the road. The road had been quiet; otherwise, we would have hit another car. Everything seemed to slow down as I watched helplessly while the car lost control. Matthew's eyes met mine as he reached out with one hand and tried to hold my body back. Even in a moment like this, protecting me was built into his instinct.

There was no time to brace for impact when a large tree on the opposite side of the road stopped the car with such force that I felt the imprint of the seatbelt bruise me and knock the breath out of me. The crunch of the metal and the sound of breaking glass echoed in my ears. My head flung backward as it came to an abrupt stop.

"Ow," I moaned as I touched my chest. It hurt to breathe. I couldn't help thinking that maybe I was injured worse than I thought. Adrenaline began to pump through my veins as I released the seatbelt.

My neck hurt and I rubbed it with my hand, trying to ease the pain. It took me a few seconds to comprehend what had just happened.

Had we hit something? Or had someone hit us?

Matthew.

I looked to Matthew. He had a gash on his forehead and

there was blood dripping from it.

The sight of blood always reminded me of the scene of my murdered parents, but there wasn't time to panic. The darkness wanted to comfort me and began to creep through me, but I fought it. Matthew was hurt. He could die if I didn't try to do something.

"Matthew," I croaked, trying to wake him up, but he wouldn't respond. Fear gripped me and I began to panic.

This can't be happening, I thought as I pressed my shaky fingers to the side of his neck, praying that he was still alive. I cried out with relief when I felt a faint pulse beneath my fingertips. He was alive.

I heard footsteps on the gravel. It had to be the person who had hit us. Pain shot through me as I turned to try and open the door.

For a moment I felt a wave of dizziness and closed my eyes, trying to let it pass over me. I felt a small prick of pain in my upper arm and my eyes flew open. Alarmed, I glanced to see a guy standing beside the car. A guy I knew.

I rubbed the spot on my arm that hurt.

"Why did you do that?" I asked, feeling more confused. It didn't help that my mind began to feel fuzzy and it was hard to concentrate. The numbness spread through my body and it became harder to keep myself awake.

"Need to...get help...Matthew," I tried to say urgently, but it came out slow and slurred.

My eyes grew heavy and it was impossible to stay awake. My eyes closed and I dropped into the darkness.

My mouth was dry and it was hard to swallow. I ran the tip of my tongue across my bottom lip as I moved slightly. A fog had settled in my mind and it was hard to link my thoughts together.

Groaning, I shifted slightly and felt the pain in my stomach and chest. When I opened my eyes, I took in my surroundings. My last moments before I blacked out came rushing back and confusion set in.

I was lying on a small bed in a basement. It was dark except for a dim, single bulb that hung from the ceiling. I winced as I sat up, holding my aching middle. As I tried to figure out what happened, I rubbed my forehead. There was a dull throb that hadn't quite developed into a headache yet.

I remembered the accident and Matthew being injured. Matthew. He'd gashed his head and he'd been knocked unconscious. The pain in my middle pulled my attention away from my thoughts and I lifted my shirt. Bruises were developing already.

My eyes scanned the damp basement. My mind refused to acknowledge the reality of what I was seeing, but then I remembered the guy who had come to the car and I remembered the slight pinprick. Why would he do that? Most people would have called an ambulance. Why wasn't I in a hospital?

I heard the door creak open at the top of the stairs when I finally understood what had happened. My breath hitched in my lungs as I watched a pair of dark boots descend the stairs one loud creaking step at a time.

Oh. My. God.

I watched in horror as my kidnapper came into view.

"Eric," I gasped as I put my hand to my mouth.

A cruel, assured smile spread across his face as his eyes settled on me.

"You've been out of it for a while," he said, as if it were the most normal thing for me to be locked in his basement as he stepped off the stairs.

One thought after another raced through my mind. Eric

was the stalker. It was the only explanation. But the most pressing question was: why?

You're my whore, not his. Fear took hold of me.

I was in a basement with a potentially crazy guy who had been stalking me. How long had I been out? Did anyone know I was missing yet? But even if they did, they had no way of knowing where I was.

Eric studied me for a moment before he walked up to me. I couldn't help pulling away from him when he reached out to caress my cheek with his fingertips. He looked displeased. My obvious rejection of him hadn't gone down well and it looked like he was trying to rein in his temper.

I never imagined I would be in this type of situation. After my childhood horrors, I never expected to go through something so horrible again and I had a gut-wrenching thought that this could be so much worse.

"Why?" I whispered. Why had he targeted me? Hadn't I dealt with enough?

"There is a specific reason why I chose you, but that talk will have to wait," he said, brushing off my question. "I thought I'd give you a chance to clean up."

I eyed him suspiciously.

"You can use the shower upstairs, but you have to promise me you won't try to escape," he warned me. The look that accompanied the words told me that there would be serious repercussions if I disobeyed him.

It was hard to believe the friendly Eric who lived in the house with Sin, whom I'd met only briefly, was the same person who stood in front of me now. He appeared the same, but the way he looked at me made my skin crawl.

I had to swallow my fear. There was no one to save me. I had to assess my situation and try to figure out a way to escape before Eric could have a chance to do anything.

I pushed the thoughts of all the things he could do to me

from my mind. If I was going to have any chance, I needed to keep calm, so I took a deep breath and allowed the fear to ease from my body.

"I won't," I assured him.

Going upstairs would give me an opportunity to get a layout of the house and hopefully I'd be able to find a way to escape. He stared at me for a few moments before he smiled.

"Come on," he instructed. "Follow me."

One moment he was a deadly foe and the next he was easy-going and friendly, like a Jekyll and Hyde.

I had to push my true feelings down and accept his outreached hand. The touch of his skin against mine made me want to yank my hand away, but I didn't. I'd already annoyed him once and I wasn't sure if he'd lose his temper if I did it again.

I was no shrink, but I was pretty sure the drastic changes in his personality indicated a more serious psychological problem. And the fact that he'd been stalking me, breaking into my dorm room, the message he'd left on my underwear, all pointed to an unstable individual who had the potential to really hurt me.

I was at his mercy. There was no rescue party. If I was going to survive this, it was going to be up to me to get myself out. The fear that I might not be able to escape brought a sting of tears to my eyes, but I gritted my teeth and followed Eric step by step up the stairs and out of the basement.

The stairs led into a small kitchen that was old but clean. My nervousness grew as he led me through a small living room and past a bedroom. I was scared of what he might do to me, there was no denying that. He stopped outside a small bathroom and let my hand go.

"There is a clean towel and a change of clothes for you," he informed me as he indicated for me to enter the bathroom.

My relief increased when I walked into the bathroom and he gave me a brief nod before closing the door. The sound of the door being locked twisted the knot of fear in my stomach and reminded me that I was a prisoner.

I took a deep breath and released it, trying to rein in the instinct that called for me to scream until someone heard me and came to find me. Keeping it together was my only hope for surviving this ordeal because there might be no one to hear my screams and I was scared it would set him off. There was no telling what he would do to me.

The thought of Matthew made me close my eyes for a brief moment and hope that he was okay. I had no way of knowing how long I'd been out of it and all I could do was hope that Matthew had gotten help. Considering the fact that he'd been badly injured and alone, it nearly brought tears to my eyes again.

Protecting me had been his job and he'd tried his hardest to fulfill it, but there was nothing he could have done to stop Eric from taking me. It scared me, the lengths Eric had gone to in order to kidnap me.

It had been my fault. The accident—I was sure—had been a setup for Eric to be able to grab me and I couldn't help the overwhelming guilt I felt.

I saw a folded towel on the bathroom sink as well as the change of clothes. What horrified me was the sight of a pair of my panties that I hadn't noticed had gone missing. It also made me wonder how many times he'd gone into my dorm room unnoticed.

Looking around the bathroom killed any hopes for escape. The only way out other than the door was a small window: too small for me to crawl through. I opened the cabinets in hope of finding something I could use as a weapon but there was nothing other than some soap and a shampoo bottle.

Still holding onto a little hope I opened the vanity, but there was nothing. Feeling frustrated, I dropped my head into my hands, trying to push the fear away so I could keep my control.

My mind began to search for signs that I'd missed that could have told me that Eric was my stalker, but I came up with nothing. I stripped naked and got into the shower. I gently soaped my aching body and then I leaned my forehead against the tiles as the water washed the soap away. For those few moments I allowed myself to cry for the first time. I hoped my allowing the release of fear and anger would help me stay calmer around him. I let the tears flow. I was angry that I was in the situation and that I had no control over it. The throbbing in my head had turned into a full-blown headache by the time I got out of the shower.

I quickly dried myself off and got into the clothes he'd given. I didn't want him to walk in on me half naked because I was scared of what he may do. The clothes—underwear, a pair of sweatpants and a shirt—fit. I was surprised that he knew my size.

It wasn't long before I heard a key turn in the lock and the door opened. I couldn't help the new wave of fear sweep over me when Eric surveyed me from head to toe. The appreciative look left no doubt in my mind that he had plans to take over Sin's role in my life. Fear gripped me.

Chapter Twenty-Four

TAYLOR

I didn't fight him as he led me back down to the basement. I had to fight the instinct to try and escape and instead I took in as much detail as I could about the layout of the house. If I ever made it out of the basement, I would need to know the quickest way out. I ignored the fear inside of me that told me I might never make it out of the basement alive.

My free arm wrapped around my stomach as it began to throb. Once he'd led me back to the small bed, I was in pain and all I wanted to do was lie down on the small bed to ease it.

"I'll get you some painkillers," Eric said when he saw the pain on my face. "Lie down and I'll be back in a moment."

I didn't let his surface concern fool me into thinking he wouldn't hurt me. I did as he said. The throbbing eased when I lay down as he left to get me painkillers. I had to stop myself from crying so I took a deep breath and released it, trying to dispel the emotions wanting to bubble to the surface. Escaping would be hard, but the fact that I was injured would make a difficult task so much harder.

The darkness at the end of my subconscious called for me to give in and let it take over. There was no hope for me to escape and the darkness would help me cope with whatever was still to come. It would be so easy to give in and let it take over like it had when my parents had been murdered, but the tiny bit of hope that I held onto made me refuse.

I had so much I still wanted to do in my life and I couldn't accept that it was over. There was no fooling myself into thinking that he may let me go. He would take what he wanted and afterward...I couldn't think about it.

As much as I hated to admit it, I hadn't seen any of this coming. The few very brief encounters I'd had with Eric hadn't been enough for me to see the dark and dangerous person I saw now. I hadn't even noticed the overpowering cologne that I'd smelled when he'd attacked me in the stairwell.

I thought about all the things that had happened to me and now that I knew who was responsible, everything seemed to fit together. The night my drink got spiked, Eric would have been there.

He was Sin's roommate so he would have known when I'd stayed overnight with Sin. A sickening feeling curled in my stomach at the thought that he'd been so close to me and no one, including me, had any idea he was the stalker.

And now I was at his mercy, his prisoner, and I had no way out.

He returned minutes later with some painkillers. I took them from him and swallowed them with a couple of sips from a bottle of water he'd brought me.

"That should help with the pain," he said as he pulled up a chair and sat down.

I was feeling tired. I didn't know if it was because of the injured state I was in or the scary situation with no idea what Eric was going to do to me.

"You are so beautiful," he said as he reached out and touched my face. His touch revolted me, but somehow I kept my true reaction hidden beneath a calm look.

"Do you want to know why I chose you?" he asked, like I was lucky to be locked in a basement with him. He really was crazy and that made me even more scared. It was hard to know what might set him off and I had to tread carefully because of what I feared would happen if I upset him.

"No," I replied softly, keeping my eyes focused on him. Trying to read the subtle indications of his mood in his face.

"I don't look a little familiar to you?" he said and I gave him a confused look. The first time I'd ever met him was at Sin's house. It wasn't like I'd had an active social life before that, so there was no chance that I'd met him somewhere and just not remembered.

"I've been told I look just like my uncle," he revealed like it should be enough for me to form a path to figure out who he was. My forehead creased as I looked at him. Why would I know his uncle?

"Who is your uncle?" I asked, still not seeing the full picture.

"I didn't think his face was something you would ever forget," he said softly with an intense gaze.

It took a few seconds for it to register. There were only two strangers' faces marked in my memory forever. I'd seen them briefly during the trial. My breath hitched in my lungs at the shock of the discovery of who Eric was related to. The fear that I'd felt before was nothing compared to the terror I felt now.

I'd seen his uncle's handiwork and I knew without a doubt that Eric was more than capable of the same. He smiled at my reaction and the blood in my veins ran cold.

"I think you need to rest," he said and the change in his demeanor and voice was so drastic that it took me by surprise.

His eyes softened. The caring Eric was back.

I swallowed hard.

"You need to rest so you can get better," he further explained as he stood up, "then we can be together."

I felt the bile rise up in my throat, but I forced it down. He didn't need to explain what 'we can be together' meant. Seeing his agitation at my reaction, I forced a smile and nodded my head, unable to get out any words. I had to keep him happy so he wouldn't get upset.

He leaned over and pressed a kiss to my cheek. I was disgusted and wanted to pull away, but I didn't.

I let out the breath that I'd been holding when I heard him close the door to the basement. Even though I was in pain, I stood up and began to investigate my prison. There was no time to waste. I needed to come up with a plan to get out of here because if I didn't, there was no surviving what Eric had in store for me.

There was a small window that was big enough for me to fit through, but disappointment filled me when I couldn't get it open. Tears began to sting my eyes at the realization that there was no escaping.

The only other alternative was to try and find a weapon of some sort that I could use against Eric. If I could knock him out or incapacitate him, I would be able to get away.

I began to look around the darkened basement. The light from the small bulb hanging from the ceiling wasn't bright, so it was still difficult to see what else lay in the room.

My pain eased slightly as the painkillers kicked in. I had to concentrate on getting myself out because there was going to be no one to save me. I'd never once suspected Eric was the stalker and doubted anyone searching for me would even look at him as a possible suspect.

There were a couple of boxes, but there was nothing in them but some old clothes and books. I couldn't exactly use a book to knock him out. Frustrated, I rubbed my hands over my face as I tried to keep the fear from taking over.

If I gave in to the fear. I was as good as dead. A picture of my parents' bloodied bodies lying in their bedroom flashed in my mind and it was enough to push me on.

I thought about Sin and my heart ached. I had so much regret. I didn't want my last memory of him to be our fight.

Connor. I felt bad that I hadn't spoken to him for a while because I'd been so upset with him. A tear slid down my cheek as I considered that I would never see him again. With a deep breath, I wiped the tear away. I couldn't give up.

I searched the entire basement but came up with very little. There was an old radio, some clothes, and books. But other than that, there wasn't anything else. I'd hoped to find a weapon I could use, but there was nothing. Nothing could keep the disappointment from creeping over me as I sat down on the bed and dropped my head into my hands.

The fear kept me from dropping off into a peaceful sleep. Instead, I tossed and turned in the small bed, still trying to figure a way out of my prison.

When I realized I couldn't think of a way out, I began to think about Eric. Why had he targeted me? Had it been for revenge? The problem was I hadn't witnessed my parents' murder, I'd just seen the aftermath of it. I hadn't seen the murderers that night.

It had been the physical evidence that had put them away for life—not me—so I couldn't understand why he'd been after me. I hadn't done anything to impact his life; in fact, it had been the other way around.

A little later I heard the door open and I closed my eyes. It was easier to pretend to be asleep than have to deal with Eric. I was tired and the fear had sapped my energy. I just didn't have it in me to try and deal with him.

The steps creaked from the weight of his steps as he

descended the stairs. The sound of the last creak told me he was close. I kept my eyes closed and my breathing regular so he wouldn't suspect I wasn't sleeping.

I heard light footsteps to the bed and then after a few seconds, I felt his breath so close to my face that I thought he was going to kiss me, but instead he whispered, "You're so beautiful."

Not moving or reacting to the revulsion I felt at his words was hard. I wanted to tell him no, I wanted to tell him that he couldn't have me, even if it was by force. You couldn't make someone want to be with you, it wasn't how the world worked.

I felt the brush of his lips against my forehead and I felt like I was going to throw up, but somehow I remained still. Fear gripped my stomach and I felt myself hold my breath for a moment before I realized he might notice, so I released it slowly.

I heard the sound of something being laid beside the bed on the hard floor before I heard his retreating steps.

By the time the door shut, I was in a panicked state and I shot up in the bed. I drew in a deep breath, trying to calm myself down in case he came back. I pressed my hand to my mouth to keep myself from crying out.

The fact that he was becoming affectionate made the dread rise up inside of me. It could only lead to one thing and I couldn't let that happen. The only person I ever wanted to share my body with was Sin.

I wanted to cry about the unfairness of this whole situation, but it didn't matter. No amount of tears and screaming were going to get me out of this. But I let the tears stream quietly down my face as I rested my head on my knees, trying to ease some of the fear inside by releasing some of the emotions that were suffocating me.

It was hard not to think about all the things that I hadn't

gotten a chance to do. But I had to keep myself from drowning in the depths of misery, so I tried to focus on the few memories that made me happy.

I brushed the remnants of my tears from my face as I remembered my first day at college and meeting Jordan. She'd been a good friend to me. I believe that, given the time, we would have built a friendship that would have lasted through the years.

Connor. I felt a physical pain in my chest at the thought of never seeing him again. I didn't want to admit it, but my death was going to devastate him. After what happened to our parents, he'd done everything he could to keep me safe, and it still hadn't been enough. He would blame himself even though he couldn't have stopped it. He'd done everything right and he was still going to lose me.

Fresh tears began to fall down my face when I thought of how I hadn't spoken to him in the last week. I'd always regret not speaking to him one last time, even it was just to forgive him and hear his voice one last time.

And to tell him I loved him.

I pressed my hand to my mouth again to suppress the sob that wanted to break free. Never once did I ever think that this was how my life would end.

I thought about Matthew and how he would react to me being missing. He was probably blaming himself because he'd been employed to protect me and he'd failed. I didn't blame him; I blamed the *crazy* upstairs.

The only other person who had become an important part of my life in the short time that I'd experienced normality was Sin. The anger that I felt toward him dissipated and all I was left with was the love that I felt for him. He'd been an enigma, but once you broke through the barriers the person underneath was still scared to get too close to anyone because he was scared he'd get hurt.

It was hard to understand him without knowing about his past. All I knew was what he'd told me and that had been enough for me to understand why he was the way he was.

Then I thought about the stupid folder that had ruined everything between us. I hadn't even been tempted to have a peek at it. It didn't matter what he'd done in the past; what had mattered was what he did now. He'd walked away at the first sign of trouble.

I took a deep breath and released it. I didn't want to cry anymore, it wasn't helping me find a way out and it wasn't making me feel any better.

Most girls in my situation would be hoping that there would be a knight to swoop in and save her. But I'd learned through my past that that didn't happen in real life—in real life, people died.

I thought about Sin one last time before I pushed all the thoughts out of my mind. I felt emotionally and physically exhausted, but at least my stomach wasn't aching as much.

I lifted my shirt to see the dark bruises imprinted by the seatbelt across my chest and stomach. It was a good sign that there wasn't any serious damage. I thought about Matthew, at the gash on his head, and I prayed that he was okay.

As I dropped the shirt, I saw the plate of food and my stomach growled. I was hungry. I picked it up and studied the food for a moment. I was too hungry to care if Eric had laced my food with something. It was pasta with meat and vegetables. It tasted great and I began to eat. I needed to keep up my strength and I couldn't do that if I didn't eat. It was also another puzzling thing about Eric. Who made food like this for their prisoner? I placed the plate back on the floor and I got off the bed.

As I began to think, I paced back and forth. He wasn't really treating me like a prisoner. Yes, he had me locked in the basement, but he hadn't tied me up.

Then it struck me that he was treating me like someone would treat a person they cared about—well, except for causing an accident to kidnap me and locking me in his basement. But I knew Eric wasn't playing with a full deck of cards. It didn't make me feel any better because I knew he would not be caring when he took me by force and I would fight back. It wasn't in me to just let him take it from me.

He was unstable. I'd already seen the small signs and I knew if I fought back he would really hurt me. There was no way to escape the basement so I would have to think of another way to get away because, if I didn't, I was not going to make it out of this alive.

I wondered when Eric had developed this unhealthy obsession for me. Had it started after the hearing or had it been later? If Connor hadn't been such an overprotective brother, would Eric have gotten to me sooner? I pushed the thought from my mind, unable to deal with the answer that I might get.

I bit down on my lip as I contemplated what I was going to do.

Chapter Twenty-Five

SIN

I was frustrated and angry. Physically putting distance between Taylor and I should have fixed the problem, but it hadn't. She was all I could think about. I dropped my head into my hands and rubbed them over my face. It didn't help that every time I closed my eyes I saw her smiling at me and I felt guilty for leaving abruptly the way I had. Granted, I'd been clear that things between us were over, but packing up and leaving had been going a bit overboard.

When I'd packed my stuff, I'd had no intention of ever going back. Now, sitting in the house I'd bought for my mom, I knew that I had to go back. I couldn't run away from the problem. The only way to deal with it was to face it head on. I eyed the offending folder that still lay on the coffee table. I hadn't been able to open it up and look at what it held, but I had a pretty good idea since I'd lived through all of it—stuff I wasn't proud of.

Feeling agitated, I stood up and began to pace the room.

She'd told me that she hadn't read the folder and I believed her because, if she had, I was pretty sure she wouldn't have wanted anything to do with me. I wouldn't have had a chance to tell her that we were over; she would have told me to leave if she knew. I'd never wanted to erase my past as badly as I'd wanted to when I'd first found out about the murder of Taylor's parents. It was only a matter of time before she found out. I thought about coming clean with her, but I wasn't sure she would want to ever see me again after that.

My phone began to ring and I pulled it out of my jeans pocket. I'd expected it to be Taylor, but it was Slater.

"Hi," I said as I answered the call.

"You need to get your ass back here," he instructed forcefully. He sounded upset and it wasn't like him.

"What's wrong, man?" I asked, knowing my best friend well enough to know that something was going on.

"Look, there's no good way to say this..." he said and I felt a sinking feeling in my stomach.

"It's Taylor," he admitted.

My heart stopped beating for a split second as I felt the fear crash over me like a wave.

"What happened?" I said tightly, already having every worst-case scenario cycling through my mind.

"She's gone," he revealed, and I felt my legs weaken and I slumped down in the chair.

"What do you mean she's gone?" I asked, my voice already thickening with the emotion I felt. I'd asked the question, but I wasn't sure I wanted the answer.

"She's missing," he said softly.

"How long?" I asked, my mind already jumping to the next action I needed to perform.

"A day," he answered. It was already too long.

"I just found out from Jordan," he added.

"I'll call you back," I told him, trying to ignore the fear I felt. I disconnected the call, not giving him a chance to say another word. I searched through my contacts on my phone and dialed a number.

"Yeah," the guy answered.

"You still tailing the guy I asked you to?" I asked urgently as I ran a hand through my hair.

"Yeah," he answered.

"Does he have a girl with him?" I asked, and I held my breath.

"No," he said and I felt my world begin to disintegrate around me.

Caleb didn't have Taylor; he wasn't the stalker. I'd put my guy on the wrong guy.

Fuck!

"You need me to find someone for you?" my guy asked on the other side of the call.

"Yes," I answered, hoping that it wasn't going to be too late. I gave him Taylor's name. He was good—he wouldn't need any more details than that to be able to gather the information he needed.

"How long has she been gone?" he asked.

"A day," I answered.

I heard him sigh on the other side of the phone. Twenty-four hours was too long already.

"You know the odds are she is dead already," he said aloud, which is what I was already thinking.

"I don't fucking care, I want you to find her!" I yelled, not wanting to believe for a second that she might not be alive.

"Sure, boss, I'll find her," he assured me before disconnecting the call.

I began to pace. My shock and fear turned to anger. I called Slater back.

"What happened?" I asked, trying to mentally prepare myself for what I was about to find out.

I didn't understand how she could be gone with a

bodyguard glued to her side. How on earth had the guy gotten to her with Matthew around? He was the best that money could buy—I'd checked. It had been the only reason I hadn't hired a bodyguard myself.

"She was with Matthew," he began to explain. "He was driving them to the movies."

I held my breath.

"A car hit them from behind and knocked Matthew out. By the time the ambulances arrived, he was conscious but Taylor was gone, as well as the car that hit them," he finished explaining.

It was unbelievable that the guy had gone to those lengths to get her. I didn't want to think about what he would do to her if he was capable of that.

"Was she hurt?" I asked, feeling the fear clog my throat.

"We don't know," he replied. "Her blood wasn't in the car, but that doesn't mean there weren't any internal injuries."

I began to pace again, not knowing what to do next. She could be seriously injured and in the hands of some crazed stalker.

"I'm on my way back," I informed Slater. I had to get back.

"Sin," Slater said, stopping me, "it wasn't your fault."

He knew me too well. I pressed my lips together, trying to stop myself from arguing about it. It was my fault. If I hadn't left, I probably would have been with her and I might have been able to stop him from getting her.

Twenty-four hours. I closed my eyes for a moment, trying to push away the voice in the back of my mind that told me she was probably dead already. I would never forgive myself for abandoning her.

"I'll see you soon," I told him before I ended the call.

"You leaving already?" my mom said as she walked into

the room. Her face was pale and she looked tired.

"Yeah, I have to go," I said as I walked down the hall to the room I'd been using.

I got my duffel bag and just started shoving stuff into it. My mind was trying to process everything I'd just found out while trying to concentrate on getting my stuff together so I could get back and find out what was happening.

Did the cops have any leads? Had anyone witnessed the accident? Did they have a description of the car?

I got my leather jacket and put it on. If I hurried, I could be back in an hour. When I reentered the living room, my mom was sitting in the chair.

"I have to go," I told her as I walked to her and dropped a kiss on her cheek.

"Okay, baby," she said, giving me a weak smile. It was still hard to link the person she was now with the mother she'd been to me growing up.

I found my mom's nurse in the kitchen.

"I've got to leave. Keep an eye on her," I said to her. She gave me a brief nod.

"You don't have to worry, Mr. Carter," she assured me kindly. "I'll look after your mom."

"Thanks," I replied before I left. I hurried to my car and as soon as I got into the driver's side, I shoved the duffel bag onto the passenger seat.

I started up the car and prayed that Taylor was still safe. I broke nearly every speed limit, and within forty minutes I was pulling up outside Taylor's apartment.

I felt a nervous fear engulf me as I got to the door of the apartment and knocked.

Matthew opened the door and looked surprised to see me. A large surgical pad covered his forehead.

"Have you found her yet?" I asked as I stepped inside. The look in his eyes made my chest hurt. It felt like a steel grip around my heart.

"No," he said, shaking his head. He dropped his gaze to the floor.

I took a couple more steps before I saw Connor sitting in one of the sofas with his head in his hands and Jordan sat beside him, trying to comfort him.

Jordan looked like she'd been crying.

I didn't want to be around them. It was like they were convinced she was dead already and I wasn't going to give up that easily, not until I saw it for myself.

TAYLOR

Being imprisoned in a dark basement, I lost track of time. My bruises were still a little sensitive and Eric kept giving me painkillers to ease the pain. I think that was the reason he hadn't tried to push me for more. He made me food and let me out of the basement into the house to go to the bathroom.

I wasn't sure if I'd been gone for two days or three. The pain from my bruises had eased and any hope of being rescued had evaporated by now. If they had any idea who had me and where I was, they would have come for me already. Did they think I was dead already? It was difficult to nurture the hope that I might escape when in reality things looked very bleak.

There wasn't a way I could find to escape from the basement. I needed to get out of the basement and into the house to have any real chance of getting away. But I wasn't sure how to do that. The only time Eric allowed me to leave the basement was to go to the bathroom and he stood by the door to ensure I didn't try anything.

My healing bruises meant that my time was running out and Eric would make a move soon.

Eric had cared for me in a crazy, fixated way. He made sure I had everything I needed. It was bizarre that this same caring had made him want to kidnap and keep me locked up. He kept talking about how we were going to be 'together.' I wasn't stupid—I knew what that meant.

The nervous dread in my stomach grew when I heard the basement door open and Eric descended the stairs.

"How are you feeling?" he asked as he smiled at me. The smile was supposed to be friendly and put me at ease, but it didn't. It scared me.

"Still a little sore," I lied. I was still trying to stall.

He studied me with narrowed eyes for a moment before he walked to the bed.

"Let me see," he instructed firmly as he bent down beside the bed. His fingers reached for the hem of my shirt and lifted it.

"Does it still hurt?" he asked as his fingers pressed gently onto the bruises.

"Yes, a little."

I was trying to buy time, but I didn't want to be caught lying outright because I feared it would anger him.

"I think they are nearly healed," he disagreed calmly and I tensed. He dropped my shirt and held my gaze. It was like he was trying to read me.

"I've been waiting a long time for you and I don't want to wait any longer," he told me and my fear was overcome by the horror that I'd finally run out of time.

"I had to sit by and watch you get it on with Sin," he spat suddenly at me, his eyes darkening with anger and I held still, not sure how to calm him down. "But now you are mine and he will never touch you again."

I swallowed hard.

"Why me?" I asked, swallowing hard. If something bad was about to happen, I at least wanted to know why he'd chosen me.

His fingers reached out and trailed down my cheek. And in a few seconds, the anger was gone and in its place was a calmness I didn't trust.

"You're beautiful and you were just as beautiful at the age of nine," he told me. So this obsession had started when I was nine?

"The murder trial tore my family apart and the only thing that brought any light into my life was the sight of you," he murmured as his fingers trailed down my throat. "You were so young and beautiful, like the sun shining through the dark clouds. I knew you were meant to be mine and now...you are."

I tried not to show my revulsion at his words. He was mentally sick and there was no negotiating with that.

"I came here because I knew you'd enrolled, but I couldn't believe my luck when I saw you arrive at one of the house parties. I didn't have to look for you, you came to me."

His eyes dropped to my lips and my horror intensified as he leaned closer and pressed his lips to mine. It took all my self-control not to shove against him. Instead, I let him kiss me.

"You are mine," he murmured against my lips as he pushed me down onto the bed.

Oh. My. God. I couldn't let this happen, I had to do something.

"I want to be yours," I whispered huskily, trying to keep the disgust out of my voice. "But this bed is a little small."

If we went upstairs, I would have a better chance of escaping. Fear gripped me. This would be my only chance. He seemed to consider my request for a moment before he smiled and stood up. He offered me his hand and he pulled me to my feet.

My mind was racing as he led me up the stairs, holding my hand. I had to do something. I held my breath as we entered the house and he led me down the hallway. My eyes quickly scanned the surrounding area for anything I could use as a weapon, but I couldn't find anything. He stopped at the second door on the right and opened it.

I tried to smile as he ushered me inside and I scanned the room, but there was nothing—just a small bed and a side table with a lamp. It was the pictures on the one wall that made me stop. There were various pictures of me through the years, starting at the trial.

My time was running out. I turned to face him and he stepped forward.

No! my mind screamed as he settled his hands on my hips and studied me for a moment.

"I've waited a long time for this," he whispered in awe as he leaned closer and I closed my eyes as his lips touched mine again.

His arms encircled my waist and pulled me closer. He backed me up to the bed. I was starting to panic as he pushed me down.

"Don't be scared," he soothed as he covered my body with his. I gave him a brief nod as his lips pressed against mine and his tongue pushed into my mouth. I opened my eyes to see if I could find anything to knock him out.

It was the only way I was going to stop him and get out of here. He reached for the bottom of my shirt and I resisted. It was going to end like this because there was no way I would allow him to go further. I would finally see the temper I'd been trying to keep at bay and it wasn't going to be good.

He stopped and looked down at me with a questioning gaze.

"I can't," I admitted, shaking my head. All the emotions I'd been suppressing came up to the surface and he could see plainly displayed on my face and in my eyes my true reaction to his touch.

I watched the change happen in his face. Gone was the depth in his eyes and I felt a shiver as his eyes darkened. His friendly smile spread into a cold and cruel smile.

"You are mine," he stated fiercely and slammed his mouth against mine so hard that his teeth cut my bottom lip.

I pushed hard, trying to get his bulky body off mine, but it was like trying to move a slab of concrete. It was then I realized that I wouldn't get a chance to fight and I wouldn't be escaping. He tore his lips from mine and then grabbed my hands and held them above my head.

"We belong together," he stated angrily. "And you will be mine."

The last bit of hope that I'd held on to disappeared and I wanted to give in to the darkness that would protect me. He pressed his body against mine and, as much as I struggled, I couldn't move. I was helpless and at the mercy of this crazy guy.

Chapter Twenty-Six

TAYLOR

Horror gripped me as I began to twist to break free while his lips crushed mine. I winced in pain at the pressure of the cut on my lips. I tried to move my head to the side, but his hand held my chin and forced it back. Adrenaline began to pump through my veins and I began to fight him as hard as I could.

For a moment I felt relief when the weight of his body eased from mine, but that relief vanished when I saw the evil inside of his soul. His fist connected with my cheek and I was momentarily stunned. It hurt and I lifted my hand to my face.

"Behave," he instructed fiercely, "or I will make you."

He was going to hurt me either way. It was the second time I'd ever seen evil in the form of another human being. My cheek throbbed. I'd never been hit before.

Taking advantage of my sudden shock, he began to pull at my shirt. The abrupt action pulled me out of my daze and I tried to stop him by holding onto the shirt. When he couldn't pull the shirt over my head successfully, he ripped it with his hands. I tried clutching the shirt, but another fist hit my right eye and the pain that exploded in my head made me scream out in pain as both my hands released the shirt to cover my eye.

"This is going to hurt if you keep fighting me," he warned in a deadly voice and I knew he meant every word, but it wasn't going to stop me from trying to stop him. Tears squeezed from my eyes as I began to struggle to get free. Another hit to my face made me cry out as I struggled to fight off the darkness that wanted to protect me from what was to come.

I felt him tug at my sweatpants from my legs before I had a chance to fight back. I was missing half my clothes and my face was pulsing with pain. He held my gaze as he stood before me and took off his shirt.

Oh no!

I had to do something now or else it was going to be too late. I scrambled off the bed and stood beside it, putting myself on the opposite side of Eric, but the problem was that he was blocking the main exit out of the room. I felt a moment of dizziness before I gritted my teeth.

Somewhere deep inside of me the little girl who had survived the horrific slaughter of her parents rose up in me and gave me the strength I needed to keep fighting and hold on to the hope that I would make it out.

He smiled at me and my blood ran cold. His eyes told me that we were far from over and there would be plenty of pain to come. I swallowed hard, trying to keep my eyes focused on him, which was becoming harder because my one eye was swelling shut.

He laughed when he walked closer and I jumped onto the bed. I shot a side-glance to the door to calculate how far I was from the door, but before I could even try and make a dash for it he was in front of the door. He locked it and put the key in the pocket of his jeans.

"You are not going to leave," he said when he turned to face me, leaning against the locked door. He said it with so much confidence that I was starting to believe him.

The only other exit out of the bedroom was a window. I jumped off the bed and went straight to the window to try and tug it open. Horror filled me when the window wouldn't budge. Frantically, I tried to see if it was locked, but I felt hands grab me and toss me back onto the bed. Before I could try and get off, he held my body down with his.

"I don't know why you're fighting the inevitable," he said, breathing hard.

"I will never be yours," I spat back. I knew saying it would only anger him, but I didn't want him to think that for a second I was going to let this willingly happen.

"But you can't stop me," he reminded me with a smile and I began to struggle again. He lifted himself off me and he punched me in the stomach. Winded and startled at the sudden pain, I clutched my stomach.

"I wonder how much longer you're going to fight me," he murmured, looking down at me like I was some sort of experiment that he was studying. There was no connection between his conscience and his actions.

"Until I can't fight you anymore," I said fiercely, struggling with the pain I was in. The blow to my stomach had been a direct hit to my already tender bruises from the accident.

He grabbed my hands and pulled them above my head. I whimpered from the pain as his mouth covered mine. He pressed his body against mine and I felt his excitement. Tasting the metal taste of my own blood I felt the sting of tears.

This couldn't be happening.

I struggled against him and he let go of my hands to grab

my hips and pull them firmly against his as his mouth slid along my throat. Through the blur of my tears, I saw the lamp beside the bed. It was just out of reach, but if I could just move a little closer I would be able to reach it.

As his hand covered my bra-covered breast, I inched my fingers toward the lamp, moving slowly so he wouldn't realize what I was doing. His hand squeezed my breast and I felt only revulsion at the act.

I wanted to push him away, but this was the only opportunity I would have to escape. I needed to stay calm. I was going to make it out of here, I swore to myself.

My eyes went back to the lamp and I inched closer. The moment my fingers touched the lamp, I wanted to cry out in relief.

Eric was trying to unclasp my bra so he never saw it coming. My hand wrapped around the lamp and, with everything I had, I swung it against his head.

"Ahh!" he yelled as he rolled off me and onto the floor with a thud.

"Goddammit!" he yelled as he held his head. Adrenaline pumped through me. There was no time to waste. I scrambled off the bed, my pain forgotten as I kicked into survival mode.

My eyes shot to the door. He had the key in his pocket so there was no way I could get out that way.

The only other option was the window that wouldn't open. I had to break it.

I grabbed the lamp and I swung it against the window, looking away. The window shattered. The groan that came from my injured kidnapper reminded me I was running out of time.

Frantically, I tried to clear as much of the broken glass as I could so I wouldn't cut myself too much while trying to climb out. I glanced back quickly to see Eric get to his knees, but he was still clutching his head and groaning.

I couldn't waste any more time so I put one leg through the broken window and I held onto the top of the window frame to keep my balance. Freedom was within my grasp.

More groaning from behind me made me panic, and as soon as my foot touched the ground outside, I pulled my other leg through. I winced as pain shot through me. My skin had caught a jagged piece of glass.

The sight of Eric getting to his feet and looking in my direction made me pull my leg through despite the pain from the glass cutting through my skin. No pain could compare to the pain he would inflict on me if he caught me now.

Once I was out, I tried to get away as quickly as I could. I couldn't run—I was too injured. It was dark, but the soft light that illuminated from the surrounding houses was enough for me to see where I was going. I stumbled a couple of times, scraping my knees. No matter how bad the pain was, I got back to my feet and kept going. My face, stomach and leg hurt, but I couldn't concentrate on that pain.

I brushed my face and looked down to see dark liquid on my hands. It took a moment to register that it was my blood. The fear that Eric was just behind me kept me going even through the pain. I felt the blood run down my leg as I hobbled along.

I didn't know where to go and a wave of dizziness hit me. The world began to tilt and I dropped to my knees on the road. I took a deep breath and closed my eyes for a moment before I opened them, hoping everything would remain still.

"Hey!" I heard someone shout and fear gripped me as I looked up to see car headlights. A car had stopped with a screech just a few feet away and a guy got out. My blurred vision meant it was hard to make out his features and I cowered away from him.

"I'm not going to hurt you," he assured me as I felt his hand on my arm.

"Please," I whispered as I looked up at him. There was so much packed into that one little word.

"What happened?" he asked as he looked at my battered face.

I swallowed hard.

"He...Eric..." I couldn't say any more without the emotion of what had just happened to me pushing through to the surface and I felt the tears begin to run down my face.

"It's going to be okay," he assured me softly and I felt the warmth of a jacket enclose my shivering form. I wasn't sure if I was shivering from the fear or the cold.

He wasn't Eric, but I still didn't trust him.

"I'm going to pick you up and put you into the car so I can take you to the hospital," he told me as I felt his hands underneath me.

"No," I tried to argue, but I was already in his arms and he was carrying me to his car.

"I won't hurt you. It will take time for an ambulance to get here. It will be quicker if I drive you to the hospital," he tried to explain.

Logically, what he said made sense, but I was so freaked out that it was hard to trust anyone. I pressed my limbs together to try and deal with the pain as he sat me down gently onto the passenger seat of his car.

The adrenaline that had pushed me began to dissipate and suddenly I felt so tired. The full force of the pain hit me and I tried not to give in to the darkness that was waiting for me.

I needed to feel safe before I'd let go.

The car started up and I heard the roar of the engine. It felt like forever but was probably only ten minutes before the car stopped. My eyes were closed, but I opened them to see where we were and relief flooded through me when I saw the fluorescent name of the hospital shining down on me like a beacon of hope.

The stranger opened my door and I looked at him. For the first time, I could see his features perfectly, my blurred vision gone. He looked mean, with his head shaved and various tattoos on his neck and arms. He looked like the type of guy who should be responsible for the shape I was in.

"Thank you," I whispered hoarsely. There were still good people in the world and, with that thought, I began to lose consciousness, giving in to the darkness. For the first time since Eric had kidnapped me, I felt safe.

When I began to stir, I felt stiff and sore. I groaned as I opened my eyes. I felt disoriented and was trying to piece together where I was.

The dark memories from my kidnapping rushed back. It was then I remembered getting away and the stranger who had helped me.

I was in the hospital, the beeping monitor and bed confirmed it.

"Taylor," I heard a familiar voice whisper and then I felt a hand hold mine.

My eyes settled on the familiar face of Connor looking at me with happiness mixed with concern. One of my eyes was swollen shut. I was safe and I felt the tears begin to run down my face.

"It's okay," he soothed, his voice hoarse with emotion. "You're safe."

He leaned forward and I closed my eye as his lips feathered a kiss to my forehead.

"I love you," he whispered like he was scared he wouldn't be able to say it to me again.

"I love you too," I whispered hoarsely. My throat was

sore.

There had been a few times when I'd been sitting in the basement wondering if I would ever see the people I loved again. He helped me sit up and tried to make me comfortable.

"I'm sorry," I murmured hoarsely, my throat burned with pain.

"What are you sorry for?" he asked, looking at me.

"For everything," I managed to say before a sob tore from my chest.

"Shh," he soothed, pulling me into a gentle hug. My body was sore, but he was gentle.

"Eric is in custody."

I tried to remember if I'd told the stranger who had attacked me. Then something dawned on me.

"How did you know I was here?" I asked, missing that piece of the puzzle.

"The guy who brought you in knew who you were."

Had I told the stranger my name? As much as I tried to remember telling him, I didn't. Had I forgotten that I'd told him? There seemed to be no other explanation. I tried to keep my fear under control. Eric's uncle's actions had taken years from my life and I refused to allow my fear of Eric to do the same to me again.

"You really hit him hard with that lamp. He had to have stitches," he informed me. I couldn't help but smile at the satisfaction that I'd given him a taste of his own medicine.

"I'm sorry," he said.

"You have nothing to be sorry for," I stated.

"I'm your older brother. It's my job to look after you."

"You did everything you could," I assured him. He'd hired a bodyguard. Then I remembered Matthew and the accident.

"Is Matthew okay?" I asked, fearing the worst.

"He is fine. He took your kidnapping pretty hard," my brother revealed. "I still can't believe the guy was Sin's roommate."

"Eric has been after me for years. It's no one's fault. He would have done anything to get me."

I was just glad that he hadn't killed anyone trying to get me. I had enough to deal with as it was. I didn't need the added guilt. I shrugged.

"I don't understand," he asked, sitting down in a chair beside the hospital bed.

"He is the nephew of one of the guys who killed Mom and Dad." I dropped my gaze to my hands as I heard the sharp intake of breath.

"I had no idea," my brother mumbled.

"Neither did I."

I'd been so excited about having a chance to live and experience things I'd never done before. There was no way any of us could have foreseen what would happen. It wasn't anyone's fault.

"How do I look?" I asked after a few minutes of silence. Connor reached for my hand and gave it a squeeze.

"You have a few bruises and a cut on your leg," he assured me. "The doctor says the bruises will fade in about a week."

I didn't need my brother to tell me about my wounds. I remembered how I'd endured every blow and cut. Dropping my gaze to my hands, I tried to build up the courage to look at what he'd done to me.

"There won't be any permanent damage," he said. He must have been able to read my thoughts. Tears seeped from my eyes despite my attempts to keep my emotions under control.

"Don't cry, Tay," he pleaded softly. "You are safe now. Eric will never get his hands on you again."

Being safe didn't erase the details of my ordeal. They would be forever imprinted into my memories. I brushed the tears from my face as I took a shaky breath.

"Please get me a mirror," I asked.

"Okay," he answered, standing up. "I'll be back soon."

The door closed shut as he left to find me a mirror. Minutes later he returned with a small compact.

"I got it from one of the nurses," he told me as he placed it in my open hand.

"I need to be alone for a minute," I told my brother, holding the compact tightly in my hand. I raised my eyes to his.

"I don't know if that is a good idea."

"I'm not asking, Connor," I told him. I needed to do this alone.

He studied me for a moment before he gave me a brief nod. As soon as he left, I opened the compact and looked at my reflection. I gasped and raised my free hand to cover my mouth.

The eye that was swollen shut was badly bruised. My whole face was one massive bruise and there were a few small cuts. I swallowed hard as I took in Eric's handiwork.

Having seen enough, I closed the compact and dropped it into my lap. Feeling the fear and anger begin to build up inside of me, I took a deep breath to try and keep the options under control.

I'm safe, I kept repeating to myself over and over again.

I closed my eyes for a moment and all I could see was the monster's face who'd put me in the hospital. I knew from the therapy that I had received after my parents died how to cope with all the feelings that were tearing through me.

Chapter Twenty-Seven

TAYLOR

Fifteen minutes later, my brother returned. He scanned my features for any sign of how I was feeling, but I kept my emotions bottled up. I wanted and needed the time alone to be able to work through them and there was no way I was going to do that in the hospital with people constantly coming in and out my room.

"There are a few people who want to see you," Connor told me as he walked closer.

I wasn't sure I was ready to see anyone, but the look my brother gave made me bite my lip.

"They've all been waiting in the waiting room anxiously to see you since we got here yesterday."

It was hard to believe I'd been out of it for so long.

"Sin is here too."

That statement cut straight through me, down to my heart, and for a moment I was short of breath. I tried to disguise my shock, but my brother never missed a thing as my eyes shot to his.

"He came back as soon as he found out you were missing," he informed me. I dropped my eyes and refused to look at my brother as I dealt with that information.

My heart began to beat faster and my palms became clammy at the thought of seeing him again. I wasn't sure if I was ready to face him.

"Did anyone get the name of the guy who brought me to the hospital?" I asked, remembering how relieved I'd been when I'd realized he was a good guy. I owed him my life.

"Yeah, his name is Jeff. He works for Sin," he revealed and my mouth dropped open in shock.

"He works for Sin?" I echoed, a little shocked at the revelation.

"Yes," Connor confirmed. But how was that possible? Sin was a college student like me. What my brother was telling me didn't fit with the Sin I knew.

"I don't understand," I said, voicing my confusion.

"That isn't my story to tell. You'll have to ask him," he said, holding up his hands. "He isn't as bad as I thought he was."

I couldn't believe the difference in my brother's attitude toward Sin. He'd been the one to do the background check to warn me about Sin and now he was admitting that he'd been wrong?

What the hell?

I felt like I was in an alternate reality to the one I had lived in. I arched an eyebrow at my brother, but he just shrugged in response.

"Sometimes there is more to a person than what's written on paper," he tried to explain. I honestly didn't know how to respond it that. Never in a million years would I have expected this.

"The nurses said it was okay for you to have visitors," he told me, pulling me out of my stunned thoughts. I didn't want to see anyone.

"I'm not sure I'm up for visitors yet," I murmured,

feeling bad that I was trying to put it off. It wasn't that I didn't want to see them, because I did, what I wasn't looking forward to were the looks of sympathy.

"I know you've been to hell and back, but those people waiting outside to see you have been so worried about you. They care about you and they need to see that you're okay."

I swallowed down the emotion his words pulled from me.

"Okay. Send them in," I replied, feeling the nervous knot in my stomach.

"They can't all come in at once. Matthew is dying to see you so I'll send him and Jordan in," he said. "I think you and Sin will want to talk alone."

I gave him a brief nod. I plastered a weak smile onto my face as I watched my brother disappear out of my room. Minutes later, Jordan and Matthew walked in.

"Oh my God," Jordan gasped as she rushed over to me and engulfed me in a hug. I bit down on my lip to keep myself together. The pain from the cut in my lip throbbed and helped me from feeling overwhelmed. The sight of my messed-up face was going to shock a lot of people.

"Hey," Matthew greeted me as Jordan released me. His eyes were guarded and I knew why. The sight of me was a lot to take in.

"It's good to see you," I said, trying to sound calm, but my voice was hoarse with emotion. I'd been so worried about him being left unconscious in the car after the accident.

"I'm fine," he assured me.

"We were so worried..." Jordan revealed, her voice breaking on the last word.

"I'm okay," I tried to reassure her as I looked to her.

"I still can't believe it was Eric," Matthew said, shaking his head.

None of us had any inkling that Eric was the unstable

stalker after me.

"It's over," I said with finality in my voice that made Matthew and Jordan look at each other.

"I just wanted to say I'm sorry," Matthew said.

I gave him a questioning look and then I realized that he was feeling guilty that he hadn't been able to save me.

"It wasn't your fault," I reassured him, reaching for his hand and giving it a squeeze. "Eric is mentally unstable and if you hadn't been unconscious, he would've killed you."

Despite my words, Matthew looked unconvinced.

"What happened to me wasn't anybody's fault and I don't want anyone to feel guilty," I stated firmly.

He lifted his gaze to mine and gave me a brief nod. I gave him an encouraging smile and he smiled back.

"Are you going to be leaving now?" I asked. I'd grown close to Matthew; he hadn't just been my bodyguard, he'd become my friend.

"I'm going to stay a little while longer," he told me. "At least until Eric is firmly locked up for life."

I pressed my lips together. I didn't like the way I felt when I heard his name. To Matthew it was just a name, but to me it held all the horrors I'd managed to escape.

"I'm sorry," he murmured, seeing the effect it had on me.

"It's okay. I need to work through it," I replied with a shrug.

"We'd better go," Jordan interrupted.

I gave her one last hug before she left behind Matthew. I was nervous and I touched a hand to my face.

The moment he walked in, I felt my stomach flip at the sight of him. His eyes fixed on my face and I saw his jaw tighten. He looked exhausted. There were dark circles under his eyes. He stuffed his hands into the front pockets of his jeans as he took a step closer, his eyes never leaving mine.

"Hi," I said, trying to sound as normal as possible. It was the first time I'd seen him since he'd walked out on me. I couldn't help feeling self-conscious of my injuries under his gaze.

"Hi," he said, taking another step closer. It was rare to see him like this. Normally he was confident and so sure of himself but now he looked nervous.

"Tay..."

"It's okay," I reassured him. "I'll be fine."

I didn't even believe what I'd just said. There was no way I was fine after what had happened to me, but I needed him to believe I was okay.

I shrugged and looked down at my hands. It was easier not to look at him because when I did I remembered how he'd told me that we were over and then he'd left. He hadn't even given me a chance to explain.

I knew why he was here. It wasn't because nearly losing me had made him realize that he was in love with me—that crap only happened in sappy romance books and movies. The reality was that he felt guilty. Eric had been his roommate, someone he knew. I think he also carried more guilt because it had happened after he'd broken my heart and left town.

"The doctors say everything will heal," I stated, lifting my eyes to see the emotion on his face. He ran a hand through his hair.

"I should never have left," he revealed, taking another step closer. He was close enough that if I reached out I could touch his hand, but I didn't.

"I know why you're here," I stated.

He swallowed hard and held my gaze.

"Really?" he asked, looking suddenly very nervous.

"Yes," I said, nodding my head.

"It's guilt."

His forehead creased as his tongue touched his lip ring.

"Guilt?" he questioned.

"Yes. You feel guilty because you left and then something bad happened. You probably think that you could've stopped it, but you wouldn't have been able to. Eric was determined, so determined that he would have left a trail of dead bodies to get me."

He was shaking his head as he took his hands out of his pockets.

"You probably also feel guilty that it was someone you knew," I added. "But it doesn't matter."

He remained silent, studying me intently.

"I'm going to tell you what I told everyone else. What happened to me rests solely on the shoulders of the crazy...who did this to me," I stated firmly, despite the way my voice broke slightly.

"You're right, I do feel guilty. I shouldn't have left and Eric shouldn't have laid one finger on you," he said. I could see anger bubbling inside him just below the surface. His eyes darkened.

I didn't want to waste time on what should have happened because it didn't erase what did happen.

"But that isn't why I'm here," he argued, taking the last step toward me as he reached for my hand.

I allowed him to take it in his and he lifted it to his lips. He dropped a soft kiss on my hand. His touch felt so good, but I resisted it.

"When I first heard you were gone, I was so terrified..." he said, closing his eyes briefly. He looked like he was struggling to contain the emotions he was feeling. "We had no idea if you were injured from the accident."

Subconsciously, my free hand went to my chest where I'd sustained the bruises from the seatbelt.

"We had no idea where you were," he continued.

They'd been out of their minds with worry while I'd

been wondering whether I would survive or not. I took a deep breath and released it when I felt the emotion start to build up again. I wished I could erase the few days I'd been a prisoner; it would make coping with it so much easier.

"I didn't just come back because I felt guilty," he revealed to me as he brushed his thumb over my hand. "I came back because I made a mistake walking away. A mistake I won't ever make again."

I shook my head at him, knowing where he was going with this.

"I know what you think you feel," I argued. "But if you really felt that way, you wouldn't have let go of me so easily."

It was harsh, but it needed to be done, like ripping off a Band-Aid. The faster you pulled it off, the less it hurt. He looked at me, a little shocked and still reeling from the blow.

"You know what I learned from this whole ordeal?" I asked softly, pulling my hand out of his. This was easier to say if he wasn't touching me. The smallest touch from him would be enough to distract me and I had to stay focused.

"What?" he asked. His eyes watchful.

"I learned that I'm stronger than I ever thought I was," I told him.

"You were always strong," he told me softly. "You just didn't realize it."

Surprised that was how he saw me, I paused for a moment before continuing.

"It also made me realize that I need more than you will ever be willing to give," I revealed. Great sex and no clearly defined arrangement wasn't what I wanted anymore. I wanted the whole relationship thing and he would never be able to be that person who could give me that.

It was probably one of the hardest things I'd ever had to say, but I needed to. I felt the sting of tears, but I fought not to break down.

"Don't put words in my mouth," he shot back as the realization of what I was saying sank in. I saw the determined glint in his eyes. "You have no idea what I'm willing to do to keep you."

I took a shaky breath and felt the first tear slide down my face as I tore my gaze from him. It hurt too much. It felt like my heart was splitting in two.

"Leaving town was a mistake and I admit that. I need you to understand why I did what I did," he tried to explain, but I was past excuses.

I pressed my lips together as another tear slid down my face and I refused to look at him. If I looked at him, I wouldn't be able to remain strong enough to do what had to be done.

I wasn't trying to bring him down or hurt him. I wanted him to realize why things would never work between us and life was too short to waste time on something that wasn't ever going to be enough.

"Sex with you is...so good—more than good—but I need more than a physical relationship," I explained to him softly as I looked at him to gauge his reaction.

"What if I want to give you what you want?" he asked, his eyes bright and nervous.

"You've never dated anyone," I argued softly, so badly wanting him to be able to be the person I needed him to be, but I couldn't expect him to become someone he wasn't. I think I was the first person he'd slept with more than once. How could I expect someone like that to change? A nagging voice in my mind couldn't stop the doubt that the guilt of what happened to me was pushing him into this.

"But what if I want that with you?"

I didn't know what to say. I held my breath as another tear slid down my cheek and I held his gaze. His thumb brushed the tear away. I wanted to believe him. I wanted to throw my arms around him and hug him tightly to my body.

"No, it won't work," I said, refusing to give him hope. His guilt was pushing him to do this.

"Why are you being so stubborn?" he said, sounding exasperated with me. "I want to give you what you want, and I don't understand why you won't let me."

"Because you left me!" I snapped, yelling at him. I'd lost the control on my temper unexpectedly. He stood back like I'd physically slapped him.

I took a deep breath to calm myself down. His eyes sought mine, but I looked away for a moment before looking back at him.

"How am I supposed to believe that you want that when, before the attack, you left me? You didn't give me a chance to explain—you just left. If you cared for me, you would have listened to what I had to say, but you didn't. You only came back because of what happened to me."

He was shaking his head at me as he flicked his tongue against his lip ring.

"Honestly, I don't think you would have come back if Eric hadn't attacked me, and that hurts," I told him as another tear slid down my face, attesting to the heartbreak I was suffering.

I hadn't planned on revealing to him how much he'd hurt me, but there was no hiding it now. The hurt was still firmly lodged in my heart. I was breathing hard and I clasped my hands together. I hadn't planned on losing it like this.

"I need to explain to you why I left," he said softly. His eyes pleading with mine.

There wasn't any explaining that was going to change my mind. I was starting to feel tired. I didn't know if it was because of my ordeal or the emotional exhaustion that was making my energy levels wane.

"And you *owe* me a chance to explain," he told me softly.

I lifted my eyes to his. I wanted to give in and take whatever he was offering, but I couldn't. After everything I'd survived, I deserved more than just settling for what he could give me. I was being selfish.

"No, I don't," I stated as calmly as I could.

"Don't do this, Tay," he warned softly.

I had no choice.

"I think you should leave," I told him, holding his gaze. He looked at me with a hard look and I saw his jaw clench. He swallowed hard as he held my gaze. A tense silence settled over us as we stared each other down.

"I'll leave," he said, "but I'm not giving up."

One more intense look and he turned and left, closing the door quietly behind him.

I let out a shaky breath as I tried to keep myself together. Tears slid down my face and I brushed them away, trying to console myself that I'd done the right thing for both of us.

Chapter Twenty-Eight

TAYLOR

Everything around me looked dull and colorless. Something had been taken from me. I wasn't sure if Eric or Sin had taken it. I tried to move on, but it was hard with the constant pain in my heart. I spent a couple more days in the hospital before I was released.

The police had come to take a statement from me and that had been difficult to relive every terrifying moment. It was then that I found out the finer details.

Jeff, the guy who'd found me, had been instructed by Sin to find me and he'd begun to investigate everyone around me, which included Sin's roommates.

What had flagged Eric as suspicious to him had been the rental of another house while he was still renting a room in Sin's house. He'd been on his way to check it out when he'd stumbled across me, beaten in the street.

I would always be grateful for Sin's part that he played in my rescue, but I'd shut the door firmly on him. He'd tried to visit me again in the hospital, but I'd refused to see him. While my heart wanted to hold on to him and never let go, my mind overrode my emotions. He'd tried calling and texting, but all he received was a wall of silence.

I wanted to be able to go back to the girl I'd been before the attack. I honestly hoped that when I got home, I would settle back into my life. But I wasn't that same person and I couldn't pick my life up where it had left off. The trauma of what I'd been through weighed heavily on my shoulders.

For the first couple of days I was still recovering, the bruises on my face stopped me from even considering going back to college. News of what had happened to me had gotten out and I was too self-conscious to walk around with visible injuries.

But even when the bruises began to fade and the physical reminders of my attack began to disappear, I couldn't bring myself to go back to school. No one around me seemed to know how to handle me. Even my brother was not sure whether to push me to go back to college or to leave me to decide when I was ready. So, for the next few days, everyone kept quiet and let me hole-up in my room, hiding away from the world.

Then one morning an insistent knock at my door jarred me from my sleep.

"Open the door, Taylor," I heard my brother demand on the other side of the door.

I groaned and turned around on the bed, putting my back to the door as I snuggled deeper into my pillow. I hoped that if I ignored him, he would go away.

He knocked louder.

"Geez," I muttered as I stumbled from my bed, brushing my messy hair out of my face.

"What?" I asked as I opened my door and pinned my bother with an angry look.

"Shower and get dressed," he instructed and I frowned. He pushed past me and walked into my room.

"What the hell?" I turned to ask him as I put my hands

on my hips.

"I can't let you do this anymore," he replied fiercely. "Go shower and get clothes on. You are going to school today."

Fear crept into me. I wasn't ready for that. I dropped my hands from my hips as I stepped forward.

"I can't...I'm not ready," I tried to argue, but he was shaking his head at me. He had a determined look in his eye that told me he wasn't going to back down.

"I left you alone, hoping that you would be able to get yourself together, but it hasn't worked," he explained. I could see that he was truly worried about me. Did he think I was going to slip back into the darkness—the place I'd fought so hard to escape?

"I'm not ready," I whispered, feeling my fear escalate. My eyes pleaded with his.

"I'm doing this because I love you," he revealed in a firm voice. "I know you're still scared, but Eric is locked up, there is no way he can get to you."

I was shaking my head at him, trying to get him to understand. Didn't he realize that it had taken so long for me to recover from my first traumatic experience only to be targeted again? I doubted I would ever feel safe again. There would always be that thought in the back of my mind that something might happen to me.

"Matthew will be with you," he reassured me as he cocked his head to the side.

Before the attack, that would have meant something to me, but the fact that Eric had gotten to me while I was with Matthew didn't make me feel any safer with Matthew. It wasn't like he'd made a mistake and Eric had taken advantage of that. I swallowed hard, seeing the determined look in my brother's eyes.

"You have thirty minutes," he informed me before he stalked out of my bedroom, leaving me staring open-mouthed in shock that he was forcing me to do this.

My hands shook as I went into my bathroom to take a shower. I quickly showered and then got dressed for class. In my bathroom mirror, I used what little makeup I had to cover up the faint bruise that was still visible on my face. All three of them were waiting for me as I walked out of my bedroom. Jordan was the first one to step forward and throw an arm around my shoulders.

"It will be fine," she said, trying to soothe me, but her words didn't ease the growing horror building up inside of me.

"Are you sure this is the way to do it?" Matthew asked Connor, not convinced they were doing the right thing. I felt hope rise in my chest as I held my breath, hoping my brother wouldn't make me leave the apartment.

"We have to do something. She can't spend the rest of her life holed up in her room," he explained.

Nerves mingled with my fear as I walked beside Matthew and Connor, with Jordan following behind us to the college. I held on to the strap of my bag and dug my nails into the palm of my free hand.

As we walked, my eyes raced from one stranger to another, trying to read their body language to see if they were a threat to me. A few stopped to stare at me and I tried my best to ignore them. Word about what had happened had gotten around campus.

A hand softly touched my back and my eyes shot to Matthew.

"It's okay," he assured me gently, his eyes seeing my fear.

I gave him a nod as I bit down on my lip, trying to keep my emotions from taking over. I didn't want to be scared anymore—I wanted my life back—so, despite my fear, I put one foot in front of the other and I walked to my first class.

"I'll see you later," Jordan said as she hugged me

goodbye. "Call me if you need anything."

I watched as she disappeared down the hallway to her first class.

"You'll be okay," my brother assured me as he hugged me.

My throat was too clogged with emotion to be able to reply, so I nodded my head.

"I'll see you back at the apartment later," he told me as he released me.

Alone with Matthew, I turned to face the door to my first class of the day and I hesitated. A warm hand enveloped mine and I looked up at Matthew.

"You can do this," he told me softly. I wasn't so sure, but I took a deep breath to try and ease the growing panic spreading inside of me.

Slowly, Matthew opened the door and walked in first. He continued to hold my hand as I took one step followed by another. My heart was pounding in my chest and it felt like I could hear my heartbeat echo in my ears. As I got closer to my usual seat, I saw Caleb notice me. He smiled and stood up.

"It's good to have you back," he said to me when I got to my seat.

Despite all the emotions drowning me inside, I gave him a weak smile.

"I'm glad to be back too," I lied. Despite my fear, I knew the only way to get my life back was to fight for it.

I'd survived the horrific murder of my parents. I'd survived being kidnapped and beaten by a crazy stalker. I was stronger than I ever thought I was and there was no way I was going to let my fear rule my life.

The first day back at college was the worst, but I pushed through it with the help of my family and friends. Each day my fear began to ease and I began to settle back into college.

The stares and whispers began to die down as well and my kidnapping became old news.

The fear would never completely go away, but I found ways to deal with it. When I felt things were becoming too overwhelming, I would try and breathe through it. I tried not to concentrate on too many things when I felt like this. It was easier to concentrate on one specific thing and try and work my way through it.

It also made me realize how lucky I was to have a brother who dropped everything to be there for me. He'd rescheduled his life to make sure he could be around while I got my life back on track. I was surprised that he hadn't tried to move me back home. It was like he'd realized that I was an adult and I had my own life to live.

Matthew and Jordan were great friends to me. They were so supportive and understanding. I didn't know what I'd done to deserve such good friends.

One afternoon two weeks after my kidnapping, I was finishing up some homework in my room when I heard someone knock on the front door. I wasn't expecting anyone and I knew Matthew, who was in the living room, would answer the door.

I heard Matthew greet the visitor, but I never heard a response. Distracted, I tried to focus on what I needed to finish.

"Tay."

The sound of Sin's voice saying my name washed over me and made me look to my doorway where I saw Sin standing there with a folder in his hands. Stunned at his unexpected visit, I stood up and crossed my arms.

"What are you doing here?" I asked, feeling my heart begin to race at the sight of him. Any time that had passed since I'd seen him hadn't eased the effect he had on me, or my feelings for him.

He looked tired and his normally neat hair was slightly messy. I had to fight the urge to touch him.

"I had to do something. You won't answer my calls or return my texts," he said, sounding a little hurt.

It took me a few moments to realize that Matthew had let Sin into the apartment. Why had Matthew done that? I would definitely be having words with him when I was finished with Sin.

"This isn't fair," I told him, feeling angry that he was trying to force something that was just going to hurt the two of us.

"Who said I had to play by the rules?" he shot back, giving me a fierce look.

He was making this whole thing so much harder. Didn't he know I was doing the best thing for the both of us? When I'd decided to shut him out, I'd done it for his benefit as well.

"And I'm not leaving until you hear me out," he told me.

I held his piercing gaze and I saw the determination in his eyes. Whether I wanted to or not, I was going to have to hear what he had to say.

"Fine," I said in a clipped tone. I sat down on my bed with my arms crossed, waiting for him to talk. It was then that I recognized the folder he held in his hands. It was the background check Connor had done on him. Why had he brought that with him? Sin closed the bedroom door and turned to face me.

"How did you get Matthew to let you in?" I asked, feeling a little betrayed by my friend.

"I called him. He gave me a chance to tell him why I needed to speak to you and, well, here I am," he explained, sweeping my room with his gaze.

So Matthew thought that whatever Sin had to say was important enough to go against my decision?

"I'm listening," I said, feeling hurt that they'd done this

behind my back.

I had no choice but to listen to what he had to say. But I wasn't convinced that anything he could say would change my mind. It all boiled down to the fact that he'd left me. He hadn't given me a chance to explain and he'd left without a backward glance. If I'd meant anything to him, he wouldn't have been able to walk away like he had. I wasn't convinced that anything he could say was going to change that. I was curious, though, as to why he had the folder with him.

"You have it in your head that I just came back because I was concerned and because I felt guilty," he started, taking a step closer.

The way he looked at me pulled at my heart. Didn't he know he was making it so much more difficult for me to do the right thing? I pressed my lips together.

"What I feel is so much more than that," he stated, making my heart skip a beat. I wanted so badly to believe.

He held the folder in both of his hands, and then his eyes dropped from mine to the folder he held.

"I know you didn't read the folder," he said so softly for a moment that I thought I'd misheard him.

"Why do you suddenly believe me now?" I asked. How could he know that now for sure, despite the fact that I already told him before that I hadn't? I remembered how upset he'd been when he'd discovered the folder in my room. He'd been so convinced that I'd read it, he'd left without giving me an opportunity to explain. It had pushed him to leave town, hadn't it?

"I don't understand," I murmured as I looked at the puzzle pieces in my mind that suddenly didn't seem to fit together.

If he knew I hadn't read the folder, why had he left? It didn't make any sense. I dropped my arms to my side as I kept my eyes fixed on him.

"I want to explain everything to you, but I think you need to read it for yourself," he said, holding out the folder to me. My gaze dropped to the folder he was holding.

He'd been so upset about it. Why would he now hand it to me and tell me to read it?

"Take it," he instructed and I took the folder from him and held it with both hands. "I want you to read it."

I studied the folder for a few moments before I looked back up at him. He was nervous. His tongue flickering against his lip ring was a tell-tale sign.

"I don't need to know about your past," I stated with a sigh. "It doesn't matter to me."

I felt the way I did and nothing in that folder was going to change that. He'd had a rough start in life so I hadn't expected him to be squeaky clean, but I knew what type of person he was now and that had mattered to me more.

"I know," he said. He looked resigned. He wanted me to read what was in the folder even though he looked scared as to how I was going to handle it.

"I'm not sure why you want me to read it now," I said to him.

"I never wanted you to know any of it," he replied honestly as he ran an agitated hand through his hair. "But you've left me no choice. It's the only way for you to understand why I didn't think I was good enough for you and that was the reason why I left. I didn't leave because I didn't care about you."

One moment of strained silence ticked into another. I swallowed hard. He looked so sure of himself and I began to doubt that I'd had all the facts when I'd made my decision to cut him out of my life. But I noticed he seemed nervous.

"Why are you nervous?" I asked.

He looked at me with sadness.

"There is a chance I will lose you anyway." I had no idea

what in the folder made him scared that would happen.

"Promise me you will read it," he asked softly as his eyes implored mine.

I felt myself nodding. My curiosity was piqued and he'd gone to such lengths to organize this, the least I could do was read it.

"I'll read it," I promised him softly. I'd had that folder for ages and I'd never once looked in it and now I was going to read everything. I wasn't nervous because nothing was going to change how I much I loved him.

"You know where to find me when you're done," he said just before he turned to open my bedroom door.

"I'll see you soon. Even if it's just to tell me you never want to see me again," he said, turning back to look at me one more time before walking out of my bedroom and leaving me a little stunned.

Chapter Twenty-Nine

TAYLOR

I don't know how long I sat there staring at the folder in my hands after Sin left. When my brother had first handed it to me, I never thought it would play such an important part in my life, but here I was, sitting, ready to open it up and read the contents.

"Are you okay?" Matthew asked from my doorway and I looked at him. He looked a little nervous.

"Traitor," I accused. The anger I'd first felt at him for allowing Sin into the apartment evaporated and all I felt was a nervous fear building up inside of me at what was inside of the folder.

"I'm sorry and I know it was underhanded, but he deserved the chance to explain," he said. "I saw how messed up he was when you were missing."

I knew that he would have been upset, but how could I be sure that whatever he was feeling wasn't being driven by guilt? I took a deep breath, not wanting to be reminded of the nightmare I was trying to forget about.

"Did you guys manage to sort it out?" he asked.

"I'm not sure," I replied honestly with a shrug. "He left

me with something that I need to read."

Although he looked curious as his eyes dropped to the folder I held, he gave me a nod and he stepped out of my room, closing the door behind him.

I opened the folder and took a deep breath.

My eyes scanned over the first couple of pages. At first there didn't seem to be anything that I hadn't already thought of when I'd first met him. It didn't surprise me that he'd had run-ins with the law. I was beginning to think maybe he'd overreacted and then I found what he'd wanted to hide from me. The reason why he'd left stared at me from the pages I held in my hand.

It didn't surprise me, but it made me understand why he'd been scared. Seeing the details of his rap sheet made me feel bad for what he had to go through. I rubbed my temple, trying to sort through my thoughts. The knowledge brought back the memories of my parents' murder and it was hard to be faced with them so soon after my kidnapping.

All the pieces to the puzzle began to fit together and now I had a clearer picture to look at. Everything began to make more sense. I understood why Sin had been so upset about the folder. It hadn't just been because he felt like I'd violated some sort of trust; he'd been scared of me finding out about his past. With this new information, I understood why Sin didn't feel he was good enough for me. He'd been so convinced that it would change how I felt about him, and it had scared him enough to leave. He knew it would only be a matter of time before I'd find out.

He saw it as something I could have struggled to see past. For the first time since he'd told me that he cared for me, I believed him. I had to take a deep breath to try and gain control of the emotions building up inside of me.

I spent the rest of the day in a daze, unsure of exactly how to handle it. I got a couple of concerned looks from

Matthew and Jordan, but I wasn't going to tell anyone.

"I would never have let him in to see you if I thought it would upset you this much," Matthew told me when he cornered me in the kitchen after dinner.

I put my dirty plate in the sink and turned to face him.

"I don't want to talk about it," I said to him. "There is stuff I need to work through."

"Sure," he said, nodding his head, but I could see he felt guilty for helping Sin.

"Don't feel bad, it needs to get sorted out," I told him, trying to relieve his guilt. He gave me a brief nod even though he didn't look entirely convinced.

I disappeared into my bedroom to try and shut out the rest of the world while I tried to figure out what I was going to do.

That night, I didn't sleep a wink. I tossed and turned, but I never felt the welcome release of sleep.

The next morning when I got up, I decided it was time to talk to Sin. I had classes, but I was going to skip them because there was no way I could concentrate on anything with thoughts of Sin plaguing my mind. I needed to talk to him.

I rubbed my eyes and yawned as I walked into my bathroom to get dressed. Dazed and tired, I got into my clothes and brushed my hair. I didn't bother with makeup to hide my lack of sleep. When I stepped out of my room and walked into the kitchen to get some coffee, Matthew smiled at me and offered me a cup.

"Thanks," I mumbled as I took it and filled it with coffee.

"You look tired," he noted as he studied me.

"I am tired," I admitted. I took a sip of the hot, fragrant liquid.

Matthew didn't ask me any more questions; instead, he

stood watching me closely.

"I'm not going to school today," I told him.

I expected him to argue or ask why, but instead he said, "Okay, where are we going, then?"

I held his gaze and said, "I need to talk to Sin."

He didn't seem to be that surprised as he nodded his head.

"Okay," he replied and I felt relieved that I didn't have to explain why. I didn't want to tell anyone else about Sin's past. Besides, it wasn't any of their business. Jordan was sleeping in and didn't have class till much later, so it left Matthew and me on our own, drinking our coffee.

"Are you ready?" he asked as he set his empty coffee mug down on the counter.

"Yes," I said. I was nervous.

The drive to Sin's house was quiet. I was lost in my thoughts and Matthew didn't try and make conversation. It was evident that I had too much on my mind to be interested in small talk. Along with the swirl of emotions inside of me, I began to feel more and more nervous the closer we got. By the time Matthew pulled the car up in front of Sin's house, I was beyond nervous.

"You sure you need to do this?" asked Matthew as he took in my body language.

I nodded my head and unbuckled my seatbelt.

"Are you sure he's even going to be here?" he asked.

"He'll be here," I answered, knowing that he was probably waiting for me to show up.

"Do you need me to go in with you?" he asked when I hesitated with my hand on the door handle.

"No, I have to do this alone," I said, opening the door and getting out of the car.

Matthew remained in the car and watched me climb the steps. In front of the door, I gave myself one more pep talk before I knocked and held my breath, waiting for Sin to answer it.

Sin finally opened the door. He looked anxious. He was still obviously convinced that I wouldn't be able to see past what I'd read in his folder.

"Tay," he said and stood back, inviting me into his house with the sweep of his hand.

I didn't like his house anymore. There was something in it that was forever tied to Eric. No matter how hard I tried not to think about him, I couldn't stop the thoughts of him or kidnapping and confinement.

"Don't be nervous," he said as he studied me. "I got rid of my other roommate. Only Slater and I live here now."

He was trying to ease my fear, but it didn't work.

"Would you rather talk upstairs in my room?" he asked when he noticed I was still agitated.

"Yes," I whispered.

He climbed the stairs and I followed behind to his room. I walked into his room and I immediately felt safe. In his room the only memories I had were of the two of us. From the first awkward encounter to when I'd lost my virginity to him. I'd fallen in love with him in this room.

He closed the door and turned to face me.

"You read the file." It wasn't a question; it was a statement.

I bit my lip as I nodded. Several seconds passed in silence. There was so much to sort out between us and I didn't know where to start. His eyes watched me for the slightest emotion to gauge how I'd taken the information.

"There wasn't a lot in that file that my imagination hadn't already conjured up," I began to say. "I know which part you were scared I would find out about."

"Dealing drugs," he finished for me and I saw the resignation in his face.

I nodded. The guys who'd murdered my parents had been high on drugs at the time they'd committed the crime. That was the reason why he'd felt I wouldn't be able to forgive him for it.

"Why?" I asked, needing him to explain it to me. A guy who dealt drugs didn't fit in with the person who'd watched me the night my drink got spiked. He dropped his gaze to the floor.

"I've told you about some of my crappy childhood," he began to explain as he lifted his eyes to mine. In them I saw the small boy who didn't know what it was like to be loved.

"While my mom was drowning her sorrows with an endless supply of alcohol, I was left to fend for myself."

It was hard to think of him as a small boy with no one to look after him. It was heartbreaking to listen to.

"Slater was pretty much in the same situation I was. His father was a drug addict and his mom could barely make ends meet. Whatever money his mom made went to pay for the drugs his father needed."

It made me sad to think that children grew up in situations like that. I'd always taken for granted my loving parents and my happy childhood up to the point where my parents had died.

"We got involved with a gang."

He paused for a moment.

"There were no options. We did what we had to, to survive," he finished.

Listening to his childhood made my heart ache.

"I'm sorry you had to grow up like that," I said softly, meaning what I said. I couldn't comprehend it.

"I'm sorry too."

He held my gaze and I watched as his tongue flickered against his lip ring.

"We didn't enjoy doing any of the things that were

expected of us," he explained. "But there was no walking away from it—we needed the money."

"Are you still working for this gang?" I asked. Was that why Jeff worked for him? I didn't know how I felt about it if he was still in the gang.

"No," he said, shaking his head. I felt relieved.

"Connor said Jeff worked for you?" I asked, wanting to know the story behind that.

I was tired and I yawned as I waited for him to answer the question.

"You're tired," he stated. "Why don't you sit down?"

I looked around before I sat down on his bed, facing him. He pulled up a chair in front of me and sat down.

"Yes, Jeff works for me," he answered.

That didn't fit in with what I knew about him and it made me wonder how well I knew this guy whom I'd fallen in love with.

"I don't understand."

He let out a deep breath as he ran his hand through his hair.

"I told you about my father," he started and I nodded.

"While he was alive I'd never met him or had any contact with him, but when he died I inherited everything he had," he revealed, watching me closely for a reaction. My forehead creased as I tried to take that piece of information in.

"His lawyer called me up out of the blue one day and told me about my inheritance."

"But what about his wife and kids?" I asked. It sounded strange that the guy who'd fathered him and who hadn't wanted anything to do with him or his mother would leave him everything he had.

"His wife died before him and they never had any kids. In his will he left me everything," he explained with a shrug.

He obviously didn't understand it either.

"Wow," was all I could say. A guy who hadn't wanted anything to do with him in life had left Sin everything he'd owned. Talk about messed up.

"I didn't want to take the money, but I didn't have a choice. Slater and I were getting deeper into the gang and it was becoming more serious. We'd gone from petty crime to dealing drugs and we knew it was going to get worse. It was the only way to get us out before we got in... too deep."

I didn't like the sound of that so I shot him a questioning look.

"I don't want to talk about it," he said, refusing to elaborate. "That part of my life is over. The money gave me the freedom to give myself a new life and I could help the people I cared about. Slater and I left the gang. Jeff—the guy who found you—left with us. Whenever I need something done, he is the guy I call."

Jeff had fit the image I'd always carried of a gangster. It had probably been the reason why I'd struggled to trust him when he'd first found me. But despite my mistrust, he'd saved me.

"I'm not judging," I quickly said as I reached out to cover his hand with mine. I didn't want him to think he had to explain to me why he'd taken the money. It didn't taint the picture I had of him in my heart.

"I never wanted to be seen as a trust-fund baby. I wanted people to care for me, not for the money I had."

His statement explained why no one had any idea he was well-off. It didn't matter to me. Money gave you freedom, but it never guaranteed happiness. His gaze dropped to my hand that covered his. His other hand covered mine and he looked at me.

"My mom had started to get sick. The years of alcohol abuse took its toll on her body. I've set her up with the best medical care money can buy. I try to visit her often, but it's hard trying to care for someone who never gave a shit about me until she sobered up."

I didn't understand that at all. Both of my parents had loved me unconditionally—the way parents were supposed to love their children.

"I want you to know that I never wanted to deal drugs. It wasn't something I was proud of," he said with sadness in his eyes. I wanted to hold him tight and tell him everything would be okay.

"I know it's a lot to take in," he said as he stood up. I stood up.

"It was hard to read your file," I replied. "Seeing what you had to do to survive was difficult to comprehend."

It made me angry that his mother and Slater's parents had done that to them—left them alone in the world to fend for themselves. It was heartbreaking.

He looked solemn as he nodded his head.

"I understand why you got so upset when you saw the folder and I understand why you ran," I said, feeling the emotions tied to those two events begin to creep up and take hold of me.

He dropped his gaze, unable to look at me anymore.

"Look at me," I whispered, needing to tell him how I felt about it.

His eyes lifted to mine and I felt my heart ache again at the broken look he gave me. He was still expecting me to walk away from him.

Chapter Thirty

TAYLOR

I reached up on my tiptoes and pressed my lips to his. His lips remained still under mine as I kissed him gently before I pulled back and looked up at him. He was holding still, waiting to see what I was going to say. He looked scared and I saw a glimpse of the hurt child in the depths of his blue eyes.

"I love you," I whispered to him. Happiness shone in his eyes for a couple of seconds but vanished when I realized he was waiting for a 'but.'

"You don't think you're good enough for me," I said, watching his expression, which was veiled so that it was hard to see exactly what he was thinking.

"I know I'm not good enough for you," he stated, still not showing the emotion I knew he was feeling.

"Yes, my parents were murdered by two young guys that were high on drugs at the time. Did the drugs put the gun in their hands and pull the trigger? No. Not every person who gets high on drugs murders someone. It wasn't the drugs that ended my parents' lives."

I paused for a moment.

"You had a tough childhood and I can't imagine what it was like. It physically hurts to think of what you had to go through," I said and reached for his hand, taking it into mine. "I understand why you did the things you did and I would never judge you."

He swallowed as he held my gaze, still unsure.

"You are good enough for me," I whispered to him, letting him know that I wasn't going to be leaving.

I watched as my words sank in and the realization hit him. In an instant his arms wrapped around me and hugged me tight. I smiled as my head rested against his chest and I allowed myself to feel the happiness that we both deserved.

I tried to pull away, but his arms tightened around me.

"Give me a minute," he breathed into my hair.

Closing my eyes, I savored the feel of him holding onto me so tightly, scared to let go. A few minutes later he pulled away and looked down at me.

"I was so scared I was going to lose you," he said, his voice hoarse with the emotion.

"I'm not going anywhere," I stated, making sure he knew that I was here to stay.

He bent down to kiss me and I wrapped my arms around his neck, pulling him closer. I felt like I was alive again in his arms, being so thoroughly kissed that it left my knees a little weak and my heart hammering in my chest.

Breathlessly, he pulled away and leaned his forehead against mine.

"I've never done this before," he said softly.

"What exactly are we doing?" I asked, needing to know what this meant to him. I needed to know that we were on the same page.

"This is going to be more than one night," he explained as his mouth tugged into a playful smile. "No hooking up with other people."

My smile faltered slightly at the fear that, despite how much I loved him and how much he cared about me, we were going to go back to our original arrangement. I wanted more than that.

"We get titles as well," he teased.

"Titles?" I asked, not sure what that meant.

"Yeah," he said as his smile widened. "Girlfriend."

He kissed me on the lips and I felt relief at his words.

"Does that mean I get to call you my boyfriend?" I asked as I broke the kiss and looked up at him.

He nodded his head at me.

"I never thought I'd ever want more, but I do with you."

"It scares me," I admitted. I loved him so much and I couldn't help but feel nervous about starting something more with him.

He'd never dated a girl before. I believed it was why he went through girls like he had, because he struggled to form emotional attachments with them. He'd never done more than one-night stands and I wasn't sure if he would be able to do the whole monogamy thing with me. I was scared to love someone who had no idea how to love me back.

"Don't be scared," he soothed. "The way I feel about you is nothing like I've ever felt before."

As nervous as I was, I felt my heart inflate at his beautiful words.

"When I heard that you'd been taken, it felt like someone had ripped my heart out of my chest," he admitted and I felt the pain in his words. "I've never been so scared in my life."

That really meant something to me. He hadn't had an easy road and I'm sure he had plenty of really scary moments in his life, but the thought of losing me had been his worst.

"I never want to feel that again," he added as he pressed a soft kiss to my forehead. "I felt so guilty that I'd left you and then you went missing."

"There was nothing you could've done to stop Eric."

I knew telling him that wouldn't erase the guilt he felt, but I still needed him to know.

"Maybe...maybe not."

He wasn't convinced by my words.

At that moment I felt so much happiness. He'd hurt me more than once, but I was willing to put my heart on the line for him again because I knew it would be so worth it if everything worked out.

"I won't lie—I have no idea how to do this, but I promise to try to do everything I can to make you happy," he promised me as he wrapped his arms around me and hugged me close.

"When I first saw you, I never imagined we would end up where we are now," I said, looking back at our journey to get to where we were.

He pulled away and looked at me.

"From the first time I saw you, I knew there was something different about you," he revealed as he held my face on either side.

"Really?" I asked. I thought he hadn't even really known I'd existed at that point.

"Yes," he assured me. "And then you came to see me, wanting me to 'take advantage' of you."

He smirked at me and I blushed. I still couldn't believe I'd had the courage to do what I'd done.

"But why did you turn me down?" I asked, still feeling the sting of his initial rejection.

"You were so innocent," he explained as he trailed his knuckles down my face. "And I wasn't. You deserved so much better than me."

I shook my head at him.

"I'm so glad you were my first," I said to him.

"I tried to do the right thing—I really did—but I couldn't stop thinking about you," he revealed. "And then I saw you drinking with Slater and I couldn't handle seeing you with someone else."

"You were jealous?" He smiled and nodded his head.

"I think I was and then I knew that, even though you deserved better, I couldn't let you go," he said softly. "I couldn't stand the thought of you being with someone else. I knew I would have to step up and give you what you wanted or I would lose you."

I was so happy listening to him talk about how much I'd affected him when I'd thought we were nothing more than a one-night stand. Listening to him reveal his feelings made me understand some of his actions.

"And then after our night together?" I prompted.

"One night with you was never going to be enough," he stated. "I was always going to want more."

"But I saw you with Slater and that girl," I reminded him as I remembered feeling so hurt. My brain knew the decision I'd made was for one night, but my heart had hurt anyway.

"I didn't like the way you made me feel. I felt vulnerable and I hated feeling like that. I tried to move on, I really did, but there was no getting over you."

"Did you sleep with that girl?" I blurted the question out before I could stop myself. I knew if he said yes that it would hurt.

"No, I couldn't do it."

I felt so relieved that I let out the breath I'd been holding.

"I haven't slept with anyone else since our first night together," he admitted softly. My eyes widened in shock.

"Really?" I asked, feeling a little stunned at the unexpected revelation.

"Yes."

I was speechless.

"When I saw you with Caleb, I was so angry," he said. I felt a little guilty for making him feel that way, but I had no way of knowing at the time how he felt about me.

"And you thought I needed a rich, preppy boy?" I asked, remembering what he'd said to me.

"I tried to convince myself that was the reason why you were with him. It would've hurt more to know that you were with him because you liked him," he admitted.

"I was trying to fill the hole that you left in my heart and I shouldn't have used someone else to do that."

Hindsight was always so clear. We'd both done so many things wrong and the chances were good that we weren't done making mistakes.

"There were more than a few times after you went missing that I thought I would never be able to hold you again," he said. In that moment, in the depths of his eyes, I saw the fear that he'd felt.

"You don't have to think about that anymore," I reassured him, taking his hands into mine. "I'm okay now."

"Everyone was getting more and more scared that you weren't coming back, but it wasn't something I could accept," he explained. I remained silent. He clearly needed to tell me.

"I called Jeff as soon as I found out you were missing. I told him to find you."

There was a solemn silence that settled between us at the reminder of what I'd been through. I looked at him as he watched me for a reaction.

"I was so scared when he found me in the street," I said, trying to block the fear that encompassed that moment.

"If the cops hadn't gotten to Eric first, I'm not sure I could've let him live for what he did to you," he said in such a deadly tone that I knew without a doubt he meant every word.

"Then I'm glad the cops got him first," I replied.

He studied me for a moment.

"If I hadn't killed him, I definitely would've made him wish he'd never touched you," he told me.

"And you would have been up for assault. With your previous criminal record they wouldn't have been lenient," I reminded him.

He gave me a look that said he would have still made Eric regret what he did.

"It's finished," I said, but the truth was it wasn't. I was hoping that Eric would just confess so I would be able avoid a trial and the press that came with it.

"But I'm so thankful that you are here with me now," he whispered as he pulled me closer, and I put my hands against his hard chest.

"Me too."

There had been so many times through that ordeal when I hadn't believed I would ever survive it. What happened just reinforced the idea of living my life to the fullest and relishing every moment I had. And now that I had someone as special as Sin to share it with, it would make every moment sweeter.

His hands settled on my hips and I waited with anticipation as he leaned closer. He kissed me. His lips covered mine and I felt the gentle sweep of his tongue on my bottom lip. As I opened my mouth, my tongue touched his and he slipped his tongue inside. I gripped around his neck tighter, needing him closer.

By the time we broke apart, we were both breathless.

"Do you want to meet me at my apartment and we can spend the day together?" I asked, knowing exactly how I wanted to spend the day with him.

"Yes," he replied with a smile that made my stomach flip. It was on his mind too. Sin walked me to the car where Matthew was patiently waiting.

"Hey," Matthew greeted us. As much as I tried, I couldn't wipe the stupid wide smile off my face. I was so happy and it was hard not to show it.

"I see you guys have sorted things out," he observed as he smiled at us. Sin gave him a brief nod and said, "Thanks."

"You're welcome."

Sin opened the car door for me and I got inside.

"I'll see you soon," he said as he pressed a brief kiss to my cheek and watched as Matthew reversed the car.

It still felt so unbelievable that everything had gone so well and that we were dating. I was floating on cloud nine and when Sin arrived half an hour later, I couldn't have been any happier.

Once we were inside my bedroom, he closed the door and leaned against it. The way he smiled and held my gaze let me know exactly what was on his mind and I had to admit I could think of little else but being close to him.

"I think you have way too many clothes on," he said as he stepped forward, and I smiled.

"Really?" I asked. "What if I'm cold?"

"Then I'll keep you warm," he promised as he reached out with one hand that settled on my hip and pulled me closer.

I didn't care that Matthew was in the next room. All that mattered was the two of us.

I let him pull me closer and I put my hands against his chest as I looked up to him and smiled. He gave me a teasing smile as he kissed me and I felt a fluttering in my stomach. He cradled my face in his hands and he feathered a kiss to my lips. I fisted his shirt in my hands.

"I've missed you," he whispered as he stared into my eyes.

"I missed you too," I whispered back. "I can't help feeling that if I'd just let you explain, we would've been able to sort things out sooner."

I felt guilty that I hadn't given him a chance to explain when I was in the hospital. I could have saved us both from being miserable for the last couple of weeks.

"Let's not think about that," he whispered, dropping a kiss to my cheek. "All that matters is that we have sorted everything out now and we're together."

He feathered another kiss to my cheek and I closed my eyes, loving the feel of his soft lips against my skin, which tingled beneath his brief touch.

My mouth opened slightly as his lips covered mine and I groaned as his tongue caressed mine. I gripped his shirt tighter in my hands, wanting more of him. As his kiss grew harder, I wrapped my arms around his neck. He lifted me by the waist and instinctively I wrapped my legs around him, grinding my hips against him.

He broke away and I unwrapped my legs. Standing on my wobbly knees, I watched as Sin reached for the hem of my shirt and lifted it up. I helped him remove the piece of clothing and then I reached for his shirt.

He removed it quickly, throwing it down on the floor. His intense eyes held mine and I felt my skin tingle under his gaze. I wanted him so much. My fingers went to his jeans and I began to undo them. They dropped to the floor.

Sin's hands went to my jeans and he unzipped them. Slowly with the slight trail of his fingers against my skin he pulled them down my legs. I held on to his shoulders to keep my balance. Standing in front of him in my underwear and bra, he glided his hands up my leg to my waist before pulling me against him. I smiled as his lips descended onto mine.

I felt his hands unclasp my bra and pull the straps gently from my arms. The feel of his hard chest was so good that I opened my hands and felt the hard edges of his toned body beneath my fingertips.

I would never get tired of the feel of his body against mine. He backed me up to the bed and he laid me down gently. I bit down on my lip as he reached with both hands to my panties and began to slowly pull them off of me. The anticipation was killing me.

He pulled me gently down to the edge of the bed as I lay down, waiting in anticipation at the sensitive touch of his tongue against my core. I gasped as I felt the insistent lick of his tongue pushing me into a frenzy of need. I threaded my fingers through his hair, unsure of how to handle the intense build up. He pushed a finger into me and I felt myself explode as a rush of intense relief crashed over me. I closed my eyes and my body trembled with my release.

He reached for the pocket of his discarded jeans and ripped open a condom packet. Once the protection was on, he knelt in front of me. I reached for him and he covered my body with his. I felt him nudge my entrance. My breath hitched as he pushed into me. I held on to him as he began to slowly move in and out of me.

He kissed me and I groaned against his lips, loving the feel of him against me. His strokes increased. I lifted my hips to meet his. I felt the build up again and I began to gasp as his movements became more insistent.

"You feel so good," he whispered, sounding like he was nearing his climax. His thrusts were harder and faster as I began to feel the crash of my own orgasm.

A few more thrusts and Sin closed his eyes as he reached his orgasm. Holding his weight with his elbows, he pressed a kiss to my forehead before he rolled off me and got up to dispense with the condom. Moments later he returned and got back into bed with me.

Afterward, we lay on my bed. I looked at him and my heart swelled, about to burst from my feelings for him. He was still breathing hard. Sweat beaded his forehead.

"I love you," I said, needing to say it again and needing him to hear it.

He let out a sigh and turned to face me. Even though we'd talked everything through and any problems between us had been sorted out, I couldn't help feeling nervous at the look on his face.

"I want to be able to say those words to you and mean them," he began to explain. I watched him struggle to find the right words to explain further. "Most people know what love means because they've experienced it, but I haven't."

I felt so sad that his childhood had been that bad. I wanted to reach out and put my arms around him and shield him from the horrible memories of his childhood.

"That doesn't mean, though, that you aren't the most important person in my life. I will do everything I can to make you happy and keep you safe," he whispered to me. His beautiful, expressive eyes held mine as he reached out and touched my cheek. His voice filled with emotion. He couldn't put a label on what he felt for me, but I knew he felt the same as I did. He didn't have to put it into words because I could tell from his actions how much he cared for me.

"I'm sorry I can't say it to you," he said and I could see the look of sadness in his eyes that he had when he spoke about his childhood.

I appreciated his honestly.

"You don't have to say the words," I reassured him softly as I leaned over and kissed him gently. "It doesn't change what we have together."

Chapter Thirty-One

TAYLOR

As soon as I walked into the apartment, I dropped my bag and kicked off my shoes. My feet ached and I was tired. I headed straight for the sofa and collapsed into the soft, comfortable leather. Closing my eyes, I savored the quiet for a moment.

"Rough day?" Sin asked. I opened my eyes and looked up to see him peering at me from behind the sofa. He leaned down and pressed a kiss to my lips. He smelled like he'd just showered and his hair was still damp.

"Yes. I'm tired," I replied, letting out a heavy sigh. My last shift at the restaurant had been brutal.

"You know you don't have to work," he reminded me and I shook my head at him.

It was my way of staying independent. I wanted to be able to make my own way in life.

There was a restaurant just off campus where I'd gotten a job. I only worked part time. Connor had argued with me about it, but my mind had been made up. Sin had assured me that I didn't have to work. He'd been on my brother's side in that specific argument, much to my annoyance. I'd refused to allow them to talk me out of it, though.

I wanted to be able to start paying my own way. I didn't earn a lot, but what little money I made was mine and that meant a lot to me. It was tough going to college and working part time, but I was managing.

Sin pointblank refused to allow me to pay him rent, so I'd offered to buy the groceries. He hadn't really liked that idea either, but I'd refused to move in with him unless I paid for something, so he'd relented.

His hands settled on my shoulders and he began to massage me. I sighed as his firm hands eased the tension from my body.

"You know, if you didn't work, we would have more time to spend together," he tried to persuade me. He'd tried using that on me before, but I'd refused to be tempted.

A month after we'd started dating, Sin had sold his house and bought an condo close to campus. I'd been relieved because I associated the house with Eric and memories of my kidnapping. I'd tried to hide it from Sin, but he'd noticed and he'd been determined to do whatever he could to make sure I wasn't unnecessarily reminded of Eric or my ordeal.

I hadn't expected him to go as far as selling the house, but he had. He'd bought a two-bedroom condo, which was really nice.

For someone who had never even dated, he'd surprised me when he'd asked me to move in with him. He'd wanted it just to be the two of us, so he'd rented another condo on the same block for Slater. Connor hadn't been happy with the idea of the two of us moving in together even though the two of them got on really well. His reasoning had been that I was too young.

Maybe he was right, but it was my decision to make even if it turned out to be a mistake.

"Mmm," I murmured as I ignored him and concentrated

on how good his hands felt on my shoulders.

"You're not listening to me, are you?" he asked and I mumbled a yes.

I protested when he removed his hands and he joined me on the couch. He was so good-looking and I took a moment to appreciate him. It was still hard to believe that he was mine.

"You like what you see?" he asked with a knowing smirk.

"Yes," I replied, smiling at him. It was difficult to believe that even though we'd been together for six months, we still found it hard to keep our hands off each other.

"Why did you stop?" I asked. It had felt so good.

"Because you weren't listening to what I was saying," he answered as he took my hand in his. I had been listening, but I didn't want to have to defend my decision again.

"It's because I can't think of anything but you when you touch me," I admitted. When he touched me, nothing else existed, only him.

"Really," he said with a mischievous grin as he leaned closer.

"Yes," I whispered as he drew closer still. My stomach fluttered in anticipation as I held my breath, waiting for the moment his lips touched mine. At the moment they did, I came alive beneath his touch, wanting and needing more. My arms snaked around his neck and pulled him closer. He deepened the kiss and caressed my tongue. I moaned against his lips. And then he pulled away and I was left breathless, wanting more.

"As much as I want to take you to bed, we have plans for tonight," said Sin, still breathing hard. I pouted as I crossed my arms.

He laughed at me and pressed a quick kiss to my lips before pulling away.

"You're no fun," I said, hating the fact that he was right.

"Come on, I'll start the shower for you," he offered as he pulled me to my feet. I was still feeling tired, but I didn't want to skip the night out. With college and work, it was hard finding the time to be together, so I was going to make the effort to go out.

I followed Sin into our bedroom and opened the wardrobe to find something to wear. It was at times like these that I missed Jordan. She would always help me find something to wear. I chose an outfit and put it out on the bed. Sin walked out of the bathroom.

"Your shower is ready," he informed me and I kissed him briefly, trying to keep my control.

I went to take my shower as I thought about how lucky I was to have him in my life. For someone who had never been emotionally attached before, he was an awesome boyfriend. He was caring and thoughtful. Sometimes I had to pinch myself to make sure I wasn't dreaming.

When I got out, I dried myself and wrapped the towel around my body before I walked back into the bedroom. Sin was lying on the bed with his hands behind his head, watching me. The look he gave me made me smile. His eyes darkened at the sight of me in the small towel and I smiled seductively at him.

I knew if I dropped the towel, we weren't going anywhere.

"Out," I told him. He studied me for a moment before he let out a sigh and got up.

"You're no fun," he said, using my line on me, and I shook my head at him.

"I'll be out soon," I told him as he left the bedroom, reluctantly closing the door behind him.

I got dressed quickly and put some makeup on. With practice, I'd gotten better at doing my own.

"You're so hot," Sin said as I stepped out of the room.

"Don't look at me like that," I warned him as his eyes caressed me. I knew what he was thinking because I was thinking the same thing.

He reached for me and settled his hands on my hips, pulling me closer. He leaned closer to kiss me, but I moved my face so his kiss landed on my cheek.

"We need to leave now or we'll be late," I told him as I pulled away from him.

"Is Jeff coming with us tonight?" I asked as I followed Sin to the door.

"No. I'll be around so we don't need him tonight," he told me and I nodded.

That was one thing Sin had insisted on. Matthew had moved on to another job and, even though I didn't feel the need to have someone to watch over me, Sin had assigned Jeff to watch me. I never went out alone—Jeff was always with me. I liked Jeff. He'd saved my life and for that he had a lifetime friend in me.

Sin opened the door and I walked out. I felt the usual nervousness when I left the safety of the apartment. Even though I knew I had nothing to be scared of, I couldn't help the apprehension that filled me when I went out.

Sin reached for my hand and held it in his. His eyes met mine for a moment. He understood and he gave me a moment to take a deep breath. I knew with time it would get easier and that memories of what had happened with me wouldn't be so vivid in my mind.

Gently, by the hand, Sin led me down the hallways to the elevator. As we waited for it, I tried to hide my nervousness.

"Relax," Sin instructed as he studied me.

"I'm good," I assured him, giving him a weak smile. I pushed through my nervousness and fear, not allowing it to dictate my life.

He pulled me closer and put his arm around me. I leaned my head against him as we waited for the elevator. I had nothing to worry about. Eric was locked up and he couldn't get to me anymore. I had to remember that. I'd been stunned when Eric had pleaded guilty. I'd been so relieved I wouldn't have to go through with the trial and relive the horror of my experience. The press would have covered it because of my past.

It was only later that I'd found out Sin had somehow persuaded Eric to plead guilty. When I'd asked him, he'd refused to tell me anything. Maybe there were some things I didn't need to know. Instead of questioning him further, I'd thanked him. The stress of possibly having to go to trial had started to take its toll on me and I was thankful I didn't have to go through it.

After Eric had been taken into custody, he'd been given a psychiatric evaluation. It didn't take a lot to see that he wasn't mentally stable and after a while they'd figured out that his mental problems had been the reason why he'd become so fixated on me. Instead of going to jail he'd been sent to a psychiatric ward.

During the trial years ago, the stress of his uncle's part in the murder of my parents had taken its toll on his family and his once stable childhood had disintegrated. It had impacted him severely and his fixation with me had begun.

I didn't know why it had been me. Maybe it was because I'd survived the event that had torn both of our lives apart.

I wanted to be able to forgive him, but I just couldn't. I knew in some way it hadn't been his fault. At eleven, he hadn't been able to handle things, but that didn't diminish the horrific things he'd done to me. There was a chance I would never be able to forgive him.

"You sure you're okay to go out? If you'd rather stay at home, I'll cancel our plans tonight," Sin offered, looking down at me with concern.

"I'm fine," I told him as I pulled away from him and took hold of his hand. The elevator doors opened and we got on.

I'd been looking forward to seeing our friends for a while, so I didn't want to cancel the evening. There would still be moments that were hard to manage my fears, but I tried to push through those times. I would get past it eventually; it would just take a little time.

By the time we got to the bar, our friends were waiting at the table. Slater and Jordan were sitting on opposite sides of the table. They could barely look at each other.

They'd made up and broken up a couple of times and they were on the outs again. I really wished they could work through their problems because they really suited each other.

Matthew was sitting beside Jordan. It was so good to see him. He was so busy with his new job that I didn't get to see him as often as I wanted.

Jordan's face lit up as she spotted us walk through the front door. I smiled at her and Slater as we walked up to them.

"You made it," Jordan said as she stood up and gave me a hug.

Sin greeted Slater and Matthew. Jordan released me and I hugged Slater.

"Good to see you," he murmured as he hugged me back. I pulled away and turned to Matthew.

"I'm so glad you made it," I said as he smiled and hugged me.

"I'm sorry I've been so busy with work. It's been hard to get time away," he said as he released me.

He didn't really talk about his new job, so we didn't ask questions. All I knew was that it was a girl. I couldn't help but wonder if he was getting attached to her because he always seemed to be on edge when he wasn't working. I wanted to ask him about it, but I'd decided I'd wait until he brought it up.

"I'm going to get you a drink," Sin said as he and Slater walked to the bar. I sat down opposite Jordan and Matthew.

"How is Connor?" Matthew asked as he folded his arms.

"He's good. He's always busy with work and stuff. I kinda wish he'd meet someone," I said, wishing my brother could experience the same happiness I had with Sin.

"He'll find the right girl one day," Jordan piped in.

"Maybe," I murmured. I think he'd already met the right girl, but things hadn't worked out. I shrugged it off.

Connor had started to ease up on controlling all aspects of my life. He still phoned regularly but not to the extent that he used to. He was learning to let go and I appreciated it because it allowed me to live my own life.

Sin and Slater returned from the bar and Sin put a drink down in front of me as he sat down beside me.

"I have a surprise for you," Sin said, whispering into my ear.

"What?" I asked, looking at him.

"Your surprise just walked into the bar," he said and I turned to see Connor walking toward us. I hadn't expected to see him. I got up and hugged him just as he reached our table.

"What are you doing here?" I asked, still feeling a little stunned that I had no idea my brother was coming to visit.

"You will have to ask your guy that question," he said as he shook hands with Sin. They shared a knowing look and I was still confused.

Connor sat down in the chair as he watched me turn to Sin for an answer. He stood in front of me and took my hands in his. Suddenly he looked so nervous.

"I have no idea if I'm doing this right or not," he said as

his eyes held mine.

I wanted to ask what was going on, but I kept quiet, giving Sin a chance to explain.

"From the moment I met you, I knew you were going to change my life. I just had no idea how much," he said and swallowed nervously. His eyes dropped to my hands being held in his.

"From the word go, I cared for you, but up until now I haven't been able to say the words to express just how much you mean to me," he said and I shook my head at him.

"I don't need you to say the words. You make me feel loved," I reassured him, not wanting him to be forced to do something he wasn't ready to do. Even if he never said those words to me, it wouldn't diminish what we had.

He let out a breath and lifted his eyes to mine.

"I love you," he said and I felt stunned. The happy faces of my friends and family faded into the background and only he existed at that moment. I felt a well of emotion that he'd finally been able to say it.

"I love *you*," I said back hoarsely, wrapping my arms around his neck and pressing my lips to his.

He kissed me back and then pulled away.

"There's more," he said, looking as happy as I felt, but he still seemed nervous.

I swallowed my emotions as I waited for him to continue. I had no idea what he still wanted to say. He turned to look at our friends, who were all smiling at us, before he turned to face me.

"I wanted to make sure our friends shared in the moment," he said cryptically as he gave me a smile and my eyes questioned his.

"Realizing just how much you mean to me made the next step so much simpler," he explained as he reached into the front pocket of his jeans and pulled out what looked like a small box. It still didn't register.

He opened the box and I was staring at a beautiful oval diamond ring. I gulped as it began to understand.

"I know exactly how I feel about you and I know you are it for me," he explained as my eyes began to water. "Will you marry me?"

"Yes," I answered as I looked at him.

His smile widened and he took the ring. He reached for my hand and slid the ring on my finger. It fit perfectly, just like us.

"I love you," I murmured as he hugged me and I heard him say, "I love you too."

I felt like I was in a dream as our friends and my brother congratulated us. Sin couldn't wipe the silly smile that was plastered to his face and I felt like I was on cloud nine. I still couldn't wrap my mind around the fact that we were engaged.

Believing in happily ever after was for kids. We knew there would be challenges along the way and we wanted to get through them together. There was no one I would rather have at my side through the rest of my life.

I glanced at Sin. He felt my eyes on him and he looked at me.

Loving someone meant loving them—flaws and all, the good with the bad.

"I love you," he whispered to me again as he leaned closer and pressed a kiss to my lips.

I would never tire of hearing him say those words to me.

"I love you too."

About the Author

Regan discovered the joy of writing at the tender age of twelve. Her first two novels were teen fiction romance. She then got sidetracked into the world of computer programming and travelled extensively visiting twenty-seven countries.

A few years ago after her son's birth she stayed home and took another trip into the world of writing. After writing nine stories on Wattpad, winning an award and becoming a featured writer the next step was to publish her stories.

Born in South Africa she now lives in London with her two children and husband, who is currently doing his masters.

If she isn't writing her next novel you will find her reading soppy romance novel, shopping like an adrenaline junkie or watching too much television.

Connect with Regan Ure at www.reganure.com